Neamat Imam

THE
BLACK
COAT

Neamat Imam

THE BLACK COAT

periscope
www.periscopebooks.co.uk

The Black Coat

First published in Great Britain in 2015 by

Periscope
An imprint of Garnet Publishing Limited
8 Southern Court, South Street
Reading RG1 4QS

www.periscopebooks.co.uk
www.facebook.com/periscopebooks
www.twitter.com/periscopebooks
www.instagram.com/periscope_books
www.pinterest.com/periscope

ISBN 9781859640067

A CIP catalogue record for this book is available from the British Library.

This book has been typeset using Periscope UK,
a font created specially for this imprint.

Typeset by Samantha Barden
Jacket design by James Nunn: www.jamesnunn.co.uk

Printed and bound in Lebanon by International Press:
interpress@int-press.com

CONTENTS

BOOK TWO

In the happiness of his subjects lies the king's happiness, in their welfare his welfare. He shall not consider as good only that which pleases him but treat as beneficial to him whatever pleases his subjects.

Kautilya, *Arthashastra*
(Fourth century BCE)

PROLOGUE

Wednesday, 17 March. Hundreds, thousands, of my countrymen are on the road today. They are marching towards the city's central public square, where the Awami League – Sheikh Mujib's party – has organized a massive, open-air ceremony on the anniversary of his birth. The Awami League-run government, which has declared Sheikh Mujib 'Father of the Bengali Nation', has deployed an extravagant number of security personnel to maintain order. They are guarding local street corners, nearby motorway intersections and strategically important rooftops, and stopping vehicles to look for dangerous items. Hundreds of party workers are assisting them; they carry rods, pipes, batons and bamboo sticks, and apply them regularly to anyone who appears to be unruly or suspicious. Dozens of loudspeakers mounted on electricity poles announce the arrival of national leaders and intellectuals, as well as acclaimed singers and musicians who will perform after the speeches.

As I sit at the stairs of the Shaheed Minar and look at the posters, festoons and banners I think back on a different time. I hear a distinctively trenchant voice: 'You have betrayed us! You have betrayed us!' It was thirty-five years ago. He was a part of my soul: a brilliant man, an immaculate heart.

BOOK ONE

1

AT THE FRONT, NOT AT THE FRONT

In 1971 I was a staff writer with *The Freedom Fighter*, a
weekly paper published in the old part of the city of Dhaka
during the Bangladesh Liberation War. It printed reports
on the progress of the *Mukti Bahini*, known as the 'Freedom
Fighters', against Pakistani military assaults. A broadsheet of
only four pages, it quickly became a hit with readers because
of its inspiring writing. Lutfuzzaman Babul, its editor and
publisher, said it was regularly smuggled into Bengali refugee
camps in various Indian territories, where the *Mukti Bahini*
received guerrilla training before moving to the front. He
added that members of the Bangladesh government-in-exile
based in India read every word of it. In the absence of Sheikh
Mujib, the leader of the liberation struggle imprisoned in
West Pakistan for treason, it was considered one of the most
important nationalist voices in the country.

I believed him. I believed in the vision of the paper. That's
why, although it was published by a small media company
with limited and irregular income, I decided to stick with it.
Sometimes I wanted to grab a rifle and go to the front, but
Lutfuzzaman Babul said I was already at the front: reporting
such a primitive war was not an easy task, it was a fight in

itself. He was sure *The Freedom Fighter* would accomplish more than killing a bunch of Pakistani soldiers could; it would redefine the entire ruling class of Pakistan by rousing its conscience against genocide. He told me to write with passion, to fill my columns with love for our people, so that every Bangladeshi, upon reading my words, would be imbued with an enormous sense of patriotism.

In all my articles, I attacked and insulted the Pakistani rulers present and past. I ridiculed them, invented stories about them, misspelled their names and designations to make them seem eccentric and trivial. They were cockroaches. Tikka Khan, the army commander in East Pakistan, should be massaged with fourteen spices and marinated for three nights before being roasted for hungry dogs on Pakistan's national holiday. We published the Pakistani flag with a Nazi swastika in place of the traditional crescent and star; superimposed mammoth, bloody, terrorizing horns on the head of Pakistan's President Yahya Khan. Using emotionally charged language, I narrated how Pakistanis had jumped upon us like beasts with sharp claws and would not give up until they had sucked the last drops of our blood and turned our country into a wasteland.

In article after article, I wrote against those who collaborated with Pakistan and smuggled out valuable security intelligence. 'Hang Them Twice', I titled one of my articles, which argued that these traitors should be hanged along with our enemies because of their misdeeds, then hanged again for betraying us while being a part of us. Bangladesh would never forgive them, I said; they were not sons of our Motherland, they were aliens, Bedouins, Jews, agents of the CIA. They were the damned, awaiting severe punishment for their actions in the people's court. When the country was free, we would find them; we would find all those zombies even if they hid under the rubble, in the bed of the silent seas, above the clouds and in the shadow of Iqbal, and hang them one by one in public squares. Traitors! We would dance in their blood.

I specifically criticized the poet Iqbal because Pakistanis regarded him as their wisest man. They called him *Allama*, 'the Scholar'. He dreamt of a unified homeland for all Muslims in the Subcontinent, thus opposing the concept of the separation of Bangladesh from Pakistan. By speaking of an integrated Pakistan, he only wanted to immortalize Bangladesh as West Pakistan's peaceful colony. I wrote that although I knew even Gandhi had sung his song *Saare jahan se achchha* – *'Better than the Entire World'* – to express his love for the Subcontinent. Iqbal died long before British rule came to an end; nonetheless, I attacked him as if he were alive today, alive and well and advising Pakistan's generals on homeland integration affairs, sitting in some fortified palace inside the Karachi cantonment. Because he was their precious poet, we needed to bully him the way they bullied our precious leader Sheikh Mujib.

In September 1971, Lutfuzzaman Babul called a meeting in his office. We gathered around his table, all eleven reporters, proofreaders and administrators. From four thousand copies in April, the circulation of the paper had grown to twelve thousand in six months; four pages had become eight. He told us there would be no scarcity of investment to take the paper to the next level once the country was liberated. By the 'next level', he meant to give it an institutional shape, to make it a real business venture so that all its employees would have a permanent job in the new country. It would not be surprising if Sheikh Mujib's government wanted to acquire it as its communications department. In that case, we would all automatically be turned into public servants. We loved our country, and becoming public servants was the best thing that could happen to us. Lutfuzzaman Babul advised us to redouble our efforts in inspiring our people to kill Pakistani forces wherever they were found. *Kill, kill, kill* – that was the message. *Kill them. Eat them alive.*

We published a victory issue of the paper following Pakistan's surrender on 16 December 1971, ending the nine-month war. Including supplements, it was sixteen pages. We printed patriotic poems and stories, pictures of children running down the street waving flags, female students at Dhaka University singing 'Our Country Has Plenty of Grain and Riches'. Noted intellectuals contributed essays on the themes of nationalism and the Bengali psyche, the evolution of Bengali cultural tradition and the history of the Bengali renaissance in the twentieth century. A professor analyzed ideas of rebellion in our folk literature.

But the main attraction was the photograph of a smiling Sheikh Mujib, wearing a heap of garlands around his neck. The article that followed praised him for his determination, conscientiousness and towering social influence. He was one leader who stated ardently that he did not want to become Prime Minister of Pakistan, and instead wanted to see Bangladesh set free. We printed details of his political career along with several pages of pictures.

Sheikh Mujib was more popular with Bangladeshis than the Prophet Muhammad; he was supported by people of all religions and creeds. On 10 January 1972, he returned to Dhaka to form a government after being released from Pakistani custody. 'There is not another leader like him in the world,' people said. 'There won't be another leader like him in the future.' A new cabinet was sworn in immediately. Military and border security forces, police and other institutions were created and organized as quickly and as adequately as possible. Mass graves were discovered in different parts of the country. The buried were exhumed and reburied. Roads were cleared. Pakistani tanks, armoured vehicles, personnel carriers, ambulances, helicopters and supply trucks – burned-out, blood-spattered and broken – were removed from the streets. Offices and marketplaces hoisted new flags. Educational institutes and courts opened. Government documents published in Urdu, the language of Pakistan, and Urdu–Bengali dictionaries were gathered together and set ablaze in the national park. *Mukti Bahini* members returned from the front, wept for their deceased fellow fighters, got married and joined in victory parades in every city. The smell of loss gradually began to fade.

Sheikh Mujib delivered a special message to *The Freedom Fighter* shortly after he came to power. He was such a busy person; the whole country was waiting for his instructions; Soviet General Secretary Brezhnev was waiting to meet him; British Foreign Secretary Sir Alec Douglas-Home was also waiting. But he made time to take pen in hand, to write a few lines on his newly printed letterhead in his most direct language: 'My brothers,' he wrote, 'the enemy is gone. It is your country now. Forget your differences. Transform your hate into action. Build this nation. *Joy Bangla.*'

That message was recognition of our hard work, Lutfuzzaman Babul said. It was an inspiration for us as well as for every man and woman in the country. Now that the country was free, he did not speak about *The Freedom Fighter* becoming the government's mouthpiece. I knew him; I had no doubt he believed a paper must be free even in a free country – *particularly* in a free country.

2
Assessing the Ash

It was now time to take a good look at the country, to record the scope of the devastation. It was time to find those who were still alive and to mourn the ones who were lost forever. The wounded and injured needed care. Those who had lost everything needed help to heal their pain. There were the stressed, the psychologically traumatized and the homeless, who needed a moment of calm. But above all, and despite all this, we needed to celebrate the heroism of our people.

I went from district to district, village to village, to understand how individuals had coped with the horrors of the war and how they now felt about living in a liberated country. I spoke with hundreds of people who had been displaced, who had lived in slums for months, but now expected something better. I submitted my reports with analysis and photographs; they were duly printed.

Sometimes it happened that I spent hour upon hour speaking with freedom fighters who had gone to the front. I wanted to know what had motivated them so elementally that they had not feared for their lives. It was an old question, but I asked it every time as if it were new. Every person faced

9

that question in his own way, in his own time, and every person must have his own answer. I wanted to know what their answers were.

They all believed in the leadership of Sheikh Mujib. They believed that if the country was not free now, under his direction, it would never be free. Some said they did not go to war for the country; they went for him. They did not know what they were doing; he said they must go, and they did. One old man, whom I met aboard a ferry on the Padma, gave me an absolute answer: 'If he calls upon you, you can't just say no, or say you're afraid to die. It is impossible. Are you an animal? Is there no shame in you? You say: "I'm here and I'm ready." You say: "I am grateful that I live in Bangladesh and that I live during the time of war." You thank Sheikh Mujib for seeking your help.' He asked me if I had gone to the front. I had not, I replied, suddenly unprepared. His sharp, penetrating eyes filled with overwhelming contempt. 'I don't speak to you,' he said as he slowly moved to the other end of the ferry, holding firmly onto his underarm crutches. 'Whoever you are, you're not a Bengali; you're not Sheikh Mujib's man. I don't speak to you.'

Some of them gave me beaten rice and cups of milk to recover my energy; some invited me to join them for a lunch of pumpkin curry and *roti*. During these meals, I tired them with my relentless curiosity and they baffled me with the details of their narratives. They wanted to speak, most of them, and while speaking they became immensely excited, as if they were still at the front, still in the war with .303s on their shoulders, crossing mountains and submerged rice fields.

In Mymensingh, I met a middle-aged gentleman who introduced himself simply as 'the Commander'. He had an excellent sense of geography. He drew a small map in the yard with a stick and gave me a visual description of where they had fought, where they had faced the most horrendous resistance and where they had swum a raging river on a stormy night to rescue their fallen comrades. He told me he had heard the voice of Sheikh Mujib in the fall of the waves and in the sound of the thunder; that had helped him overcome his fear during the battle.

It was obviously an exaggeration. I looked at the Commander. He was a strong man with short hair, a cobra tattoo on his back and a clean-shaven face, wearing heavily aromatic aftershave – quite the opposite of the sort of bearded village elder with a Qur'an clutched to his chest, who might believe in superstition. I left the yard, confused and lost, and stood on the path facing the open south. One of the Commander's disciples followed me there. He said he knew I did not believe the Commander, but it did not matter now because the war was over. He said he had also heard Sheikh Mujib's voice several times during the war. 'You may not believe me either, but you may believe in God. At this moment I can only tell you that if you believe in God you must believe in Sheikh Mujib.'

In early 1973 I was assigned to visit Gangasagar in Akhaura, to write a piece on Mostafa Kamal. He was a martyr of the war. When he and his fellow fighters came under heavy attack from the Pakistan Air Force, he decided to give his men the opportunity to escape. Pakistani soldiers shot him, then bayoneted him to death.

Raihan Talukder, whose brother Wahab Talukder had also been killed in the Gangasagar assault, offered me a bed for the night in his hut. With an eight-hour return journey before me, I decided to accept his hospitality. He took me around the village, introducing me to his neighbours respectfully. 'Khaleque Biswas, eminent journalist from Dhaka,' he told people, 'and very close to Sheikh Mujib.' I did not know what prompted him to introduce me like that; probably he thought everyone interested in history and politics and living in the capital was close to Sheikh Mujib. I remained silent. If the invisible presence of the prime minister made my life easier in a remote village, who was I to complain? In the evening, I worked on my report by the light of a hurricane lamp. Raihan Talukder went to sleep in the inner room, but got up every few minutes to enquire whether or not I needed another glass of water or perhaps a cup of tea, or if the hurricane lamp had enough kerosene and finally, if he should tell me the stories of Gangasagar once again to make sure I had all the necessary information for my assignment.

I asked him if he was aware that the Bangladesh Army was preparing to decorate Mostafa Kamal with the title *Bir Sreshtha*. 'Are they?' he said. I asked if he knew what that title meant. He looked at me with wonder.

'Mostafa Kamal is one of the seven great heroes of our Liberation War,' I explained. '*Bir Sreshtha* is the army's highest recognition of bravery.' Still, it did not seem to make much sense to him.

'There are more than seven great heroes in the Gangasagar area alone,' he said. 'What about those who died with him? Did they die any less than he?'

I realized it would not be easy to make a philosophical point about death and heroism to him. Telling him that there were levels of valour and that there were many kinds of good deaths, even if all of them happened in the same place at the same moment, triggered by the same hazard, would end in futility: he had already accepted death as the Great Leveller. The simple solution was to ask him if he thought there were differences between himself and Sheikh Mujib, though both of them loved our country. There were, he said immediately; many. 'What kind of a question is that?' I knew that would be his only response.

'Sheikh Mujib is not an average human being like us,' I said; 'he is special, superior and incomparable. The same way, there is something special about Mostafa Kamal that separates him from other martyrs.' Raihan Talukder accepted my point thoughtfully.

After he left, I put out the hurricane lamp and tried to visualize the very moment when Mostafa Kamal had decided to take charge of the situation. I wanted to enter his heart. I wanted to be a blood cell in his veins, to see what his eyes had seen in that enormous chaos. I wanted to experience how a simple moment – a moment in a small village of horror and ferocity – had defined a whole life and made everything else insignificant. I wanted to imagine I was him, a non-commissioned soldier, telling my comrades that I was their protector, their most dependable and dynamic guardian angel; I could bargain with death and successfully deny or postpone or defy it for them. Then I wanted to see how my end crept up on me, inch by inch, following my decision: a decision that he had taken for me, a decision that I had taken for him.

I woke up early and walked dreamily to the spot where Mostafa Kamal was killed. It must have been the place itself that had influenced him to take his decision, an influence he could not ignore. I walked around with my shoes soaked in the dew, and filled my chest with cold, translucent air. I walked from side to side, corner to corner, stepping on my footprints, looking around, looking for something I did not know existed but hoped would explain to me the very heart of the place. I found nothing. It was a place of nothing; it had been a place of nothing, for everyone, today and yesterday, and it would be a place of nothing for centuries: that was what I understood. I was not Mostafa Kamal, I thought then, to satisfy myself. I did not have his eyes to see, his heart to feel, his moral stature to commit to serving the life force. Whatever I would see or feel would be mine, completely mine, not his. I felt a small vibration in my fingers, a mild increase in my heartbeat, and my footsteps became slower and more lethargic and finally stopped. That was mine, I knew. It was not vast, definitely not as immense and overwhelming as Mostafa Kamal's feeling, but it gave me something.

The sun came out, making the surroundings luscious and flamboyant. Raihan Talukder joined me. I asked him what time of day it had been when Mostafa Kamal was killed – whether it was a morning like this, or a dark, cloudy day, or an evening retiring fast into night. He did not answer, as if it was no longer necessary to know what time of day it had been. Mostafa Kamal would have made the same decision no matter what. Raihan Talukder sat at the foot of a bamboo clump; I sat beside him, and we looked at the field before us as if something was happening there: the past was unravelling, and Mostafa Kamal was advancing towards the very moment of his non-existence like an oyster creates a pearl, little by little.

Back in Dhaka, I examined the entire Liberation War from Mostafa Kamal's perspective. I considered his final moment as a long moment that lasted nine months, the entire course of the war. I believed it could last longer, until eternity if need be, until all the dictators in the world fell and all discrimination came to an end. Together Mostafa Kamal and his fellow fighters made one large moment of truth. Their eyes did not see, their nerves did not feel, their rational faculties did not function, but their human spirit worked without fail. By engaging with that moment, they knew they were serving the most valuable and inevitable cause in human history: the cause of freedom.

I posted a copy of the article to Raihan Talukder. I was grateful to him for his hospitality and friendship, I wrote in a note. The first-hand information he had provided was absolutely invaluable. If he ever came to Dhaka, even for a day, he must see me; it would be a pleasure to buy him a cup of tea.

Life moved on. I did not hear back from him immediately; nor did I bother to send him another letter, because I had new stories to focus on, new assignments to complete. Until one morning a young man appeared at my door and gave me a letter.

3
NUR HUSSAIN

Raihan Talukder had received my message, the letter said, and everything was well in Gangasagar. Strangers came there almost every week looking for their lost ones. They walked where the battle had taken place, sat in the tea stalls, asked villagers about the dead, if they had been of a certain skin colour, age, body shape and height, if they had left anything behind: letters, shoes, clothes, combs, spectacles, handkerchiefs, wallets, rings. They gathered at the graveyard, prayed for the unidentified valiant fighters, then left with tears in their eyes. Some of them returned again and again; they brought fish heads, cow shank soup, sweet fried rice balls, green chillies, ripe palm fruits and scallions for the villagers, invited them to their houses and attempted to create lasting bonds with them. Sometimes journalists came; they came from different newspapers, radio and TV channels, sometimes from as far as the Indian city of Kolkata. They took pictures, interviewed villagers and bought goat's-milk yogurt before leaving. It was encouraging to see that Gangasagar had drawn the attention of so many good people from across the region.

But fame had not made life any easier for the village's inhabitants. Raihan Talukder used the rest of the letter to introduce to me one Nur Hussain, its bearer, who desperately needed employment. Raihan Talukder described him as a 'loyal, patient, sociable and diligent young man'; he believed that among all his acquaintances, only I was in a position to help Nur Hussain find suitable employment. In the last passage, he also gave hints about what that suitable employment might be. Nur Hussain could serve in a responsible position in the government, he wrote. The nation-building process was painstaking and challenging; the government needed honest, dedicated people to work in its various departments; there would be many positions in the newly created ministries for which Nur Hussain would be fit. He would work with devotion; I would never have cause to regret helping him out.

I removed all the old newspapers from my storeroom and placed a single cot there for Nur Hussain. I gave him a mat, a bedsheet, a pillow and a pillowcase. In the village, people slept on *hogla* mats or mats of jute fibres or rough, wooden floorboards. Their pillows were often greasy and stank, filled with cotton compressed by years of use and moisture. I had seen people use bricks as pillows and straw blankets as quilts. By comparison, I made comfortable arrangements for him. There were mosquitoes, hundreds of them, but I never spoke about this. From my bed inside a net, I frequently heard Nur Hussain slapping them. 'He'll get used to them,' I said to myself as I closed my eyes. 'He'll have to. A person can accept anything and everything when he faces the question of survival.'

Dhaka was not an easy place to conquer. I told him this in our first serious conversation, a day after his arrival, when I thought he had recovered from his trip. Dhaka had too much going on, too many people involved in too many things at the same time. But he shouldn't worry; the city had a strange capacity to accommodate anyone from any background. He, too, would settle in. At least he had a roof over his head, which many newcomers did not. He would eat with me, stay with me and, in due course, would have enough money of his own to rent a flat as big as mine, if not bigger.

Gradually, I learned that he had no transferable or marketable skills. Skills were the currency in the new labour market, in which employers looked for more than knowledge and credentials. He could not speak standard Bengali, let alone English. He never browsed the newspapers I brought home with me every day, not even the sports pages or the entertainment advertisements. He was just not interested. Raihan Talukder had said he was a fast learner. I did not understand what he meant by that. In the evening I made Nur Hussain tea and asked what level of schooling he had had.

'Please don't feel embarrassed by my asking this,' I said. 'I need to know exactly what you can do, so that I can find something that will suit you.'

'Fifth class,' he said, then sat for some time with eyes cast downward, perhaps wondering if it was actually fifth class.

'That's great,' I said, quietly, though I felt uncomfortable. 'I know loads of people who have never been to school, but they are raising their families like everybody else.' Then I asked if he knew how to stitch clothes, lay bricks, work with wood or iron; if he knew bicycle mechanics, welding, plumbing, digging, scaffolding ... anything. He did not. All I understood was that he could sleep all day and all night without ever asking for food. When I invited him to dinner, he ate silently, and ate only what I put on his plate. He was shy, introverted, principally a useless human being in a city of four million human beings.

It was not easy to approach someone about a job for one who had lived all his life in his father's bamboo shed without caring to fix or learn or earn anything. He might be intelligent with goats, know their body language, grazing and foraging strategies and reproductive cycles, but there were no goats in the city. Here, people had to deal with people – hard, solid, rubbish, despicable people with very low or no self-esteem. They must know how to give commands or how to live under constant commands without whining all the time. Nur Hussain gave me a serious headache. I had no idea how he would fit into the highly competitive and ambitious culture of city life.

Just to give him the impression that I was looking for a job for him, one day I told him we had an opening for a staff reporter position at *The Freedom Fighter*. The salary was good, the job was interesting, and, most importantly, he would meet many political and business leaders as part of his professional duties, which might open further career opportunities. If recruited, he would travel to remote corners of the country, to the hills and borders, to collect information, to investigate favouritism, conspiracies, poisonings, murders and mass killings, to report on various developmental activities, to interview people in a range of different circumstances for human-interest stories, to build reliable contacts, to collect facts on developing incidents … and the paper would pay all his expenses. Wouldn't he want to enjoy such an exclusive opportunity?

It was an honourable job, too, I said with emphasis, mimicking my editor Lutfuzzaman Babul; but I immediately added that it might not be ethical for me to recommend his name, because he did not have a proper education or the technical knowledge for the job. Writing a report is an art, I explained. One has to begin with a clear idea about the purpose of the report and end it with an equally clear point of view. Understanding the difference between mundane and significant points is one of the guiding factors.

Besides, he was not well informed about what had happened to our country in the past few years, I said, as if I had known him all my life. He had seen the assault on Gangasagar; after the war he might also have seen the evidence of atrocities committed by Pakistani soldiers in the surrounding twenty villages. But did the war begin in Gangasagar? No. Did it end there? Absolutely not. That meant many more causes and decisions were associated with it. Until he could explain them one by one, his knowledge of the war was limited, and his analysis of it irrelevant and dangerous.

By contrast, a journalist with *The Freedom Fighter* knew what the war was about. He knew its typology, its ambiguous complexity. He knew when a difficult time was approaching, raising its horns like an angry bull. He remembered at all times which minister said what, what Sheikh Mujib's six-point demands were, where they were written and declared, who the British attorney was who helped get him out of the Agartala Conspiracy Case, which song George Harrison sang at Madison Square Garden in New York in support of Bangladesh. I also pointed out that Nur Hussain was not aware of what was happening at the moment. He did not know, for example, who Dr Kamal was, even though Dr Kamal was engaged in writing a full, workable and acceptable constitution for the country.

It was not his fault, I finally said. He lived in the countryside, where people survived on agriculture, traditional neighbourly goodwill, religious values and ethics, happy to know of only ordinary matters; the rules of political engagement, statesmanship and diplomacy did not apply there. They did not watch TV, listen to BBC broadcasts, read newspaper editorials or attend weekly discussion programmes at the National Museum on aspects of our cultural life. I did not expect him to be well-prepared for a profession he had never heard of.

Another day I said I had a friend who needed a locksmith: not a prestigious job like being a newspaper reporter, and the payment was probably meagre too, the working hours odd and longer, but good enough to begin with. I asked him if he had seen those black, electroplated 300-gram keyless pin-controlled locks hanging from the doors of banks. It was the technology of the future. Who would want to carry a set of rusty keys if they could do without them? He said he had never seen a bank, and that the only lock he had ever seen was the one used to protect their cow from thieves. That would be a small, nineteenth-century solid padlock with an iron key made in India. The key must turn 180 degrees to undo the hook. Those locks were out of fashion now. Thieves knew too much about them.

I gave him a concise description of the steel Taiwanese locks that had three columns of digits from zero to nine with almost unlimited resettable combinations, perfect for home, business, garage, school or post office. From my cupboard, I brought mine out. 'How strong do you think it is?' I asked. 'You think you can unlock it with a piece of wire? There is no hole to slip a wire into it. There is no way you can tamper with it or damage it.' He gazed at it for at least thirty seconds.

'Hold it, here,' I said, and gave it to him. The country was developing fast, I told him as he played with the digits, and every locksmith must know how to operate new locks that provided maximum security and protection if they wanted to remain employed in the future.

4

AN EMBARRASSMENT AND A DREAM

His prospects looked grim. I did not know what to do. Telling him I was busy, I spent two days without speaking to him. I kept a newspaper on the dining table and read it again and again while we ate. Then I went to my room and closed my door.

I could not ask him to leave. That would be too embarrassing, considering the fact that in my mind I had always believed I was an immensely powerful person. More importantly, it would be a social crime. It would destroy my reputation with Raihan Talukder. He would think I had let him down. You're an educated person, he would say, how could you do something like that? If you yourself were not enough, couldn't you talk to Sheikh Mujib? Nur Hussain had to leave of his own accord. I could only make things so complicated and confusing for him that he would give up and say goodbye.

Today or tomorrow, he was going to accept that Gangasagar was not only an easier and better place for him to live, but that it had also been a gross mistake to leave it for Dhaka. Perhaps one day he would understand why I had failed him, and would be able to forgive me.

Two more weeks passed. He did not appear unhappy or distressed. Instead, I noticed, he had adjusted to the wild attacks of the mosquitoes and the untarnished solitude of the flat, as if he was on a pilgrimage and would accept any hardship. The only change was that he was more silent now, more detached and more preoccupied with himself. When it rained, he sat at the window the whole day, leaning against the wall. He coughed a few times as the humid air entered his nostrils and grew slightly frightened when thunder struck nearby. Then once again that awful silence, his eyes upon the rain. I gave him one of my woollen hand-knitted pullovers. He accepted it without a word, wore it over his T-shirt, crossed his hands and looked at me with gratitude. Then, stretching his neck, he watched me as I tidied the living room – but he never rose to help me, not even when I struggled to lift the sofa to clean underneath it. Probably he did not want to do anything that I might consider foolish, insane or disturbing, or he had noticed the sharp anger I had to hide day after day. I was angry not because of my failure to find him a job, but because he was there every moment to remind me of that failure. 'He has no right to embarrass me like this,' I kept telling myself. 'Why on earth did Raihan Talukder send him to me? I would never have accepted his hospitality if I'd had the faintest idea this would happen.'

The only option I could think of was to engage him as my caretaker. I did not need a caretaker; in fact, I hated the concept of enslaving someone to secure my own comfort.

That was obvious exploitation. But he needed me. If enslaving him protected his existence, I should happily go for it. I decided that he would cook for me, sweep the house, wash my clothes, go to the grocer and guard the door in my absence. If there was time, he would collect water from the market when tap water was unavailable. His compensation would be regular meals, clothing and lodging. I asked him if he wanted to do it, if he *really* wanted to do it. 'I won't be unhappy if you don't do anything for me,' I said. 'If you find it condescending, that is okay, I'll understand. Many people value dignity over comfort. I consider that a sign of character and strength. I just wanted to help.'

He nodded. He would like to begin right away, he said.

One or two evenings he chopped onions, washed the dishes and proved himself disqualified. He was absent-minded. He was not hygienic. He did not know how to peel potatoes or handle a knife safely while cutting through the spine of a three-inch freshwater fish.

Did I want to see blood on my floor?

Absolutely not.

On one of those nights, as I was lying on my cold, moonlit bed, tired from trying to think of someone who could employ Nur Hussain in a temporary but real job, I dreamt of Sepoy Mostafa Kamal. I dreamt I was a young boy, younger than Nur Hussain, in Gangasagar, just outside Raihan Talukder's house, and that I was watching Mostafa Kamal fight against the mighty Pakistani military. Hiding behind a high mound of earth, soaking in my sweat, trembling with fear and anger, I saw how fiercely he chased the enemy with his machine gun. The colour of the sky changed from white to grey, darkness fell in the surrounding rice fields, the wind brought rain, stars shone and sank in the morning lights; but the battle continued. It continued for seventeen hours, and for seventeen hours I observed him from my hiding place.

'I see you,' he said to me between chases. 'Don't stay here, go away, go away; leave this place. Fighting is not fun; it favours nobody; it wants everything – your body, your mind, your heart. Go away right now. There are just too many of them; they are in the sky, in the water, on the land; they've taken hostage the whole universe. Hear that noise, that striking, brutal, monstrous noise, ruthlessly echoing in ten directions? That is from a twin-barrelled, self-loading mortar; soon the whole area will be covered with a dense white smoke spiralling to the sky. Through that smoke they will come like ravenous beasts, searching for prey and glory and meaning. But I will not give up; I will not let them steal even a drop of water or a small leaf from this land. They will not touch any of our flowers, our fish, our beautiful evenings, our songs and waterfalls. You stay away, go to a safer place, find yourself something to eat, sleep well; there will be fights for you too, many of them, after this fight. Fights never end.'

I stood up, shouting through the smoke: 'I can't leave you alone! I've to learn fighting; I've to learn it watching you. Let me stay here, please; let me know what blood is when it is warm, what hate is when it is good, what endurance is when it is indispensable.'

'You make me happy, kid; you make this war more inevitable and pleasing than it has been; you make this gun fire by itself. But staying here won't do you any good. This is my fight; it was mine long before I was born, before my mother uttered her very first word. Let me win it or die. Here they come. Close your eyes.'

I stayed. I did not close my eyes. I saw the destruction. I saw the elation of the human devils as they stood before him, pointing their weapons at him.

After he was bayoneted, and the earth became red with blood and then black, the air smelled of sulphur and the military left, laughing like hyenas, spitting in his face, feeding his testicles to hungry crows, I took him in my arms, wept for several hours and carried him to the nearest deserted char land, where I buried him in the sand. It is useless writing an epitaph on the grave. The sands do not remember for long. There are heavy dust storms, which irritate the ground, sweep away sea crabs and their skeletons and fill every snake hole. Frequently, tidal waves come. But I wrote his name. I wrote his name in letters twelve yards long, perhaps expecting someone from the sky to look after him.

It was not a complicated dream. Its suggestions were also not complicated. I believed that the war in 1971 had happened for me and for me alone. It happened to boost my spirit, to keep me rational, to make me responsible. Mostafa Kamal died only for me. He became history, so that I would know exactly how important it was to remain motivated. I believed it was my turn now: I must do for Nur Hussain what Mostafa Kamal had done for the country. I felt ashamed of myself for not looking for a job for him.

So I began.

5
A NEW PICTURE

Too many people had moved to Dhaka after the war: those who were directly affected by the war; those who could not find any employment in their villages, like Nur Hussain; those who suddenly became ambitious because they were now citizens of a free country. The homeless made up the largest group. They came from all areas of the country, but mostly from districts that had seen repeated natural disasters. Homes lost; entire crops damaged; cattle mad or dead. The only hope was the railway that ran between cities. They got on the trains, crowd upon crowd – children, the elderly, the newly married, widows, widowers, anyone who did not think life was limited to the confines of their village. In Dhaka they slept on pavements, in railway stations, in hospital corridors and abandoned buildings. Every morning they came out into the streets, begged from pedestrians, robbed them, squatted openly on the sewerage and then slept in their filthy clothes, only to prepare for next morning's struggle. Innumerable tent cities rose on unclaimed plots and public parks, next to newly built multi-storey office buildings, glitzy five-star hotels, dazzling mosques and temples. Smoke from their portable earthen kitchens blackened the Dhaka skies day and night.

Until then, I had been engaged in finding a superior meaning to the freedom that had come to us at the cost of thousands of lives. To be honest, I had engaged in theorizing about that which did not exist, and which we had never known: stability. I saw people coming to Dhaka, but I did not know why Dhaka was the only solution for them. Now I saw what I did not want to see. I saw hunger, dissatisfaction, rampant poverty, looting. It was only eighteen months into Bangladesh's independence, and the country was falling into a deep pit of brutality.

Seeking a job for Nur Hussain I went to a friend, who sent me to another friend, who sent me to yet another friend. I went to my distant relatives, to their relatives, *their* relatives and *their* relatives. I spoke passionately about him. He had already made a serious effort by coming to the capital from the remote countryside, and dared to live with a stranger to better his luck; I thought he deserved my reference. He was a gentleman, I said. He was caring and never got involved in arguments of any kind with me. Anyone who hired him would be doing themselves a favour. It was not easy to find someone who would not steal from his master or disappear suddenly without trace. He would not do that.

Nobody took any notice. Those who did, did so negatively. 'Do not come with any such requests, please,' they said. 'We are worried we might lose our own people. We have no time for one who is already lost.' What happened to these people? Has freedom made them heartless and selfish? How can they be so apathetic? Every night I returned home and ate my supper with him in silence. Every night I looked at him less and less, and yawned more and more, to give the impression that I was terribly tired. I could not forget I was failing scandalously in a very simple matter. I was failing before someone as trivial as Nur Hussain, who knew nothing and understood nothing.

Perhaps he did know something. He began to chop onions regularly with me in the kitchen, trying his best to make every slice fine and equal. He washed his hands before and after touching food, swept his room every day, cleaned the kitchen and my bedroom, scrubbed the walls and the floor of the toilet and dried his underwear in the privacy of his room. He made the pile of newspapers tidy, arranged them according to date, and one day pointed out that I was wearing a soiled shirt – a shirt without two lower buttons, its collar damaged by sweat and salt.

I gave him money and he bought our groceries. At the end of the month, I gave him letters to post, bills to pay. He did everything as directed, and returned home immediately. He walked quickly – and I guess sometimes ran – through the sad, distracted, unmoving crowd to finish his work. He had no interest in the city; he didn't care what went on there. His world was my flat, with its uncomplicated compromise between space and furniture, and his contribution to my life became wider and stronger.

I visited Lutfuzzaman Babul. After a brief introduction about the daily state of affairs, I told him I had thought about it a lot, and every time I thought about it I knew I had to do something. He looked at me with wonder.

'What do you mean? Haven't you been doing what you wanted to do? Don't you enjoy it anymore?'

I told him I wanted to write something different.

'Different?'

'Something new,' I answered. 'Substantial.' My country was suffering. Good-for-nothing politicians were playing games with people. There was emptiness in people's stares. It was rapidly contaminating those who were still active and dreamt of a better life in the future.

I gave him a detailed account of my recent experience across the city.

'And what difference would that make?'

I did not know. 'Freedom is freedom when it surfaces as a lifestyle for people,' I said. 'The first step is to ensure food for everyone, then a place to sleep. At the end of the day, everyone must go home. Where is Sheikh Mujib? Where is the Awami League? Don't they see these people?'

Lutfuzzaman Babul remained silent, although he looked troubled. I understood that, as an editor, he had to consider the circulation of the paper before implementing any major policy shift. His daily bread, along with that of the whole team, depended on it. Change would not come in a day. But I reminded him that the paper actually originated from a highly devoted political project, and that it had achieved its present position only because we had presented the truth persistently, irrespective of our political affiliations. We wanted our people to go public about the most burning problem of our time: to be free or not to be free. Was daily bread everything? I asked. Didn't we call our paper *The Freedom Fighter*?

He stared at me for some time, then abruptly ended the meeting. Within a week, he made the decision to lay me off. 'Financial constraints,' he said.

I became like Nur Hussain.

6

MY VALUED COMPANION

Not entirely like him. I had experience, I told myself; he did not. I had a month's salary in my pocket and some savings that I had put aside over the last two years. I saved money by quitting smoking, by walking from place to place instead of hiring a rickshaw, by taking buses for long-distance trips instead of renting a taxi, by not inviting friends to my flat on social occasions. By contrast, Nur Hussain was penniless.

Besides, I knew people; I had connections that could be of immense help. He had nobody. My friends had not done anything for him, but I was sure they would do something for me. At least they could make some phone calls to potential employers in their circles. They could spread the news: 'One hard-working, vibrant, dutiful, far-sighted and forward-looking journalist with an extraordinary writing portfolio, Khaleque Biswas, is now available for hire.' They would be happy to stand as referees for me. If they could not do that, what was friendship for? And I had ideas, I told myself. Finding a lucrative job would not be that difficult for me. By contrast, Nur Hussain was stuck; he would go nowhere; his life was created to be wasted. My accidental caretaker, then somebody else's professional caretaker and then one day, after a few seasons, an old man who couldn't even take care of himself. He would disappear as nature's unplanned production.

I stayed at home for a week, coming up with a strategy. I must begin to network seriously, to be well-organized, with the specific purpose of landing a suitable job. There must be a crack somewhere in the industry. I must find it and enter through it. Then I would make my presence felt, using my energy, intelligence and perseverance. I would move so fast that that crack would soon turn into a tunnel leading to a golden gate. My colleagues would be astonished at my capacity.

I prepared my résumé, revised it several times to perfect its wording and to rectify all spelling errors, used bullet points to highlight my aptitudes and clearly stated what I was going to bring with me to my new workplace: leadership, management, investigative skills, the ability to produce an extraordinary piece of writing within a short period of time. I then wrote customized cover letters for every appropriate position I could think of. The newspaper industry was expanding rapidly. It had drawn an obscene percentage of new investment in the private sector. Money was pouring in from everywhere. Who could tell before the war that we had so much money in our country? Who could tell that, in a country with only a twenty per cent literacy rate, people would love and respect the print media so much?

Soon, thanks to my good luck, I met two editors of daily papers and had a long, unhindered, stimulating conversation with them. They were rising non-academic political thinkers who kept away from salacious trivia. I knew they were jealous of the extraordinary growth of *The Freedom Fighter* – I had insider information. Wouldn't they want to know what had made that growth possible, and the secret to making that growth sustainable in the post-war period? I had my thoughts about a well-governed society, but I did not want to overwhelm them with my arguments, especially in our first conversation. I wanted them to go home and think about me, look at my résumé when they were free, and then decide how I would add a new dimension to their papers. But I could not resist mentioning one point. I said the time of process journalism was over; it was important that we offered readers news as it happened, so that people believed we were on their side. We could not hide anything. People had become conscious, and they had proved it during the Liberation War. Guns could not terrorize them. Tanks could not stop them from marching. Wave after wave of carefully fabricated propaganda could not break their determination. The only way for us to go forward was to respect our readers and countrymen.

One of the editors lit a cigarette, releasing a large spiral of smoke. The other walked to the kitchen and poured a glass of water for himself. I have been able to torture them, I thought. I have put them on the sword. They are now suffering. They will suffer until they have heard the rest of the story from me. My strategy was working.

Everyone I spoke to in the press encouraged me. They understood my plan. Some who hesitated to support me before their superiors patted me on the back in private.

'Extraordinary,' they said. 'Smart thinking. Go ahead. We're with you.' They would do anything to help me out. They were real people, I thought, people with brains and vision. They sensed danger before everyone else.

I was satisfied with my progress. I needed only one opportunity, and I had unshakeable confidence that it was going to come from one of the papers. It was only a question of time.

At home I began to share more and more hours with Nur Hussain. He could not talk about anything other than Gangasagar and its seasons, its landscape and marketplace, its animals and vegetation. But I accepted him with kindness. I spoke softly. We went to the market together to buy stuff. We ran in the school field together and went to the lake to swim.

'There is a famous song in Gangasagar,' he said one day. 'Everyone seems to like it there.'

'What is it?' I asked, seemingly curious. 'Can you sing a line?'

He sang the opening four lines of *My Golden Bengal, I Love You*. He did not even know that it was our newly declared national anthem. I let him sing the lines twice and then said, calmly: 'Yes, that's a lovely song, a very lovely song indeed; no wonder people love it so much there.'

When he got to the story about the bamboo bridge that connected the village to the main road, and the fact that it broke down every year because of the huge current in the canal during the monsoon, I knew that was the end of his stock. He always ended there. That bridge brought the whole country to the village; it thus had symbolic significance, which did not escape his attention. Nostalgia choked his voice.

I, on the other hand, could tell him stories of the whole war, dividing it chronologically month by month, dissecting it analytically incident by incident, area by area. In fact, I told him the story of the Subcontinent beginning with 1757, when India fell to the British imperialists. The British had bribed *Nawab* Siraj Ud-Daulah's military chief, Mir Jafar, and with his help had captured and brutally killed the *Nawab*. I spoke about their barbarism, which had lasted almost two hundred years. They enslaved us to produce raw materials and then compelled us to buy their processed goods. I also narrated how they divided the Subcontinent in 1947 on the eve of departure, and what happened in Pakistan in the two decades that followed. With reference to the general election of 1970, I told him how Pakistani dictators did not bother to democratize the country when the grand occasion came, and how they wanted to control us with might in our own home.

It was not clear how much of it he understood, but he respected the passion I put into my story. As I did not go out every day, I told him the story of the war again and again, and he heard me again and again with the same reverence in his eyes.

My savings were dwindling fast. It was not my flatmate I worried about now; I worried about myself. In particular, I worried about losing the flat, becoming one of the homeless, the utmost tragedy at this time. It would be too much to bear.

When I did not hear from any of my potential employers and no offer came from my friends and colleagues, I reflected on my conversation with the editors. I could not understand what had gone wrong. If they were future keepers of our democracy, they would have needed me. Then I read their papers. Their columns were boring. They created a surreal world with words and pictures. They filled page after page with rubbish, as if they had surrendered willingly to the stifling control of the government instead of attacking it. I supposed they considered me an enemy of the people. One who goes against the government is not an enemy of the people; those who accept their government's limitations in silence are the real enemies. I had never felt so disheartened.

The situation compelled me to go back in time, to refocus on Sheikh Mujib's speech delivered in Dhaka on 7 March 1971.

It was a historic speech – the seed of our independence. It had the unique power to motivate Bangladeshis from all walks of life to stand up for their right to self-determination. It kicked off the celebration of our Independence Day. *The Freedom Fighter* regularly published a quote from it in a box in the upper-right corner of the front page. *This is the struggle for independence*, it read; *this is the struggle for our freedom.* Now that we had achieved nationhood, I wanted to understand what Sheikh Mujib had in mind for me as an individual citizen.

I played part of the speech on my cassette player, listening to every sentence carefully. I played it at morning and at night. I played it whenever I could not decide what else to do. I listened to it quietly, and spoke along with it so that the words could not cheat me and I felt them in my heart. Sometimes I carried the player in my hand and walked from my bedroom to the sitting room, where I sat for hours listening to it. I pressed the auto-reverse button. The speech ended and began again, only to end and begin again.

Nur Hussain understood the trouble I was in. He had instincts, if not knowledge.

'You're a good person,' he said. 'Soon someone will understand you and offer you a place at the table.' Then he sat beside me silently, probably thinking he had said almost too much and put himself in trouble. He took small breaths. His hands and feet did not move. Then, after a few minutes, he turned his face to me and smiled to cheer me up. Though I was much older than him, and was supposed to take his responsibility on my own shoulders, day by day he was becoming my most valued companion.

7

HE BEGINS TO SPEAK

One evening, a few days later, after a long, purposeless walk across the neighbourhood, we took a break in the Shaheed Minar area. Nur Hussain suddenly began to recite from Sheikh Mujib's speech. His voice was artificial, but nevertheless it was deep, loud and passionate. Sitting against the reddish daylight, he spoke slowly, uttering one or two words at a time, as did many of our countrymen who attended political campaigns and were so carried away by grandiose slogans that they repeated them in their sleep.

He did it, I believe, to amuse me. It was a joke; I could tell by looking at his smiling face. When I turned away from him, he stood up.

'What are you doing?' I asked out of irritation. 'Nur!'

It was clear he had no idea why I had played the speech on my cassette player. He thought I enjoyed it and sought inspiration from it. Now, in the absence of the cassette player, he became the speaker for me.

He looked away, down the street.

I was not used to passing time in the company of the kind of bad-mannered, drunk, reckless and lowly people who loitered around the Shaheed Minar. They smelled of burned meat and rotten tomatoes. All poor people smelled that way, I thought. It wasn't because they hadn't had a bath in weeks. The insides of their heads were rotten. Like the inside of my own head was rotten now. My feet were soiled. There was a layer of dust on my cheeks and neck. It was madness to leave the flat, but I was bored. Though I was sure most people would not recognize me, I did not want to broadcast to them that Nur Hussain and I were together, and that at that moment I belonged exactly where he belonged.

'You are drawing attention,' I said. 'Sit down. Sit down right now, or I am leaving.'

My warning had no effect on him.

He was not an introvert after all – at least not as introverted as I had thought. He walked away from me, stood before the columns of the Minar with glimmering eyes and continued to speak. Every word exploded in his mouth and came out through his lips with an extraordinary vigour. He spoke only the part I had played on the cassette player. Then he sat down beside me and said it would never happen again; but seeing I was still gloomy, he got up to speak once more, as if he would not stop until I smiled. Small slum-children sitting on the dusty ground raised their heads to him, and a few rickshaw-*wallahs* pulled the brakes gently and stopped to listen. Some pedestrians paused to join the crowd, and shopkeepers pushed their heads through windows to see what was going on.

He had an extraordinary power – I felt it under my skin. Though he spoke only a few sentences, it seemed he was able to rouse his audience exactly as Sheikh Mujib had done. He ended with '*Joy Bangla'* and the crowd shouted back: '*Joy Bangla!'*

As he came to sit beside me, I pulled away. 'You don't know me,' I said to him. 'Don't pretend that you do. The person you see before you now is not the real person I am. You want to embarrass yourself, go ahead, do it; nobody will stop you. But don't you ever do things that I am uncomfortable with. You understand me?'

A woman I had seen collecting empty glass bottles from city drains and drying them on the concrete pavement slapped her two little boys when they began fighting. 'Tell us about the Liberation struggle,' she then said to Nur Hussain. 'Tell us something about our future.' Though he did not speak, she opened the knot of her *sari* and threw a coin at his feet as a token of her respect for him. 'Take this money, please,' she said. 'Protect our Motherland.' Others in the crowd followed her. They threw whatever little money they had. I watched Nur Hussain as he bent down and collected the coins one by one, frequently looking up at me with a worried face.

I wished I had never allowed him into my house. Who would steal from a beggar? I sat there, hiding my face behind my palm, disgust filling my throat. A small line of sweat appeared on my nose. I could imagine people were looking at me instead of at him, although he had been doing the speaking. Who is this person, they were asking in their minds. Is he suffering from a serious mental disorder? What is he doing here with that imbecile? I could not raise my eyes to look at them, to answer their contempt for me.

Then we walked home, silently, I before him, following the narrow neighbourhood street lit momentarily by the lanterns on passing rickshaws. Through that light, I looked back. He was pressing the coins to his chest.

At home he poured the coins on the kitchen table and went to his room. He did not count them. Neither did I

– until after supper, when I was sure he was asleep. I did not know what was happening to me, but I found myself closing the kitchen door, cleaning the coins on a wet towel and counting them several times. The coins, many of them featuring Sheikh Mujib's portrait, shone in the light.

That night, and three more nights after that, I sat at the table until midnight. My head ached. Too many thoughts surfaced there. Was it pity in people's minds that compelled them to throw their money at him when they needed it more than he did? He had not actually extended his hands to them to receive their coins, but was he indirectly begging from them in the name of Sheikh Mujib because I was not in a position to help him anymore? Did he feel real love for Sheikh Mujib when he recited the speech, which helped him imitate his voice so enthusiastically, while I felt nothing as I listened to it on my cassette player?

When I looked at Nur Hussain the following morning, I thought he looked rather like Sheikh Mujib. My heart shook, but I quickly gathered myself. After a few hours, I looked at him again in the daylight as he stood at the window. He did have a certain resemblance to Sheikh Mujib, I had to admit. I believed the woman was right. She did a very natural thing: she admired him. I believed the crowd knew what they were doing when they sacrificed their precious coins.

I played the speech again, this time not to understand the inner meaning of Sheikh Mujib's words, but to see if Nur Hussain was present in his voice. I did not have to play it for long. The opening sentences were enough. He was there, in an unbelievably unambiguous way. It would not be easy to separate them by listening to their voices only, I thought. Nur was Sheikh Mujib's copy – a true, honest, reliable and enviable copy.

'I am sorry for what I did,' he said on the fourth day. 'I did something that was very painful for you. I should have controlled myself. If you want, I can go back to the Shaheed Minar and return the money. Maybe the exact same people will not be there, but whoever is there would be grateful to receive one or two coins.'

He rose, for I did not answer. He took his shirt, slowly collected the coins in his pocket and prepared to leave.

'It is not necessary anymore,' I said. He looked back, surprised. 'Yes.' I sat on the sofa, looking for an easy way to communicate with him. 'I do not know what I am thinking,' I said, after a long pause, 'but I am thinking something. I cannot tell even if you as a person would like to be associated with it, though it is about you and involves you. But I will explain it to you in detail, so that you know what is what, and you can pull me back if I appear unreasonable and crazy. Come. Sit.'

8

THE SPEECH

From my pile of books I pulled out a booklet published during the war. It was called *Motherland* and contained Sheikh Mujib's entire speech. I separated the relevant pages and glued them to the wall. Nur Hussain began to read immediately.

I could see he was not good at reading. Sometimes he sounded out every syllable of a word, but could not connect them together to pronounce it correctly. He even forgot the sentences he had known by heart when he enunciated the words syllable by syllable at my request.

'Minor problems,' I said, like an experienced adult-education instructor who knew numerous tactics to counter learning disabilities. He should not worry. It was only a few hours' job. I told him I would read the speech end to end so that he could see it was not intimidating at all as a piece of text. There was nothing to panic about. I took several deep breaths and began. He sat attentively, looking at me. I would show him how Sheikh Mujib spoke it in his own way.

Sheikh Mujib did not pronounce all the words correctly, following the standard rules of our language; but was able to produce beautiful music in the speech, which helped people appreciate his spirit. His commitment appeared heartfelt to them. He used judicious repetition, short sentences and striking but easily relatable images to make his content easier to grasp.

When I finished, Nur was delighted. It was the first time he had heard the speech in full.

'Can you memorize the speech?' I asked.

'Absolutely.'

He wanted only three days. Every comma and semicolon would be in the exact place, he said, and began reading.

He did memorize the whole speech in three days, startling me further. I sat before him and heard him several times. I made notes. It was not easy to capture the tone of such a speech in its entirety, especially when there was no audience before us. But he made it, though with some limitations. 'Here you must pause,' I said. 'Give your listeners time to digest your words. It is noisy out there, and not everyone can think quickly. Listen.' I played the sentence on the cassette player. He spoke again, and paused. 'Longer,' I said. 'A little bit longer, please. If people do not understand you, they will not respond correctly. If they do not respond correctly, the purpose is lost.' I reversed the cassette and played it again for him. 'You see?' He paused longer and asked if that was enough. 'Not enough,' I said, and replayed the tape before saying the sentence myself.

He laughed at himself for using shorter pauses. He laughed, and then became serious and finally terrified, as if Sheikh Mujib would not forgive him for misreading his speech. 'Becoming an orator needs patience and humility,' I said. 'Empathy is a great virtue.'

When he had the pauses right – sooner than I had anticipated – I turned my focus to getting him to speak faster or slower, to create a sense of enthusiasm, and adding easily executable dramatic effects where applicable. It was no use explaining to him what adjectives or adverbs or prepositions were, or how Sheikh Mujib had used them in his speech as tools of persuasion and dynamism. He would not be able to analyze the structural components of a piece of writing as a professional grammarian would. Nor was it necessary. He did not need to know what complex political, philosophical, psychological, historical or patriotic causes or traumas compelled Sheikh Mujib to produce his words. The style was already decided. The meaning was already set. I wanted to go through the words with Nur, again and again, so that he received them experientially. He was an audio-kinaesthetic learner, as far as I could discern; hearing was his best method. We had the cassette player, which was helping us greatly; now we needed to maintain some movement: probably walking around the room, or speaking in the dark, standing on the road.

'Excellent,' I said in the end. 'Well done. Today you have accomplished something that will define the rest of your life. Today you are ready to please anyone anywhere in the country with your ingenuity. You are not just a boy anymore. You are in contact with the heart and the soul of this land. There is no wall before you. Nothing can slow you down.'

But he must continue practising, I said. He must know where he was guiding his audience. On the one side were the Pakistanis who discriminated against us by imposing their will, and on the other side the dream of a free Bangladesh, the right to choose our destiny – Sheikh Mujib utilized this compare-and-contrast system of communication so effectively that seventy million Bangladeshis could not help but begin waging a passionate and immediate struggle for liberation. He had given them a choice. They knew instantly what to do.

One of the aspects of the speech I thought would be difficult to explain actually took very little time. 'How many voices do you notice in that speech?' I asked.

'Why, one,' Nur said. 'Wasn't it Sheikh Mujib who delivered the whole speech?'

That was not a correct answer, but that was also not an unintelligent answer. I was ready to explain.

Sheikh Mujib delivered the whole speech, I said, but if Nur looked carefully he would see several Sheikh Mujibs in action: one of them was sympathetic, one was analytical, one a rebel and one a villager who spoke in a local dialect. (I had told him before of Sheikh Mujib the poet, who spoke with infectious enthusiasm.) All those voices came together and created an organic whole – Sheikh Mujib the person. To produce the speech successfully, one would need to give careful attention to all those voices. I wanted to give him an example by quoting a specific sentence from the speech, but he interrupted and said: 'For example, *I have come before you today with a heavy heart.* Wasn't Sheikh Mujib sympathizing with the people of Bangladesh in this opening line? Wasn't he suffering because people in general were suffering under Pakistani rule?'

He practised all day long. His words echoed off the walls and bounced off my ears. I knew he was sure to win the confidence of his audience. I could visualize people clapping, coins coming out of their pockets.

9
AT THE BARBER'S

My objective was to present Nur Hussain in the most effective manner possible before the target audience, so that at the end of the day even the most destitute among them would feel they were taking something home in exchange for their coins. As far as I could understand, he had completed only one major requirement by memorizing Sheikh Mujib's speech. Although he had exceeded my expectations, it would really not amount to anything until the other requirements were duly fulfilled as well. If people wanted to hear Sheikh Mujib speak, they could play cassettes of his speeches. These were available in every electronics shop and convenience store. Even vegetable stalls sold them. If people did not own a cassette player, they could sit at a restaurant, order a cup of tea and enjoy the speech for a few minutes. No restaurant manager in the country would dare refuse to play that speech for a customer. That was not what we were planning. We were planning a live presentation. A life-size Sheikh Mujib would stand on the podium, walk, move his arms, automatically raise his voice, empathize and speak from his heart.

Therefore, the second requirement: attending to his look.

This included changing hairstyles. One must not think it was someone speaking like Sheikh Mujib; he must be present through Nur Hussain. After all, we were talking about a man whom everyone knew, who was agreeable, ardent, confident and calm. Imitating his speaking style would not be easy. It would not be like singing for people's entertainment in a noisy, crowded market under a gloomy sky to sell poisonous pesticides or smelly aphrodisiacs. There would be no instrumental accompaniment, no unconnected songs from Lata Mangeshkar, no monkey dance, no snake charmer in action, no jokes from Gopal Bhar, no displays of the sort commonly used to evoke pity by showing shockingly deformed and bizarre human faces. Nur Hussain would have to please people all by himself.

I took him to the barbershop down the street. I told him not to be nervous; it would be done before he knew it. We were not shaving his head. 'Relax. We only need some minor adjustments.'

Then I explained to the barber what type of cut we wanted. 'Look at that picture,' I said, pointing at the portrait of Sheikh Mujib over the looking glass. 'Look at every line, every curve and every shade minutely.' Did he see how Sheikh Mujib had his hair pushed back in the front, clearing his forehead? And the sideburns, those Victorian ultra-conservative sideburns, that balanced his facial features?

'That is what we want. Like the hair of Sheikh Mujib; nothing more, nothing less.'

The barber, confused and hesitant, looked at me and then at Nur Hussain and finally at the portrait. Whenever anyone requested a particular hairstyle in this neighbourhood, he said, it was of a movie actor, for example, Razzak or Raj Kapoor, or something from the English catalogues – say,

Elvis Presley's ducktail and high pompadour. He could not believe the stoic Sheikh Mujib might occupy someone's imagination because of his hairstyle.

Sheikh Mujib has no hairstyle, he said, with a certain irritation. Were we joking? He had been a hairdresser all his life – no less than twenty years now – and in all that time there had not been a single moment when Sheikh Mujib's hairstyle had drawn his attention. Then he explained: Sheikh Mujib had no ears, no cheeks, no jaw, no nose, no mouth, no brows and no forehead. He was just a face, a face without features. When he looked at Sheikh Mujib, he saw himself. That happened to every citizen in the country. It was the person inside the heap of flesh who mattered. Besides, he elucidated, if Sheikh Mujib had a hairstyle, his barber would have been famous by now, considering his extraordinary rise through the years. Had anyone ever heard of any such hairstylist?

He was a rogue. A rogue with a quiet, gentle face. I had seen many in my life. 'You do whatever we ask you to do,' I told him. 'We are aware that Sheikh Mujib is not a fashion-conscious man, but we want his low-maintenance style.'

He sat on the stool, had a silent moment and then asked if we were not going to change our minds later. A man with Sheikh Mujib's hairstyle, but without his substance, would look awkward, if not funny, he warned.

Awkward or serious, he could leave that to us to consider. 'Keep your thoughts locked within your mind, if you have one. We are not here for idle curiosity alone. We have a purpose. You may go ahead.'

The barber observed Sheikh Mujib's portrait more closely and then sharpened his scissors on leather strips before beginning his job. Nur Hussain sat on the stool, closed his eyes and bent his head from side to side when the barber directed him to do so. I sat on another stool in the corner, where I could monitor the progress of the scissors.

Perhaps the barber thought he was doing an audacious job by creating Sheikh Mujib's style on someone who was not Sheikh Mujib. Perhaps he thought nobody should try to be like Sheikh Mujib, because that would undermine Sheikh Mujib as a person, as a leader and as a head of state. His face remained dark as he worked. He stopped several times, looked out the window, filled his lungs with fresh air and consulted the portrait before returning to his task. 'I don't know,' he muttered, 'I don't know. This is outrageous. This can't be happening. A very unusual day for a barber.' But he seemed to be comfortable with his work as he removed the black cape from Nur Hussain. He moved backwards, to the rear of the room, to look at him from a distance. Then he came back and lifted a mirror behind Nur to show him the back of his head.

Instead of looking in the mirror, Nur Hussain looked at me.

'That's the best I can do for you,' said the barber. 'If you don't like it, I'm sorry. You may find some other hairdresser next time. There are many on the main street.'

'You yourself should move to the main street,' I told him after observing Nur Hussain's head from a 360-degree angle. 'Or better yet, go to the Gulshan or Dhanmondi residential areas, where people buy style with heavy cash. You've done a fantastic job.'

The barber turned the mirror towards himself and looked at his smiling face.

Nur Hussain's own face became bright.

'Now give him a quick shave, will you?' I said. 'We don't have all day.'

He found a Balaka blade from the drawer.

'Look at me,' I said. 'Look at me. Do we look like two cheap village rascals arriving at the city port for the first time? Throw away that rubbish. Use your sharpest double-edge classic razor.' I also directed him as he opened the creamy lathering tube and poured water in a cup from a jar. I said: 'No, no, that is not going to work. Cold water? That would make his skin hard and beard stiff. Splash some warm water on his face, will you?'

He did not have a hot-water system at the shop, so I advised him to collect some from the tea stall next door. He had already considered us the worst of his customers, but I did not give him any chance to say a word. A man like him needed to be kept under constant pressure.

'Very good,' I said, when he returned. 'Now skim the brush back and forth across his cheek. Change to a circular motion. Good, good. Create a rich lather. Don't rush. Don't you irritate his skin. We don't want any shave bumps. That's it. Rinse your razor after every stroke. What are you doing? Are you crazy? Remove the clogged hair. Hygiene is the most important part of a man's grooming. Didn't anyone ever tell you that? Be very careful at the neck. Don't play with those pimples on the jaw. They are not ready to be popped. Now look at the portrait; observe, wait, think, remember. Time to trim his moustache. Comb it down, slowly. Don't be a butcher. Trim it there with gentle, downward strokes. Be extremely precise, will you? Haven't you eaten anything this week? Why is your hand trembling? Left side will be shorter – more, more – so that it is as high as the right side. Bravo. Now apply some aftershave balm.'

10

THE COAT

Now, the next requirement: the coat, the Mujib coat:
Sheikh Mujib's signature style.

It was a sleeveless black coat to be worn over a white
punjabi. Every Awami League supporter, worker and leader
had one. They wore it during party conventions, public
meetings and election campaigns, or just any time they went
out, at the tea stall with neighbours, at a marriage ceremony.
It was a demonstration of a person's loyalty to the Awami
League as a political party, and to Sheikh Mujib as its leader.
During the war we considered it a symbol of patriotism.
Only those opposed to independence would speak ill of it.
More recently, people had started to wear that coat when
they went to pray at the mosque. They wore it during Eid
festivals and even bought it for their children, who did not
know why they had to wear a black coat on a beautiful,
festive day. Some mosque assistants who called for prayers
had also been seen to wear it; some said it made their voice
deeper and sincere, like Sheikh Mujib's, something much
admired within the spiritual community.

The coat gave Sheikh Mujib a graceful look. It made him
look wise and solemn. Wearing that coat, he could easily

59

stand beside Gandhi, Castro, Mao Tse Tung or any other world leader of similar stature. Nations of the world first saw it when he spoke at the UN General Assembly. Some called it an opportunity to spread his revolutionary image abroad, to internationalize his call for independence for all oppressed peoples of the world. A few weeks after the assembly, a front-page photograph in a Bengali newspaper showed a farmer in rural Bolivia cultivating his land, wearing a Mujib coat. The country looked like our country: the water, the fields, the trees, the winding village paths and the sky. Only the man's skin colour was different; he looked whitish. But that difference was lost under the charm of the Mujib coat. The coat had the power to make all men look the same – strong and unafraid in the quest for freedom.

Another newspaper in Dhaka had published a feature article on the coat in its fashion section. Women's *salwar*, *kameez* and cloaks were pushed down to the bottom of the page to make room for it. The paper printed a picture of Sheikh Mujib sitting on a sofa in the comfort of his living room, the coat buttoned to the neck. There were two other pictures beneath it. One showed him sitting with noted Awami League leaders, all of them wearing that coat. That was to suggest the coat's social acceptance – it was as professional as any coat worn in the West. It was dressing with a message: unity among colleagues. Another picture showed a folded coat with a Montegrappa Privilege Gioiello Peacock silver fountain pen and a pair of spectacles placed upon it. That picture of luxury depicted the coat as a component of a sophisticated lifestyle. The writer of the article, titled 'Men's Wardrobe', also placed the coat into historical perspective. Whereas all other coats were designed to be worn with ties, the Mujib coat was *never* to be worn with a tie; and it was the only coat that was sleeveless. 'From Bangladesh to the world – a style to admire,' read a caption.

I took Nur Hussain to a young tailor known for being inexpensive. As far as I could tell from the outfits he had on display, he specialized in tailoring for ladies. There were *lehengas* swinging from wooden hangers; there were *ghagras* and *cholis*. But when I asked him if he could make us a coat, he agreed graciously and said he had had the good luck to examine the tailoring techniques of a Mujib coat not long ago, when he was an assistant at another tailoring house. It would not be difficult to make one by himself. I agreed. He measured Nur Hussain's chest, neck and the distance between his neck and the waistline, and gave us a rough idea how much the cloth and tailoring might cost us. It was not a fortune, I found; quite within my capacity. I knew that if I wanted to present Nur Hussain before a crowd in a professional manner, I would have to be prepared to invest a little money. It was a must.

All the same, I pressed the tailor to lower the price, citing his inexperience. 'The Mujib coat is not the dress of the past,' I argued. 'It is the dress of the future. There may come a time when you will make only this type of coat, nothing else. You will forget what a *lehenga* is. You will say that only non-smart tailors make ladieswear; a tailor like you goes for something extraordinary. I am offering you a chance to do exactly that. I am giving you a chance to see your future. It is up to you to accept it or not.'

I told him I could spend only seventy per cent of what he was asking for. He pushed a little, and we settled for seventy-five per cent. The coat would be ready in a week, he said. He had a bridal dress to deliver first. I bargained again: 'A *week*? You cannot be serious. Why do you need a week? Just fold the piece of cloth, cut it with scissors and then quickly put a couple of buttons down the front; anyone can do that before afternoon tea. We liberated fifty-six thousand square miles of homeland in nine months; now he wants as long as seven days to make a two-foot coat!'

He understood my impatience and halved the delivery time.

I could not wait that long, either. I went to him the evening of the second day to ask if he was working on it, whether or not he needed to take more measurements; on the third evening I went to see if he had finished, if he needed a hand to fix the buttons. He was displeased to see me and said I was slowing him down by visiting him without notice.

On the fourth morning I woke up, and the first thing I did was remind Nur Hussain it was our delivery day; we must be at the tailor's as soon as possible, and would eat breakfast upon our return. The breakfast would taste more delicious if we had the coat with us. He got ready instantly.

It was not the most ideal coat I had ever seen. It did not fit him at the waist. There were also just too many buttons, and the distance between them was not equal. The material was too soft for a coat. The two bottom pockets were saggy. But the coat was black, and Nur Hussain liked it. It was his first coat ever. Naturally, I silenced my dissatisfaction. 'Thank you,' I told the tailor as he sat on his cot with great satisfaction on his face. 'Thank you, you've done a terrific job. You have been able to hide your age under your craftsmanship. You will make many more coats after this, I am sure. Once Sheikh Mujib knows it is you who have made this coat, he may order a pair for himself. Then you will be recognized across the country. Never be nervous to welcome new challenges.'

Then we went to the clothing store to buy a *punjabi* shirt. I sat before the cashier, money in hand. One of the assistants spread several *punjabis* before Nur Hussain. He tried a couple and chose one from the Mohammedia brand. I paid the money.

At home he put on the *punjabi* and buttoned the coat up to his neck. When he pushed his hair back with his fingers and stood before me, I knew we were almost there.

11

THE SPECTACLES,
THE PIPE AND SOME NECESSARY ADVICE

That same day, I bought Nur a pair of spectacles with thick black frames from a newly established optician. The automatic glass door opened before us. Soft music played. We walked on the thin carpet and went directly to the sales counter. The salesperson was an old man with long hair, a long beard and a white gown over a white collared shirt. He asked if we had a prescription, and whether or not we were looking for vision correction.

'Prescription? Vision correction? What are you talking about?'

He gestured at the 'Schedule an Exam' poster on the wall. It read: *When it comes to protecting your eyes, our eye care specialists make your experience easy.* 'Eye exam provides a comprehensive picture of your visual ability,' he said. 'It is key to your proper eye health. Your vision may change significantly but you may not feel the slightest pain in your heart.'

I liked the fact that he behaved so politely with us. Manners of this standard were not seen in many places nowadays.

After walking across a whole country and witnessing all the destruction caused by the war, you came to him and found he was living in a sane world. There was no problem here. Everything was clean, professional and scientific. Optometrists were working hard to treat people's vision problems. Brand-name spectacles, designer and prescription sunglasses filled the revolving shelves. The benefits of freedom had started to show.

'No,' I said. 'Just for everyday comfort, for eye protection against flying dust; full-frame with supporting pads on the bridge, if possible. No smoky quartz or reading stones.'

'Any history of myasthenia gravis, diabetes or athero-sclerosis?'

'Does he look like he requires assistance with walking? What do you people think you are? For God's sake. No, nothing of that sort.'

He thought for a few moments and then directed us to one of the cabinets in the front.

The vintage-style plastic spectacles sat on Nur Hussain's nose like a beautiful ornament. They flattered his face. The black-toned arms clasped his ears perfectly. An absolute fashion statement, I thought. Once combined with the whiteness of the *punjabi* and the blackness of the coat, the specs would shine.

'Our bestselling item,' the man said. 'Suits freethinking, creative individuals. Comes with a manufacturer's warranty. If you are not hundred per cent satisfied with your purchase, bring it back within ninety days. No questions asked. And what about you?'

'What about me?'

'You don't wear glasses?'

'Why would I wear glasses?'

'To see clearly. To protect what you are left with.'

I drew near him. 'Listen,' I said, 'I do not want to upset you by criticizing you for your attitude. I also do not want to say that maybe, maybe you are too old for this job. Consider this: first you tried to invent a disease for him which he did not have, so that you could press us to undergo some unnecessary tests. For courtesy's sake we have overlooked it. And now you are saying I do not see clearly, I need to get glasses. What do you mean to say?'

'Nothing,' he said, as his face turned gloomy. 'Nothing.' He walked quietly to the main sales counter and spent a long time producing a receipt for us. Then, as we were ready to leave, he smiled suddenly. 'I do a lot of push-sales,' he said. 'That's why they say I am a good salesman. Hope you didn't mind.'

A person of that character did not deserve to be honoured with a response.

Next I bought Nur Hussain a nine-inch, handcrafted walnut-wood tobacco pipe. Sturdy, thick, clean-looking, its bowl was one inch in diameter and one inch deep. It was detachable into three sections for easy cleaning. The seller said the pipe might smell strongly of smoke after being used, and needed to be cleaned more frequently than other pipes, but I did not want to spend a lot on this either. Nur Hussain was not going to smoke tobacco. Our main purpose was to mount a charade. I showed Nur a photograph of Sheikh Mujib holding a pipe between his lips.

'That's what you'll do. That's what people want to see. You want to try? Go ahead.'

The pipe made him look older than he was. How old was Sheikh Mujib at the time he gave the historic 7 March speech? Fifty-one, if he was born in 1920. The pipe made Nur Hussain look at least forty. He would put it in his mouth after he had finished the speech, and would not remove it until after the crowd stopped throwing coins at his feet and we had found a rickshaw to take us home.

The hair, the moustache, the coat, the *punjabi*, the spectacles and the pipe – all the elements were there now, a purposeful combination ready to function and serve. Whatever their standard, they were there. All that was left was to lay down a few important rules, without which the props would not bring the expected results. First: Nur Hussain must control his desire to speak after delivering the speech. 'No socializing,' I said. 'Absolutely no socializing of any sort.' Sheikh Mujib had a hundred things to do every day. He would not speak with people individually, and anything important he had to say would have already been said in his speech. The public must be satisfied with hearing just that. If they wanted to speak to him, to tell him about their problems, they had to follow official protocol or contact the relevant department of the prime minister's office. We would tell them where that office was. Obviously, it would be our flat.

The second rule I set was that he would not eat anything in public – for example, in a restaurant or tea stall. Nor would he bite into a piece of sugarcane while on the street, something young people like him did unknowingly. 'Any eating must be done at home, in private.' Nobody ever saw Sheikh Mujib eat. Nobody knew how he looked while eating.

Being seen eating would reveal the fact that Nur Hussain was not, after all, different from anyone down the road. Eating in public would also raise the question of what kind of food Sheikh Mujib ate, Prime Minister that he was. If he ate what refugees ate, there would be no difference between them; rigorous confidentiality must therefore be maintained.

The next rule was that he would not eat fish with hard bones that could get stuck in his throat, causing choking and bleeding. Attempting to remove the bones with his fingers could cause further damage. He must also chew his food properly before swallowing, which would aid proper digestion and keep him in good health to deliver the speech most attentively.

He must go to sleep on time, and sleep enough to maintain a balanced temperament.

12

COUNTING COINS

We made a good team, he and I. I made the plans, he delivered the speech. I selected the venues, he followed me without question – even when it was too hot and the humidity was high and the *punjabi* was damp with sweat and the coat proved the most impractical piece of clothing to wear. I collected the coins, counted them three times and told him how much we had made; he went to bed peacefully, with trust.

Soon the time came when I selected his food and checked the size of the potatoes; he ate only after I approved them. It appeared to be simple fastidiousness on my part. I was controlling his life, he might say. I was standing between him and self-determination. But I believed it was my duty to make sure he realized how precious his voice was for us, and how quickly we might turn into nothing if we did not proceed carefully. Destruction was never very far from us. We saw it every day when we went out to speak, when we spoke, when we returned home after speaking. We had to be extra-cautious. He understood me; that was why he never disputed my decisions.

We went out almost every day now, and within a few weeks covered all the local areas, some more than once.

Then we moved out farther, closer to the bus stand, the overpass on the highway, the district court building, the old book market and the pharmacy square. We attended every day of the week-long city fair and spoke on the same spot several times, always to the great elation of our audience. With every delivery Nur became better, more comfortable and natural, and every time he spoke our pockets filled with coins.

The unit controller of the city fair treated us with respect. Why wouldn't he? He wanted his part of the fair to be filled with visitors, especially in the morning hours, when the city refused to wake up. He came to us on the third evening and proposed we come early the following day and speak. With his delivery, Nur Hussain could pull the limited number of visitors from other units to this part of the fair. That might help the businesses make some good money right at the start of the day.

'Our pleasure,' I said. 'We'll come here at nine sharp tomorrow, when the fair opens. We'll do the speech as many times as needed. But you may ask your business partners to be generous to us. They might send someone with a few coins for us before night falls. Wouldn't it look odd if they made money because of us, but did not share it *with* us?'

Nur Hussain always kept a copy of the speech in his pocket. Sometimes he read it loudly between his performances, usually while sitting in a rickshaw. That happened when he remembered he had skipped a sentence or a paragraph during the speech. Even though I had heard him many times, and had read the speech many times before, I did not notice what he had skipped. My attention was locked on the space before him, that small, warm circular space where the crowd would throw their coins. I had seen him look at that solemn space once or twice while standing with the pipe in his mouth. That was all. It was my space; I knew what was happening there. I had to make sure that it protected us, and that it was well-protected. I kept it clean and threw some coins from my pocket onto a handkerchief before he began speaking, so the crowd knew what to do.

But he was a perfectionist. Failing to maintain the proper sequence of paragraphs in the speech worried him. That anxiety came from his heart and covered his face with irritation. I had seen him refuse food or drink when it happened. Consulting the copy in his pocket did not always remove the irritation. I told him he mustn't speak *like* Sheikh Mujib, because he *was* Sheikh Mujib. I told him he must speak without worry, without bothering about what he had skipped. If Sheikh Mujib was worried, he would not have been a pioneer. He would have scared his audience. His political disciples would have thought he was not in control, that he was not the man they wanted to trust with the future of the country.

'I cannot control my mind,' Nur said, worrying me more. 'I speak a sentence and I look at the people before me. I get angry when I see the same people sitting before me hour after hour. If they follow me carefully, they may understand I am speaking the same paragraphs in many different ways.'

He sat looking at me, searching for a solution. The crowd did not have the speech memorized by heart, I said, and they were not there to test him. They gathered before him because of the feeling they had experienced when Sheikh Mujib spoke on 7 March. His job was to feed their imaginations, to recreate that exact Mujibesque feeling by adding words to words, by stacking passion upon passion;

minor changes in the order of paragraphs, or speaking an incomplete paragraph, did not harm anything. He was doing a great job, I said, and to give him courage I scratched out some sentences from the speech and let him read it.

'See,' I explained, 'even after those brutal deletions, the message of the speech remains the same.'

He looked at me with utter disbelief, as if nobody had the right to modify the words of Sheikh Mujib. I had to respond reasonably. 'Does the Awami League play the speech in full on Victory Day?' I asked. 'They do not. They repeat the most effective passages from his speech whenever they need to. They have edited him more brutally than anybody else. Then why should you concern yourself about losing a few sentences?'

'It wouldn't bother you if I skipped something?' he asked.

'Not at all,' I said. 'Not at all.' I could not tell from where he had got the idea. I was surprised, but there was no time to show my surprise at that moment; he needed to be reassured immediately. 'Who cares about Sheikh Mujib,' I said, 'when we are in the field? I do not. This is business. I do not care even about the people who sit before us. They are nationalists and will accept the Devil as a prophet if Sheikh Mujib recommends it. Becoming a nationalist is not a matter of decision; it means one has locked one's mind forever. No reason or practical advice or evidence is strong enough to unlock it. These people are in a trance – the indolent, seductive trance of Bengali nationalism. We are creating a trance within that trance so that they reach into their pockets. Whatever you speak or do not speak will not move them from it.'

Because of my intervention, Sheikh Mujib's speech became shorter and shorter in Nur Hussain's voice day after day.

Sometimes he began with *'Joy Bangla'* and ended with *'Joy Bangla'*. Sometimes he continued chanting *'Joy Bangla'* until he believed the crowd had thrown enough coins. A few times he ended the speech in the middle and then, going back, uttered some popular quotations before chanting *'Joy Bangla'* to end it. That happened towards the end of the day when he felt tired, but I would push him hard, telling him repeatedly that we had at least three more groups to speak to before going home. Sometimes it happened that he chanted *'Joy Bangla'* in the middle of the speech to draw the attention of people who had stopped on their way, and started again from the beginning. Then there was the rain. It came suddenly. Sometimes it came with thunder and lightning, when he was halfway through the speech. He had to chant *'Joy Bangla'* immediately, so that the crowd had enough time to throw coins before running into a shop, a tea stall or the nearest post office.

I told him that he was sure to satisfy the crowd as long as he delivered the passage where Sheikh Mujib said: *'We had given blood in 1952, we had won a mandate in 1954, but the Pakistani military government continued to enslave us year after year.'* Did he think a longer speech generated more money? My calculations did not say so. More money depended on visiting more places, speaking to more crowds. Smaller crowds were better, I said; people standing at the back of large gatherings did not come forward to throw coins. Except for one or two, they moved on once he finished the speech.

Every time he spoke to a crowd, I surveyed the people and watched who threw coins. I applied a value system to their clothes, their sense of cleanliness and their ways of expressing excitement. I could tell if they were moved by his speech, if they believed in what he said, if they were having some sort of conversation with themselves.

By observing the formation of the crowd, I came to a conclusion. If the crowd consisted of poor, illiterate, working-class people, unemployed, rootless people, people from slums, rescued from mudslides, devastated by cyclones, we earned more coins than when moneyed, middle-class, educated people working downtown stopped to listen. I saw shopkeepers extend their heads out their windows, but never saw them put their hands in the cash counter to take a coin out for us. At best, they saluted us when we passed and offered us *paan*. I also noticed, regretfully, that only the poor heard the speech from beginning to end attentively and applauded Nur Hussain after it ended, while the educated stood at some distance, listened to a sentence or two and then went on their way.

The poor sometimes became tearful; they wanted to touch Nur Hussain's hands to receive his blessings. Some even ran closer to embrace him, wearing their filthy clothes. Often I had to stand between him and them. I had to tell them he had another speech elsewhere, that his coat mustn't be soiled. They would not give up until I embraced them on his behalf.

I hated those who did not throw coins at us. Most of all I hated the clean ones, who gave me the impression that they understood our trick. Sometimes I thought they were accusing us of cheating people. They stood for one or two minutes, then left. Why did they stop for such a short time? Because of the magnetic power of the speech. Then why did they leave? The only answer I could come up with was they did not need a sovereign country; they did not need Sheikh Mujib's leadership. They did well during the British period and under Pakistani dictators, and they would do well if the country fell to dictatorship again. They were egoistical and snobbish. I believed they had not gone to war, and had never spoken to a freedom fighter as I had.

My observation affected our strategy to a large extent. I selected smaller streets, shantytowns and the most polluted and densely populated areas of the city, instead of the popular markets where petty-minded, condescending, well-off people shopped.

It worked.

13

A STORY FOR THE PRESS

As selecting a venue was my responsibility, I would
sometimes go out alone. I would walk from street
to street, neighbourhood to neighbourhood, looking for
places with floating crowds. I would survey which spot in
the slum was most easily accessible, where homeless people
gathered to pass their idle noon, where they sat to play cards.
Sometimes I would take a bus and sit in a corner seat looking
through the window, watching people milling about on the
pavement, walking into stores, waiting in the sun for buses.
I would take notes in a small notebook and review them
before going to sleep, selecting the most suitable venues for
the next few days.

Sometimes, while on these tours, I would have a conversation with myself. I would take a hard look at my life,
at my career, and then review what I was doing with Nur
Hussain. Just months earlier, I had been a journalist. I had
responsibilities, a set of properly defined tasks to perform
every day. I had a dream, and I could speak about my dream.
I was surrounded by people who understood what I thought
– at least I believed so. There was excitement in it, if not
satisfaction.

Now I had no plan. Most shamefully, I was living off someone else's ability to earn. I could well be on the street tomorrow, one more rootless person in the company of thousands of rootless people, without a future, without any goal. In addition, I was playing with people's helplessness. With a fake Sheikh Mujib I was manufacturing dreams for them. I was convincing them that the future was behind us. It had frozen the moment Sheikh Mujib opened his mouth in 1971; now we must live in the past forever. We must rot there year after year after year.

As the bus moved past the slums, I imagined myself living in one of the tents I saw, passing a fortnight without a bath, looking hungrily at colourful food in nearby luxury restaurants, stealing from someone just as hungry as I was. I envisioned myself walking in the rain, waking up in the rain in the middle of the night, then running to look for shelter for my children – perhaps inside abandoned sewer pipes, beneath the unsafe railway bridge, in the deserted stables behind the hospital morgue, all places I had seen crowded with hundreds of ill-fated people.

Sometimes I thought I saw someone sitting on the pavement looking at the sun, disconnected from the chaos around him and forgetful of his clothes. His brain chemistry had changed. His ability to cope with stress had been reduced. No war, abuse, disaster, violence, accident or medical emergency could distract him. He would not know if the high wind from the northwest stole his body parts one by one, finally evaporating him one sunny day. I believed I knew that man, had known him for years. He lived with me, wore my clothes, used the same toilet, drew his eyes across the same newspaper columns, knew everything about me. I looked at him more closely as the bus moved forward. It was a flash, just a flash, but I knew I was looking at myself. My body became cold with fear, my heart ached, and after that I saw nothing until the bus reached its destination and the conductor freed me from a pathological state of numbness by shaking my shoulder.

Sometimes I would buy a copy of *The Freedom Fighter* and scan it from end to end, reading the reports, features, editorials, comments, columns. I would take my time. After all, this was the world I knew best. I turned to the last page and checked the masthead at the bottom to see if Lutfuzzaman Babul was still its editor. He was. Why was it so difficult for him to see what I saw? Why couldn't he recognize the ever-changing political reality of the nation?

I went to *The Freedom Fighter* that week. Lutfuzzaman Babul was in; he greeted me warmly and led me into his office.

We spoke about the weather: how hot the summer was, how chilly the winter was going to be. He offered me tea for old times' sake and pushed his pad and pen aside, as he used to do when he was in a good mood.

He knew what I was doing. He hesitated to talk about it, filled the silences by scratching the backs of his hands, cleaning the surface of the table with a feathery brush, checking the time on the wall clock every second minute. Finally, he broke his silence when I told him that I was not ashamed of myself: 'Everyone has to do something for survival, but that something does not have to define the real character of a person. I am what my head tells me I am. I am what my feelings say I am. I do not depend on anyone's approval.'

'Exactly,' he said. 'That's what I tell my staff all the time. A person cannot be anything until he knows what he is, and he can be anything when someone inside him says what he is not. But they are rude, immature, very unprofessional people to deal with; they do not believe me. They say: "Why is Khaleque Biswas doing this? Has he lost his mind? Does he want to embarrass all journalists in the country? If he cannot find employment as a reporter, let him serve as a compositor, a distributor, a news-stand man, a paperboy. Is it good for him to leave the industry without looking for an opportunity because he can earn more money by entertaining beggars? Lutfuzzaman Babul, you're praising him for what he is not. You are just wasting words. Maybe you can send a message to him. Maybe you can explain to him that the last thing the country now needs is confusion, speeches about authority and governance. People have suffered a lot; let them have some rest now." I tell them they don't know you as I do. I tell them they should not underestimate Khaleque Biswas; he'll always be worth a piece of gold, not like them – shallow, cheap, foul-mouthed fraudsters. I tell them Nur Hussain is a brilliant addition to our political scene. His is an extraordinary story. It is not about rags to riches – what they all expect it to be, so that they can make big headlines – but about anonymity and remembrance. He questions our collective memory, and highlights the tension between our political aspirations and political reality. It is interesting to notice how geniuses find their way into the world and stun a whole generation of people with their vitality and imagination.'

I told him that meeting Nur Hussain had been an extraordinary event for me, and that he had extended my horizons: 'Without him I might not have seen what I now see. It is because of him that I understand what it means to be one of the people, or even deeper – to see how their minds work, and why they dare to trade their last coin for a slice of an obsolete dream.'

He looked for something in his drawer, but seemed to have not found it. 'When I heard the story from one of my reporters,' he said, 'I told him: let us follow Khaleque Biswas. He may not be working with us anymore, but we know what he can accomplish; let us follow the story closely. Maybe we'll hire him back; we won't be in this downturn for long.' He searched his drawer again, and again he failed. 'If there is any chance that we can help him to say what he wants to say, it is our duty to help him. He was one of our founding reporters and he did so many good things for us during the war.'

I grew irritated; what was he trying to do, blind me with these sugary words? 'I'm not here to talk about myself, though I've done a lot of that,' I said sternly. 'I want to talk about Nur Hussain. He's the speaker and far more important than me. I want to talk about what his speaking means for me, for you, for anyone for that matter, including Sheikh Mujib.'

If it had been during the war, he would have locked the door immediately and pulled his chair closer to mine. He would have asked, in whispers, as if we were engaged in some clandestine projects, what amazing new ideas I had come across, what my point was, if I had enough information, if my sources were genuine, if he should send a photographer to take a quick snap, how fast I would be able to give my thoughts written shape. I would not be allowed to leave my desk until the story was ready, he would have added; if it was to be a late night, let it be a late night. What was one person's suffering compared to keeping a whole country waiting? But now he sat with his hands together, fingers between fingers, boorish, unmannerly.

I gave him an article I had written about Nur Hussain. 'This is an exclusive,' I said. I put the envelope before him and told him I had contextualized Nur Hussain within our broader national background, analyzed him as a man on the road who had no clear idea what freedom meant for him and what his life would be like a few years from now. I had concluded that a fake Sheikh Mujib like him was an indication of our political malady; that the number of fake Sheikh Mujibs would rise if the real Sheikh Mujib failed to act, to prove his worth. People had not fought to live on pavements; they had not sacrificed their sons and daughters in a devastating war to go hungry and to remain unattended in sickness. The course of events had cast huge doubts over our country's leadership. Nature did not understand what it was doing to people by increasing the heat of the sun; nature did not have feelings. Pakistanis had not understood what they were doing by oppressing us, because they never understood the real value of freedom; they had always lived under generals and dictators. But Sheikh Mujib must know what harmed people, because he was a leader of the people; they trusted him, believed in his ability to lead and provide. An unthinkably dangerous situation would arise if Sheikh Mujib failed to administer the country as a visionary leader, reflecting the desires of its people. We might even end up in a civil war.

'I wanted to show you the instructions I gave to the reporter whom I've advised to follow you,' he said, 'but I can't find them at this moment. A newspaper office is a no-man's-land, things get lost pretty easily around here; you know that. But I can assure you of this, Khaleque Biswas, whatever you've produced is good enough to be printed in *The Freedom Fighter*. I will give it to one of our specialists to look into and prepare a final version. In the meantime I want you to know that I think Nur Hussain can be our springboard for revisiting and pinpointing the role of political and intellectual leadership during times of national crisis. Through him we may be able to determine the bargaining capacity of an effective leader as well as the potential consequences of his failure. It is the responsibility of all concerned to keep real vigilance against the manifestations of failed leadership, in order to divert a national disaster.'

I noticed that he did not mention Sheikh Mujib's name, not even once, but I was happy when he said he would make sure the story was printed without delay.

He did print the story, in the next available issue of *The Freedom Fighter*, but as a small, one-column six-inch item on the seventh page. Sunk among the classifieds, with their clear headlines and catchy texts, the story applauded Nur Hussain for the originality of his effort. He was further proof of how solemnly the people of Bangladesh had taken Sheikh Mujib into their hearts, it said. All the observations and statistics about people's suffering, and all the recommendations I had made for reshaping our present and making our future meaningful, had been thrown out. The item ended by predicting that sooner or later all Bangladeshis must become Sheikh Mujibs; that was the only way to show him our sincerest appreciation for his leadership.

14

MEETING MOINA MIA

Sometime in December 1973 Moina Mia, a local Awami
League leader and Member of Parliament, sent his
personal assistant to us. The man introduced himself as
Abdul Ali and told us we were expected at Mia's residence
the following afternoon. He would not say what the meeting
would be about, how Moina Mia knew us, why the rush.

'Have you come to the right people?' I asked. 'The number
on the gate is not clearly visible. The number plate has seen
at least twenty winters. The name of the road is nowhere to
be found. Are you sure you are looking for us?'

He said yes, there was no mistake about it. 'When I do
a job for my boss, I have all the time in the world to make
sure that I have done it properly. I don't care about my own
suffering, illness or exhaustion. I don't care if house number
22 comes after house number 16, and if house number 16
follows house number 36. I care about what I am supposed
to do for the MP, and that I have done it according to his
expectations.' He told me my name was Khaleque Biswas,
that I had a *talented* young man living with me whose name
was Nur Hussain, and that together we delivered Sheikh
Mujib's 7 March speech in various public forums. 'You may

stop me if I am mistaken,' he said, 'but I am sure you will not stop me, because I will not be mistaken.' To make himself clearer, he took from his pocket a clipping from *The Freedom Fighter* and showed me the small item on Nur Hussain that had my name as the byline.

'Would you like some tea?' I asked. 'It won't take more than two minutes.'

'No,' he replied. 'Thank you; there is no time.'

It was a surprising invitation, because we thought that only street people knew us, people who did not know right from wrong, who were still under the illusion that Sheikh Mujib's voice heralded a new era and healed them from the inside out. Now we knew we had gone beyond the boundary of the slums and reached the minds of people who were powerful, who decided on national executive policies and were responsible for lots of people like us.

I had my reservations about the invitation. After Abdul Ali left, I was besieged by questions and doubts. Perhaps he looked down upon us. He could very well do that, as he was an MP's assistant; at this moment in time, nothing could be more worthwhile than working for the Awami League. Then I wondered if we had angered the party by delivering Sheikh Mujib's speech without its permission. What if he had been instructed to invite us as naturally and calmly as possible, so that we did not suspect some violent punishment awaited us at Moina Mia's residence?

I buried my fear. I did not want Nur Hussain to be affected by it. I was glad to see he took the invitation easily, without thinking much about it. As long as I was with him, it was clear that he felt he had nothing to fear.

We went to see Moina Mia at his house, which was only a few blocks away from our place. It stood alone and had high boundary walls with wire barricades above. Inside the walls, builders were working on a new construction that already had three storeys completed and would rise even higher. The wide, complicated but aesthetically pleasing wrought-iron gate, and the image of a lion on the railings, reflected the kind of people who lived there. Not many houses I had seen had such a distinguished combination of security and theatricality.

Seeing us, the gatekeeper – whose name was Ruhul Amin – went inside and came out a moment later with Abdul Ali behind him. Abdul Ali advised him to take a close look at us in order to recognize us when we came next. Sounding as mechanical as the previous day, he told him we would be 'frequent visitors' there and should be given immediate access at any time of day. Ruhul Amin saluted us; it seemed he had understood our importance before we ourselves did. 'Come on in,' he said, 'please.'

Moina Mia was in his Mujib coat. He was ready to receive us. He walked to the door, embraced Nur Hussain, shook my hand and led us to the sitting area. 'There you are,' he said, 'what an auspicious day.' Abdul Ali exited the room, leaving us alone.

I had seen him before. In fact, I suppose I had seen him many, many times, when he campaigned for the parliamentary election in early 1973. He was a veteran Awami League leader, and although he was not in Sheikh Mujib's cabinet, it was said he was 'close to him personally' and 'had advised him on various occasions about national security measures and enemy property affairs'. He had been in charge of recruiting freedom fighters for the war, and was considered one of the most illustrious of the fighters not to be adorned with medals – only because he was never part of the military. After the war he organized the *Jatiya Rakkhi Bahini*, Sheikh Mujib's private militia – a tough, formidable, totalitarian-minded armed force – and helped him in his nationwide political campaign. It was he who had arranged the massive reception for Sheikh Mujib when he returned from Pakistan in 1972. About 150,000 people had gathered at Tejgaon Airport that day.

As the shopkeepers did in the market, Moina Mia addressed Nur Hussain as 'Sheikh Mujib' and asked him directly if he would be interested in working with him. The job, he explained, involved speaking to various crowds within the local constituency – something we were already doing. Nur Hussain would appear at the meeting spot well ahead of time and deliver the speech again and again to prepare the crowd for the main attraction of the day: Moina Mia's own speech. He was aware of the public displeasure I had observed across the city. He wanted to address it before it took a dangerous turn. Nur Hussain would help him do exactly that.

I intervened. 'Forgive me,' I said. 'Would you mind telling us a little more?' I asked if he would give us a hint as to the fee. I did not want to sound mean, but Nur Hussain needed to know how much money he would earn from his speeches. He admired Sheikh Mujib as much as anybody else in the country, there was no doubt about that; but he had no other means to support himself apart from delivering the speech. We were now going out almost every day, and were not limited to one constituency. If we were to work for Moina Mia instead of doing what we were doing, we would have to know the monetary part of the proposal in detail.

No hint was necessary. Moina Mia smiled, as if he had expected this. There would be a deal between us, he said, a solid and transparent deal. We would work sincerely, and be compensated sincerely. There was nothing to worry about. As long as Sheikh Mujib was leading the country, there would be no scarcity of money for any patriotic work. He had freed the country; he knew how to fight hardship. Bad times had arrived, but they would not stay long. The Awami League being in power meant all the people of the country were in power. They knew exactly how to take proper and pragmatic initiatives, to build the country from its foundation upward. Such initiatives would be taken in every constituency, and Nur Hussain was an indispensable part of that effort.

Then he mentioned an amount. It was so huge compared to what we were earning in coins that I did not deem it necessary to consult Nur Hussain before giving consent.

'We are in,' I said promptly. 'We'll be waiting for specific directions regarding where to go, when to go and what to say.'

Moina Mia slipped us an envelope from the breast pocket of his coat. 'An advance,' he said. 'Just to buy two cups of tea to entertain yourselves tonight. Two very good cups of tea.' The rest would follow. Even if there was no meeting to deliver the speech, we would not miss our payment.

The deal done, two servants – both of them of Nur Hussain's age, but thinner – came in with tea and biscuits. They walked cautiously, served us silently and took a few steps back to stand in the corner of the room. Moina Mia noticed the deep surprise in their eyes as they watched Nur Hussain constantly. He smiled and whispered: 'This is a miracle. Tell me this is really happening. This is exactly what I needed. I don't have any doubt anymore.' He looked at us with a smile on his lips. 'You say nothing,' he whispered to us. 'Just watch.' He added an extra direction for Nur Hussain:

'Watch, and just be yourself. Don't worry, I am not testing you; I am testing them. I've already accepted you. Ready?' Nur Hussain looked at me before nodding.

'Basu and Gesu,' Moina Mia said, 'come here.' The servants took a few steps forward and stood there, keeping a respectable distance from us. 'What do you think you were doing, standing there? I am very disappointed. Didn't I tell you not to look at my guests eye to eye?' Basu and Gesu began to tremble as he spoke. 'You only work for me; you're not my friends or my guests' friends, you know that?' They knew that completely. 'I can dismiss you right this moment for such deplorable behaviour, and also forfeit your salary this month.' They knew that too; probably it was a condition of their verbal agreement to work for him. 'But I forgive you this time, because the Prime Minister of the country forgives you. Don't repeat this. Ever.'

It was a surprise for them. Perhaps they had wanted to meet Sheikh Mujib face-to-face from the very first day they had heard his name; but under the constant commands of Moina Mia, they did not know how to show proper respect to him.

'Will you stand there like two fools, or do something appropriate?' Moina Mia asked, giving no sign of controlling his anger. They fell to the ground instantly to touch Nur Hussain's feet. 'What did I teach you?' Moina Mia shouted. 'Do it properly. Three times every time; no concession!' They touched Nur Hussain's feet three times and touched their chests and remained on the floor for further commands. 'As he is our bravest hero, you respect him again,' said Moina Mia. They touched Nur Hussain's feet three more times.

'They're not always like this, Your Honour understands that,' Moina Mia said to Nur Hussain. 'I am ashamed of their conduct today, but I can assure you they are very loyal servants. They are not loud or greedy, and they do not disrespect anyone. Other servants may have issues with their masters; they may have their heads full of conspiracies to harm them, out of hate and jealousy; but these two are different. They know every moment what I want from them. They are very good servants, Mr Prime Minister; I hope you did not find them rude.' He gestured to Nur Hussain to touch their heads, which he did without hesitation. Basu and Gesu, still looking at the ground, stood up. Nur Hussain's touch was reassuring; now they were less nervous than before.

15
MY RAGE AND FRUSTRATION

The development schemes the Sheikh Mujib administration had introduced were miserably inadequate. No strict mechanism was in place to determine whether or not they worked, or how fast they worked. This was because there were thugs everywhere, in every office, in every profession, thugs who had been freedom fighters but were now destroying the very concept of freedom. No specific policies were introduced to protect citizens from them. They came like bloodsucking Pakistani soldiers, looting and then disappearing. Then they came back again.

Whoever these thugs were, my anger was directed against Sheikh Mujib. And I was right. Because, although the thugs came with different names and with different levels of power, they all came wearing the Mujib coat and raising the 'Joy Bangla' slogan. They all introduced themselves as his relatives, his dear friends, his dedicated supporters, and professed to sacrifice their lives for him. Then they looted. They attended his public speeches, worshipped him as the founder of the nation, and looted. They hung his picture in their offices, sitting rooms, bedrooms and waiting rooms, and looted as much as they wanted. And he knew everything.

Still, he employed them, supported them, gave them power, shared his prayers with them, as if without them he could not exist.

Obviously, I could not share my anxieties with Nur Hussain. When we were in our respective rooms, I wanted him to come out, join me and relate how his day had gone. That would give me an opportunity to ask how he thought his days could be better, how he felt about any specific political direction the country was taking and what he wanted to do about it. We would discuss the relationship between politics and paranoia, exploring layer by layer the complex construction of social dynamics in a new society. Freedom belonged equally to all citizens, yet some citizens alienated others so much that it was not really a society now; it was a primitive clan. We could spend hours and days interpreting our feelings.

But he never came. He went to bed early and slept all night, snoring deeply, and woke up a happy man, ready to deliver the speech. He made the *koi* fish crispy when he cooked, and the beef was soft enough to open fibre by fibre when chewed; he ate a good amount of rice in every meal. When his hair grew after one and a half months and altered his appearance, he did not mind going to the hairdresser by himself after I said I was not feeling well. He took his shirt and some money from the tin pot in the kitchen where we kept small amounts for everyday expenses, and walked down the stairs humming a tune. Upon his return he took long baths, the same tune rising and fading and rising again. On days when we had no speaking schedules, he borrowed my cassette player and played the speech repeatedly in his room. The sound barely came through the door, but I knew he was honing his style, moving towards the highest level of perfection possible.

Although I knew nothing would come of it, I sat with him a few times. I had to try, if I was honest. If I began the conversation, I thought, he might come forth and express himself. With images and arguments I might make him confront his woes, his vulnerabilities, thus making him dream and reform his beliefs, attitudes, feelings and actions. He might not be able to understand instantly why pro-Awami League Bengalis were so politically submissive, but at least he would be able to see how Awami politicians had played with his and the rest of the country's sense of deprivation and dissatisfaction under Sheikh Mujib's rule. Gradually, he would understand that action must be taken to challenge the status quo, to carry out redemptive social change. I sat with him, and spoke and spoke and spoke, and he listened.

Then, when I stopped – drained and frustrated – he talked about unrelated things, leaving me alone in my dark world. 'There is a cave there, you know,' he said, 'a very dark cave, hidden behind the thorny trees of the Red Earth Mountain. We were told that every once in a while the cave opened its mouth and pulled little children and grazing cattle into its wide stomach. We were never allowed to roam in that part of the village alone.'

And another day: 'When we are out and see a black cat crossing the street before us, we return home. There is no way we take that street that day. It would bring us misfortunes, plagues. The problem deepens if the cat belongs to a widow or a lonely old woman. Then it has to be burned.' He spoke about Gangasagar, told me stories of fairies and demons and witches and monsters that he had heard in his childhood. Despite the fact that he was in Dhaka now, and had been for almost eight months, he had not taken the city to heart. He knew nothing of it.

I forgave him. How would he know what was in Sheikh Mujib's mind, or in my own mind? He had come to the city for some kind of employment; he found some kind of employment. He did not care if it was the work he wanted to do for the rest of his life. The whole country did not exist for him, as long as he remained alive.

16

DANGER AT THE DOOR

One of the conditions of working for Moina Mia was that he would have absolute control over Nur Hussain's speaking schedule. The purpose of Nur's performances would be to bring people under the umbrella of the Awami League. At no time could that agenda be undermined.

There was no need to speak at the market anymore, as Moina Mia kept his monetary promises and paid us a generous fee for our services, though I noticed that Nur Hussain often felt like talking whenever the fishermen or rickshaw-*wallahs* threw the *'Joy Bangla'* slogan at him. 'How is Sheikh Mujib doing today?' they would ask, and when he did not begin the speech – after I had given him a hard look – they would ask if he was not in the mood, if he was suffering from a stomach ache or constipation.

'All right, another day. Maybe when the wind falls and the mangos ripen.' Then they would move on.

Many times he would start delivering the speech as we returned from one of the appearances scheduled by Moina Mia. He would not look at me, thus categorically avoiding me. He would look back to make sure no other rickshaw was following us, then recite: *My brothers, I have come here before you today ...* He would continue until he finished with: *I look back on the past twenty-three years, and I see nothing but a history of bloodshed.* He would repeat 'bloodshed' several times, the word turning softer and softer each time before getting lost between his lips. The rickshaw would continue moving, the rickshaw-*wallah* pedalling silently – probably he did not want to distract Nur Hussain – and we would sit next to each other, quietly. No noises on the road, no familiar music coming from roadside shops, no neighbourhood policeman, postal officer, banker or teacher could move him from his silence. He would sit as if he had lost the will to live, as if the material world did not have the ability to touch him again. Arriving home, he would retreat to his room, and I to mine. The night would pass in uninterrupted silence.

Sometimes he spoke at home. He would say a few paragraphs and then take a long, long pause before speaking again. Did he fall asleep momentarily? Did he faint? I would run to look at him. Then he would speak another paragraph, or a few lines, and lie down. Sometimes he spoke behind the closed door. I understood that he was not sure what I might think of him. Well, I did not think anything. If I thought anything, I thought about the unfathomable fear I had that something bad would happen to us very soon, and we would be undone. I could see it coming, speedily and dangerously, but I did not know how fatal it would be. Let it come. But before it came and washed us away with its ruthless terror, let us live fully. So I gave him freedom in the flat.

One day I advised him not to wear his Mujib coat when we went out to buy groceries, or for evening walks, or when we went to watch the neighbouring children play marbles on the street. 'Just for a few days,' I said. 'Maybe a few weeks, after which we'll evaluate the situation.' He would wear the coat, I said, only when we went to collect a crowd for Moina Mia. He did not ask why. He never asked questions. But I had to be frank with him. I had to educate him so that I did not need to explain every little thing we might encounter every day.

There might be some wicked characters lurking in the crowd who had no common sense and who did not appreciate what we were doing, I told him. Some people might behave badly simply because they had not been trained to be courteous when they were children. Some might be insane or just rude to the world because they cared for nothing. Some might seek a different society because they believed in something that Sheikh Mujib found hard to endorse and fight for – for example, a country based singularly on the concept of the dictatorship of the proletariat, as advocated by the likes of the Soviet revolutionary Leon Trotsky. Those belligerent hotheads, who could not be identified easily among the crowd, might get violent with us. They might want to stifle us whenever there was an opportunity.

My fear was not baseless. Of late, people had become rather stubborn and inconsiderate. They would not concede favours to anyone, for anything. Society as a whole was turning increasingly desperate and confrontational. Often there were fires in neighbouring areas, in the market. Some of these incidents could be traced back to angry, mentally unstable individuals, a few of whom were suicidal, but most of them remained a mystery. They did not happen by chance, I told Nur Hussain; someone must be behind them, someone who knew exactly what he was doing. That someone could be anybody from the neighbourhood, the tea stall, the street corner, the bus or even from Friday prayers.

A bank teller was arrested one day on the high street. Allegedly, he was carrying a canister of kerosene and a matchbox. He was old and experienced, a respected man in the community, but would not speak when asked about his intentions. 'I am guilty,' he said. 'Do whatever you want with me, but remember: I will not be the last one to carry fire.' There were confrontations among rickshaw-*wallahs*, some ending in serious physical assault, blood on the dust, gouging of eyes, stabbing. Traders yelled at one another more frequently; there was no courtesy. The rules of fair competition were buried for good. Excessive price hikes had their curses. Public property was stolen or vandalized at record rates. Households were burning with anger. One could not walk along the streets without being distracted by quarrels among agitated neighbours, siblings. Sometimes women's voices drowned out men's. I saw drunken women crawling on the road, their husbands yelling at them from the dark depths of their tiny houses.

On top of everything, an increasing number of anonymous artists were now going out every night with paint rollers, brushes and aerosol cans to create graffiti in various sizes and colours on city walls, storefronts, abandoned vehicles, railway compartments, public buildings, monuments, construction fences, hospital boundaries and high bridge railings. They were hard-working people, I must admit. They had plans. Despite the vigilance of law and order officials, they found their ways. One night they worked on the north side of the city; the following night they moved south.

Although the municipality's cleaning squads removed the graffiti as soon as possible, some of it stayed for days, or even weeks, spreading previously unheard-of radical political messages among the public. Because its removal required special expensive procedures, some of the graffiti was left completely untouched. 'Be Prepared to Die', read graffiti on the railway route leading to Dhaka, along with: 'The Famine Is Coming'. Between the two warnings, the artist had painted two skinny boys with big mouths and bloated bellies, staring into the horizon. Highly decorative graffiti that I saw only once – 'No Rice to Eat? Eat Awami League Leaders' – was stencilled onto the General Post Office building. It was removed within a day. Later I heard that the same graffiti had surfaced on many buildings at various locations throughout the city, and that the municipality had given up trying to remove it. It engaged its resources in removing graffiti that was larger in size and which appeared in prominent areas.

During this time I came across many banknotes defaced with slogans like 'Leave Now'; 'Prime Minister for Sale'; 'Death to the Dictator'; and 'Who Is this Person? What Is He Doing in Our Country?' On some of the notes Sheikh Mujib's eyes had been blinded with fountain pens; some showed him with bloody vampire teeth, some with his face crossed out. Some had scribbles next to his portrait: 'What is the value of this banknote? Zero. Don't let Sheikh Mujib turn Bangladesh into a wasteland,' read a five-*taka* bill. The local grocer handed me a one-*taka* bill that was completely hidden underneath scribbling from end to end: 'Believing in freedom is not a crime, but believing in Sheikh Mujib is. Because he does not stand for freedom. Not anymore. Give me my country back. Give me my rifle back. God condemns the Awami League.' When the writing on the banknotes went out of control, the government forced the Central Bank's director to go to the media to declare that bills with such writing, stamping or additional tampering would be considered invalid. In a press release, the government also declared that possession of defaced banknotes could lead to arrest and imprisonment.

It was apparent that a good number of individuals or underground organizations were out there, and did not want to let time pass without a fight. I was sure they were active not only in the capital, but also in other cities and towns. They were doing what nationally circulated newspapers and magazines had failed to do. Their intentions might be to serve the people, but at the moment they were instigating action by the authorities against them. I did not want us to be victims of such a fight.

17

AN ENORMOUS CAMPAIGN BEGINS

Winter was exceptionally cold that year. The temperature went down to ten degrees Celsius, the lowest since record-keeping had begun several decades earlier. Scores of people died in the capital's shantytowns and slums. More people died in the countryside and especially in the northern districts, where villagers lived in small bamboo huts and did not have sufficient warm clothes to wear. People died in December, January and February.

March 1974 saw better weather. Evenings, nights and mornings were not so cold now. Calves came out early in the morning and jumped in the yard. Chickens walked in the fields, and geese flew into the ponds without hesitation. Snakes ended their hibernation.

Still, people continued to die. They died even in the south, where the lowest temperature recorded was eighteen degrees. They died by the hundreds and thousands. They died every day, in every town, in every village, though Sheikh Mujib was far from admitting it.

In the city, more pavements were covered with tents made of old *saris*. The *saris* soaked in the night fog and dried in the sun during the day, and soon began to look as colourless as the faces of people who lived under them. Because of the lack of proper sewage facilities, the city air became sticky with bad smells. Blind people, people with elephantiasis, people wounded in the Liberation War, people who were disabled or paralyzed, found their stations on the road. In many areas, old and new refugees broke pipes to collect water. They cooked on the road, quarrelled among themselves, attacked one another and torched one another's tents. Their sons learned the art of picking pockets, breaking into stores, threatening one another with knives and hockey sticks and assaulting anyone who came their way. Their daughters and wives lost all shame and learned the language of the street; desperate for some coins to buy food, they gradually found it natural to invite strangers into their tents.

In April alone, Nur Hussain delivered Sheikh Mujib's 7 March speech a total of seventeen times. It was an extraordinary number, even by our standards. It seemed that the more people died from starvation, the more Moina Mia needed to convince his constituents that we must not forget the enduring spirit that had made us free, that the food crises would end soon and that every family would be happy.

Most days we had to leave early in the morning for the venue set for Moina Mia's rally. We ate our breakfast there, with local Awami League activists. We cleaned the venue, raised banners depicting Sheikh Mujib and mounted the stage before midday. From time to time Nur Hussain delivered a few sentences from the speech to test the microphone, and to let the neighbourhood know a public meeting was planned there that day.

I did not have any experience of manual labour. As a result, I grew tired easily. I would take a nap sitting beside the piles of posters and leaflets behind the stage. The area would be dark and full of mosquitoes; the floor would be damp and even slippery. Sometimes I would see rats running from one end to the other, spreading the sewage smells. One or two would stop next to my feet, seeking a little warmth. When I jerked my feet, they screeched and scurried away. Sometimes I would wake up hearing the booming voice of Nur Hussain at the microphone. I envied his energy. His voice was always the same, loud and clear, as if he had just got up from sleep and uttered his first sentence of the day. Probably it was because of the microphone. He loved speaking into it. He freed it from the stand and walked around the stage, speaking. Sometimes he ran from end to end like a pop star and spoke in various acrobatic poses, providing the crowd with some extra entertainment. It was not necessary, I thought. It was absolutely an exaggeration. Not part of our deal. He should not do it.

His impromptu physical movements happened before the actual meetings began, and definitely before Moina Mia arrived with a contingent of the *Rakkhi Bahini*. After his arrival, everything would happen very fast. Nur Hussain would deliver a few lines from the 7 March speech. Awami League workers would chant *'Joy Bangla'* a few times, followed by some moments of high tension, whispering, impatient waiting. From there Moina Mia would take the crowd on a tour through our history. He would begin in the style of a conversation, asking the crowd how they were doing that day; Awami League activists planted within the crowd would respond loudly that they were doing excellently.

Moina Mia would not pause long, in case some starving troublemakers took a chance to ask some embarrassing questions. Every new day was a great day for the Bengali nation, he would say with satisfaction, because every new day was a day of freedom in the account of our lives. He would then relate how we fought against the British, how we resisted the Pakistanis' efforts to make us speak their language instead of our own, and finally how we defeated them in 1971. 'Couldn't Sheikh Mujib, who created history by freeing his people from the yoke of slavery, also feed those people?' he would ask rhetorically. He could, Moina Mia would say, and he would. 'Yes! Yes!' the gathering would break out in a chorus. Sheikh Mujib would stand by his people, and no conspiracy was going to change that. Moina Mia's favourite quotation came from the 7 March speech: *I call upon you to turn every home into a fortress*, he would say in the voice of Sheikh Mujib, and then explain that while the fortress in 1971was against our Pakistani enemies, the new fortress was to stand against the food crisis.

The purpose of those meetings was to communicate the very important fact that Sheikh Mujib was not sitting inactively in his palace, oblivious to the conditions of our people; that he was not sleeping while the whole country suffered, as I believed he was. He was doing everything in his power to feed the hungry. Diplomats were being sent to different corners of the world with his special message, seeking emergency food aid. The response, too, had been extraordinary. A large number of containers had already arrived at the port in Chittagong, with ready-to-eat food; more were on their way. Once they were released, after official customs formalities, they would be sent immediately to every city and village, so that not a single Bengali suffered from starvation. In Sheikh Mujib's country, nobody would be allowed to die of hunger, Moina Mia would say decisively, even if nature was against us and brought us relentless drought and cold for an unforeseeable period of time.

At the height of his speech, he would ask the crowd if they believed in Sheikh Mujib. They answered in the affirmative. Then he would take a step forward and ask them again, saying he had not heard them, that for some reason he was not hearing well that day. The crowd would now speak louder: 'We believe in Sheikh Mujib! We believe in him!' He repeated his question until the entire crowd raised its voice to the utmost, screaming that they believed in Sheikh Mujib's vision for the country, that they would give their lives to fulfil his dreams.

After the speech, he would sit on a chair behind the stage, take a few deep breaths and drink a glass of water. He would give specific directions about his next schedule. It was now time to ask about his performance. Who would he ask? Definitely Nur Hussain, with whom he seemed to have begun a competition. 'So what do you think?' he would say. 'Do you think they will hate us a little less than they did yesterday?' He would laugh after that, though nobody else would.

18

DINNER WITH SHAH ABDUL KARIM

In May 1974, hundreds of refugees took over the
Mrittunjoyee Primary School in our neighbourhood. They
occupied the school buildings, which had been devastated
during the war and still lay in ruins. Those who did not fit
inside the buildings pitched small tents in the field, against
the boundary walls. They dug the ground to make temporary
ovens as well as holes for toilets; they made small canals to
wash dishes and clothes, hung their ragged quilts from ropes
in front of the tents and reserved a corner of the field to
dispose of their daily rubbish. It was obvious that they had
just arrived from the villages. Their clothes were cleaner
than those worn by migrants who had been living in the
city for some time now. They lived a rather reserved life, as
if trying hard to distance themselves from the world, from
people who looked at them with curiosity and considered
them extra trouble in a city already burdened with hundreds
of thousands of refugees. They would not have moved
to the capital had they been able to support themselves in
the villages.

One of the new refugees was Shah Abdul Karim. He was a
sixty-year-old singer who played a yellow *ektara* folk guitar.

I had heard him at night when passing by the school field, and had stopped on my way and stood still, listening to his music. There was something in his voice that I could not ignore. Standing in the dark, close to the edge of the refugee camp, I had heard him sing how a terrible madness had come down from the sky and turned our dreams into pebbles. We could only look at them, collect them in our hands and burst into endless tears. We had tried for an eternity, but could not turn them into dreams again.

One day I saw him at the Shaheed Minar. He was singing before a gathering, jumping around inside a small circle, raising his guitar in the air. I went ahead and sat with the crowd. *All will die,* he sang under the yellow sun, *all that lives and suffers. There is no escape. Neighbours and friends, let us sit face to face, and be kind to each other. Lovely shadows, let us play, the night is near.* Then: *Everyone, everywhere. No place to hide, no God to pray to, no air that is soothing. My heart, I have not known it, is burning, falling to the dust in undisputed pains.* The songs were not long, but every time he finished a stanza he repeated the intro twice and played the guitar for some time.

When the crowd applauded, he responded with some extra tunes. He smiled and stared at me. After that, he looked at me several times, I suppose. I clapped too, but under his gaze I felt numb. I felt he wanted to speak with me, and that he had a lot to say. So I stayed until after he had finished blessing the refugee children by touching their heads.

He had seen Nur Hussain and me working at one of Moina Mia's meetings. He thought I would not come to hear him because he had no good news for Sheikh Mujib. I understood instantly what he meant. I told him, frankly, that I was living two lives. Though I was attending Moina Mia's programmes along with Nur Hussain, helping him reach his constituents as effectively as possible, I was in fact not a part of Sheikh Mujib's private militia or the Awami League's vote bank. I was selling my services to the Awami League in order to survive; that was all. There were specific conditions that had to be met for me to provide my services to them. When I thought those conditions no longer served my interests, I would withdraw them or make a new deal with a new set of conditions.

He told me he had walked over three hundred miles in the last few months to sing for people. He had composed many songs, but most of them were lost because he did not keep copies. Words came to his mouth and tunes came to his guitar. He was the medium that brought the two together. If it were not he, somebody else would, he said; the songs would have been sung, the music would have been created. Along the way he had made friends with strangers, had lived in their huts, in their kitchens, and shared their last handful of rice. He had participated in many burial prayers too, watched many bodies placed in one grave, saw bodies rotting on the side of the road and in the waters of the canal, bodies being eaten by dogs or forsaken in deserted houses. Our neighbourhood was one of many such stops. When asked how long he would continue to walk, he smiled and began a tune on his guitar.

We went to the Mrittunjoyee Primary School, which he called home. He did not have a tent there. He lived on the veranda of the school building. There were many around who had had to accept the same fate. It was not a place for a human being to live, and definitely not a place where someone could invite guests, but he would invite me, he said. We sat together, a yard apart, and watched the refugees who cooked in the field, their children playing in the dust, young ones crawling in any direction they liked, eating mud, cow dung, guava seeds, sundried banana peels. A few yards away a woman of eighty was caning her fifty-year-old son. He had assaulted his wife when she refused to go and look for work. The wife sat on the dust and wept. She said she had looked for work day after day, but could not find any; she had offered to work the first day free for the second day's payment; that was also not enough. Now she was showing her mother-in-law the bruises on her knees.

Abdul Karim said he wanted to continue singing as long as he lived. An entire life devoted to music would not convey the sorrows he had seen, so deep were they. He had seen death in all possible shapes and colours. One did not need to walk three hundred miles to see death, he said; death was at our doorstep, happening every day, exposing itself concretely to the elements. He walked because he could not stop walking. The more deaths he witnessed, the more pressure he felt to move on. If nature could teach him how to overcome the thought of self-annihilation, he would stop somewhere. Unfortunately, it did not. He gave me some peanuts from his bag and threw some at the children, who tumbled upon them. They were a gift from an admirer from the market, he said. The admirer regularly offered him something.

What one was going to eat for supper was the most awkward question at the time. It was more deeply personal than the question of faith. I did not want to embarrass him. If he would be kind enough to give me company for an hour, I said, I was going to eat something at a restaurant before going home. Of course, that was only if he was not busy; I did not know whether or not he had other engagements.

He was not busy, he replied, but he must return at sunset to sing for them – he pointed to the tents. 'Good people,' he said, 'very good people; sadly enough, many of them won't survive another evening to listen to my music. Their souls will fly to a world fairer than the one we live in, so tomorrow is always a better day than today.'

We walked to the restaurant, where we sat at one of the front tables. I ordered *paratha roti* and *bhaji* with tea for both of us. There were not many customers in the restaurant at that time, so we were served our food quite quickly. As we ate, I told him I had been a journalist and had worked with *The Freedom Fighter* for over two years. He had never seen or heard of it, so I gave him a brief description: when it began, who the editor was, its role during the war and why it thrived so well compared with other journals of the day. I told him one day I would have my own paper, which I would call *The New Sun*. I would write in it whatever I believed the times demanded. I would be its editor; I would change the job description so that no editor could become rude and inert. I would talk about how life was *now*, real life, from the very first issue. I would recreate it as it had been for a long time; I would recreate it in all its ironies, pitfalls, pretensions and sensations. I was keeping notes of everything I thought and everything I saw, I said to him, and in that paper I would print it all in very straightforward language. I would not wait for history to judge. If I waited, it would be too late. I would use my own judgement. How could we disregard something that was so obvious? I would say it was the fault of Sheikh Mujib, who did not see people dying, because he did not want to accept that death could exist in Bangladesh as long as he led the government.

I could have gone on and on and on, but I just wanted to give Abdul Karim an idea of the intense fury I carried in my heart. I did not want my country to be ruled by a morally bankrupt fascist force like the Awami League. By working for Moina Mia I was saving money for that purpose, I told him finally. Once I had enough money to print a four-page newspaper, even if only once a month, I would not stay idle for a day. 'Believe me,' I said to him. 'I am not kidding. This is the single most important thing I aspire to accomplish.'

He still looked hungry after eating his second *paratha*, so I ordered one more for each of us. He ate and then burped several times – an indication he had enjoyed the meal.

'I feel so good now,' he said in the end. 'As if I have become innocent again.' He burped noisily. 'Ah, what a feeling! I need to sleep.' He smiled.

'Sure.' We both stood up. 'Please.'

'Don't forget to stop by.' He looked back from the door as I paid the bill. 'You know where to find me.'

After Abdul Karim returned to the school, I walked down the street. At the crossing I saw a woman sitting with a little boy lying as if dead before her. She was weeping inside her veil. Rickshaw-*wallahs* passed and pedestrians passed her, looking at her indignantly.

I had seen her many times before, in various places – in front of the mosque, at the market, at the mouth of the refugee camp, at the bus stop, under the flyover, at the yard of the local two-storey Hindu temple. She always wept with the same sadness. Every time I saw her, she had the boy before her. Although I knew he was not dead, only pretending, I gave her a coin and left without question.

At night I spoke to Nur Hussain. I told him it was my great desire to invite Abdul Karim to live with us. 'He is a harmless person, as harmless as a singer could be,' I told him. 'He will eat whatever food we have and sleep in the living room. As he is a wanderer, he does not have any luggage; just a small bag that we won't even notice. If he lives with the refugees, he will not survive for long. It will be a mistake to let such a visionary person perish. What do you say?'

Nur Hussain remained silent, which angered me. He could remain silent even in the face of the worst atrocities happening in front of him – such an ignorant, mean, worthless person! Simply irritating. Our country desperately needed people like Abdul Karim – didn't he see it? Soon there would be nobody around to provide us with higher knowledge. For its regeneration, a nation actually needs knowledge that is *not* useful, rather than knowledge that is. A nation needs to get back its own heart. Only people like Shah Abdul Karim could bring it back to us.

It was useless to consult Nur Hussain – not only about the singer but about anything, whether important or unimportant. He would choose silence over words, as if he never spoke. He would look into my face, as if I would not have asked the question had I not had it answered already.

He did not care.

He had no feelings.

19

A GUEST IN THE HOUSE

Abdul Karim loved sleeping on the couch, leaving his bag and guitar next to his pillow. He relished the tea that Nur Hussain or I made in the morning, and with great appetite he ate every item of food we put on his plate. We would leave him at the flat when we went to work for Moina Mia. Upon our return, we would find it clean and tidy. He wanted to show his appreciation by providing small services for us. I turned to Nur Hussain and said: 'See? I told you. He's a person with a conscience. He knows how to be courteous. How many people of this stature do you see around here, and how many of them are as humble as he is?'

Frequently, he entertained us with new songs. In one, he sang: *How shall we escape the claws of misfortune? The snake is there, waiting / and the rhinoceros, its rocky mouth eager to strike.* And in another: *What evil is this? The heart, stiff, and memory, mechanical / the ceremony of formal feeling is over / what continues is eternity, with all its great pain.* He had an outstanding ability to compose serious songs with very ordinary words that, in his voice, became musical; they came out of the gloom we had imposed on account of the sad life all around us, and became beautiful. He played the guitar with one hand and slapped his forehead with the other; he sometimes also hit his chest, as if by torturing himself he might evaporate the expanse of sorrow inside him. A few times he woke up early and left the flat for the refugee camp, to see his new friends there, to sing for them under the morning sky. By singing and talking he was able to erase much of the dismal mood of the day. He forgot to return home at night; he returned only when we went to look for him. He saw us and instantly remembered he was living with us. We could tell by looking at his face he had not eaten the whole day. That his friends always fed him was a lie. At home we would give him food, and then he would take up his guitar to sing for us out of gratitude. Nur Hussain or I would take the guitar away and prepare the sofa for him. 'You are tired,' we would say. He would fall asleep within minutes.

Nur Hussain and I did not speak to each other a great deal. I should say, rather, that we did not speak much outside our business needs or small, everyday matters. He knew his job and I knew mine. We trusted each other so much that our silent physical presence was sufficient for communication. But he spoke a lot with Abdul Karim, and I guess he also bonded deeply with him within a short period of time. Together they sat in the living room, ate meals and drank tea. They went out together; from the window I could see them walking side by side, talking, stopping in wonder to look at each other. I would watch them until they were lost behind the walls or trees. At night, sometimes Abdul Karim started a song, and when he returned to the intro Nur Hussain would add his own voice. He swung his head while following the notes of the songs; the songs seemed to pierce his heart.

I suppose Shah Abdul Karim gave him what I could not: ease and friendship. He made him feel at home in my home. By contrast, I crushed Nur under the weight of life's obscene necessities. I reduced him to a shiny coin on which I engraved my own portrait. He was mine, I thought. His energy was mine. His words, his silence were mine. His future was mine. It was my future now. He had nothing for himself. He would be mine – the same stuff, the same creature, the same nothingness – as long as I needed him. That was not what he had expected when he came here. Probably he was at a loss with me, and did not know how to get out of the situation – if he had known, he would not have come to me in the first place. All these things made him silent around me.

At the same time, I also did not know what else to do, what else a person could do at such moments. I had lost much of my self-respect. If an accident were to occur during one of Moina Mia's assemblies – say, an explosion – and I was killed, newspapers would publish feature stories on how a journalist ended up accumulating wealth by taking advantage of society's most destitute people. They would print my picture with a caption: 'The most unpredictable end of a very predictable man.' This was not what I had believed my life would be like. I had never thought that one day I would have to accept such a pitiful condition.

What was happening to me? I asked myself this when Nur Hussain was not around. I sat before the window and reflected on how abrupt and impolite I was to him. My responsibility was to give him courage, to inspire him, to make a better human being of him, or at least to try and get him to explore his potential so that he could attain his own goals. In times of crisis we needed to cultivate virtue with greater perseverance than ever; we needed compassion and generosity. Instead, I seemed resolved to do the opposite.

Abdul Karim lived with us for only three weeks.

He behaved strangely during his last few days. He began cooking for us, and gave us some beautiful advice about life, as though he was our father and had just rediscovered his role after an early retirement.

'Do not burden yourself with problems you do not understand,' he said. 'If you do, then only the problems win. Human life becomes a tragedy.' Or: 'No man is more of a stranger to you than you are to him. Receive him with trust.' Or even this, which he said as he took us by the arms: 'Look beyond your self-importance and pain. You will know yourself better.'

I could not stop myself from asking him about Sheikh Mujib. He said: 'Love or hate for Sheikh Mujib will not end this. Who is Sheikh Mujib? Is he imperishable? Can he tell when seeds will wake up, when the sky will shine? The answer to hunger is in our hearts, not in food. It is not in politics, but in our feeling, in divinity, in the very essence that makes us human. Our hearts must weep to end our tears. Our minds have to be free in order to end this suffering.'

I understood there was a sphere beyond politics and famine, where he lived as a man free from illusions. When he sang, he came down from that sphere, became an ordinary man, soiled his feet and crawled in the dirt willingly, after which he raised himself again to his ideal dwelling place. There was no government in that sphere. It was not cluttered with human complaints and sighs.

One day he arose early in the morning, drank tea with us, gathered his bag and guitar and sang one last song before stepping out.

'I'm leaving,' he said. 'Don't look for me.'

That was all.

20

YOU GIVE ME GOOD MONEY,
I GIVE YOU GOOD PUBLICITY

Moina Mia told us one evening that Sheikh Mujib was not satisfied with the way the Awami League was handling the party's public relations. It wasn't that the Awami League could not define itself in the post-liberation period, or that it did not know what to do with the country after fighting to liberate it. The Awami League had always been the Awami League: an up-to-date political party with a clear vision and objectives. In fact, it had recently taken on a long-term key project called 'Bread, Water and Electricity', which was going to play an extraordinary role in the party's rejuvenation. A group of wise men from within the party had already been selected to execute it. However, the party's traditional public-relations strategies were ineffective in conveying its message in these new times. As a result, the Awami League faced potential danger.

The responsibility of helping the party grow, and of keeping its popularity alive, lay first with its executive leaders and then, in descending order, with regional leaders, local leaders and, finally and most importantly, at the microcosmic level with individuals such as we, who worked directly with the people. We needed to serve the party's interests more aggressively and, if necessary, to invest more time in it. Moina Mia believed that we needed to find a way to engage and persuade a particular segment of the populace so that it did not have the opportunity to damage our 'unity' and harm our nation with its 'anti-people agenda'.

'Nothing is wrong with the country,' Moina Mia said with emphasis, 'but Sheikh Mujib is losing popularity among people because of these naysayers. They are tainting his name by saying that he is not relevant to our future. They say this because he fought to liberate the country while they opposed liberation, and because they want to plunder us and control our lives. They say food aid is not distributed properly, though all aid is evenly distributed, to the last grain. They are torturing people in the villages to force them to relocate to the capital in order to humiliate the government. By showing the world that our capital has an ugly face, they want to prove that we have failed in our mission.'

His voice rose further. 'What about the floods?' he asked. 'Did Sheikh Mujib hit the clouds in the sky so that rain came pouring, causing the rivers to overflow? Did he make this summer hot, hotter than all previous summers, so that the crops dried before the harvest was ready? Certain people actually believe all this. Certain people who admire these heinous conspirators will never accept Bangladesh as a stable nation – not even fifty years after our independence.'

He looked at Nur Hussain's Mujib coat and became upset. 'The coat does not look black,' he said. 'It does not look pure black. Have you overused it? Nothing is really useful if it is not pure. Let me give you an example. What do you feel

126

sitting before a colourless sunset – excited? It is not to be seriously admired, is it? If an Awami League representative does not know how to keep his clothes in order, how will people think that his party will be able to keep order in the country? We have to be more cautious about everything we do, especially about small details such as wearing a coat, keeping our shoes shiny, hanging the portrait of Sheikh Mujib in a spotless and expensive mahogany frame, choosing an effective typographic style for banners, choosing images with warm colours for the posters. These are things that are easily overlooked, though they make the first impression.'

He asked how many coats Nur Hussain had.

Why, just one, we replied, was that a problem?

'Only one?' He could not believe us. We were to buy half a dozen immediately, he said, if possible that very day, so that if one was damaged or discoloured or lost, Nur Hussain had another ready to wear to work.

'It is his voice that is important, not the coat,' I said resolutely. I did not hesitate to argue, as I felt a bit embarrassed by his interrogation. 'It is the way he delivers the speech. Anyone can buy a coat if there is money; but hundreds and thousands of beautiful coats would not enable people to serve the Awami League the way Nur Hussain does.' I looked at Nur for support. He was as lifeless as a yellowed picture in a frame. 'Besides,' I said, 'coats are worn over the *punjabi*; they are meant to be discoloured, aren't they? There is the sun. There is humidity. And a world of dust out there. They cannot glisten all the time, can they?'

Moina Mia understood my point. He brought out some money from the soft interior of his pocket and handed it to me. 'The purpose of having money is not to save it. It

ROSCH

is to complete a job efficiently.' He asked if we understood what he had just said. We nodded. 'Good. Also, buy a pair of *punjabis*. A new coat without a new *punjabi* is meaningless. It means we respect neither the coat nor the *punjabi*.'

21

THE NEWCOMERS

A new wave of refugees came to the city in September 1974. It was probably the worst thing they could do. In the villages, they could collect herbs, catch birds in the fields, steal eggs from turtles and uproot a banana tree to extract its white skeleton. There were hundreds of thousands of canals and ponds full of fish. Such opportunities were not available in the cities. Still, they came.

What pushed them to set out for Dhaka at that critical moment of our national history, I asked myself once again, if not a conspiracy of Pakistani collaborators, as Moina Mia had said? I came up with several answers. First, they were not landowners. These people were rootless, so it was easy for them to decide to set out for a new place; they had nothing to lose. Second, they were not going anywhere. They were just wandering the way they had wandered year after year, generation after generation, before the liberation as well as after it. And in the course of that wandering they found themselves in Dhaka, which happened to be the capital of the country. Third, they were scared of seeing more death. Death came every day. They looked for the most densely populated area in the country. They thought they would be able to hide themselves among Dhaka's crowds, where death would not find them. Fourth, they did not want to die meaninglessly; they did not want to be shadows of lives without enjoying the promises of the new country. They had lived year after year in slavery, burdened by discrimination and shame. Now they were free. If they could survive a few more days, they might be able to live with honour. By going from place to place, they wanted to buy time.

I revised my answers again and again, until I believed I knew exactly why the refugees chose to come to Dhaka. For other refugees at any other time, I would not have used the same arguments. I was sure these refugees set out on the road to Dhaka one morning compelled by a higher cause.

They wanted to get as close as they could to Sheikh Mujib. That was it, I thought; definitely. That was why they were here. He was their man. They wanted to draw his attention to their suffering. What better way was there to do that than by coming to the capital, becoming his neighbour, burying the dead at his doorstep, bowing down before him and saying with unshakeable conviction that even after thousands of deaths they would not lose confidence in him? He was not going to go see them in their villages. They had waited and waited and seen death after death; still, he did not come, even though he had promised in his speeches to look after them. So they came to him.

I saluted them. They were strong people. They had made it this far through the famine. Soon they would be at his house; they would be his uninvited guests and speak their minds, calling for his attention.

If I lived in a village and the famine had hit, I asked myself, would I have the courage to come to Dhaka as they had? Would I dare travel those drought-stricken miles and raise a tent next to a burial ground under the open sky, knowing that one day after my death from acute starvation I would be buried by strangers in a strange place, or left on a street corner to be eaten by dogs and vultures? Would I be able to think clearly about such a long and critical journey? Would I do something else entirely, like killing people who stood in my way, or who hid food in their backyards and did not sell their wares because they waited for a price hike? It was good that I was alone, with no children or elderly relatives; good that I had no parents to look after. If I had, I would have left them behind. I would have snatched their food to feed myself. *Every life has a duty to live, you know; every life is precious, but at this moment my life is more precious than yours* – this is what I would have argued. It would have been reprehensible.

I became exhausted whenever I asked myself these questions. I struggled for breath. I struggled to look normal, to appear to Nur Hussain as though I was perfectly fine, fit to accompany him to Moina Mia's gathering, although I knew in my mind that I was falling into an endless abyss.

In 1974 alone over one and a half million people died in Sheikh Mujib's liberated Bangladesh. How big was that number? Five times the number of Bangladeshis killed by Pakistani forces during the entire period of the Liberation War in 1971. No natural disaster had claimed so many lives since the beginning of our national calendar. No ruthless tribal landlord or maharaja in our history had been the cause of so many deaths on the Subcontinent. No religious clash, territorial disagreement or deadly disease had subjected our people to witnessing helplessly the untimely demise of such an astronomical number of lives.

22

A Coat for All

Abdul Ali was waiting for us at our door. There was no chair or stool in the passage, so he must have been standing the whole time. 'Where have you been, so long?' he asked, almost angrily, as soon as he saw us climb the stairs. He had come to call us to an urgent meeting with Moina Mia; one we mustn't miss, he said.

As we followed him silently, he drew our attention to his Mujib coat. How did he look, he asked; did he look like a real supporter of Sheikh Mujib? He told us that because of a step taken by Moina Mia recently to strengthen public support for Sheikh Mujib, from now on he would have to wear a coat; the gatekeeper, Ruhul Amin, would also have to wear one, and Basu and Gesu would have to wear coats as well. Moina Mia's initiative did not end there, he said. Although it was not election time, new measures were being taken to raise huge wooden boats – the insignia of the Awami League – in the market, at important intersections, at the gates of the refugee camps and at other significant public venues. There would be at least sixteen boats across the constituency, and the first one would be raised over the gate of Moina Mia's residence.

I could not tell if he looked like a real supporter of Sheikh Mujib or not, I said, but I could tell for sure that he looked interesting. 'What do you mean by "interesting"?' he asked immediately, sounding concerned. 'Are you trying to insult me?' He stopped and refused to walk any further until I explained myself. His expression of delight was ruined, and I imagined I could cause him immeasurable trouble with such a comment. Where this trouble came from, I could also guess. He should not worry, I said softly; if Moina Mia knew what a person felt in a coat when wearing that coat was compulsory, he would not have imposed it in the first place. He wanted to arrange a pageant, with hundreds of people across the constituency wearing the coat. His purpose would be served. He could boast to the Awami League council that he had gone beyond traditional means of popularizing the party; he had made an extra effort to protect Sheikh Mujib's legacy. Nobody would bother to read what was written in the hearts of those wearing the coat. They might be real supporters, but if they were not, it did not matter. Abdul Ali could look like a monkey in that coat, or a crow without a tail, but to Moina Mia he would still be a loyal colleague, a valuable fighter for Sheikh Mujib, an indispensable element of his pageantry.

'Do I look like a monkey in the coat?' Abdul Ali asked, as he took the first step onward. 'Do I really look like a crow, so ugly?'

I asked Nur Hussain what he thought. 'Why don't you answer him?' I said. 'After all it is not a meaningless question.'

He took a moment and then said: 'Protect your heart. Forget the rest.'

Did he learn that from Shah Abdul Karim, I wondered?

20

YOU GIVE ME GOOD MONEY, I GIVE YOU GOOD PUBLICITY

Moina Mia told us one evening that Sheikh Mujib was not satisfied with the way the Awami League was handling the party's public relations. It wasn't that the Awami League could not define itself in the post-liberation period, or that it did not know what to do with the country after fighting to liberate it. The Awami League had always been the Awami League: an up-to-date political party with a clear vision and objectives. In fact, it had recently taken on a long-term key project called 'Bread, Water and Electricity', which was going to play an extraordinary role in the party's rejuvenation. A group of wise men from within the party had already been selected to execute it. However, the party's traditional public-relations strategies were ineffective in conveying its message in these new times. As a result, the Awami League faced potential danger.

The responsibility of helping the party grow, and of keeping its popularity alive, lay first with its executive leaders and then, in descending order, with regional leaders, local leaders and, finally and most importantly, at the microcosmic level with individuals such as we, who worked directly with the people. We needed to serve the party's interests more aggressively and, if necessary, to invest more time in it. Moina Mia believed that we needed to find a way to engage and persuade a particular segment of the populace so that it did not have the opportunity to damage our 'unity' and harm our nation with its 'anti-people agenda'.

'Nothing is wrong with the country,' Moina Mia said with emphasis, 'but Sheikh Mujib is losing popularity among people because of these naysayers. They are tainting his name by saying that he is not relevant to our future. They say this because he fought to liberate the country while they opposed liberation, and because they want to plunder us and control our lives. They say food aid is not distributed properly, though all aid is evenly distributed, to the last grain. They are torturing people in the villages to force them to relocate to the capital in order to humiliate the government. By showing the world that our capital has an ugly face, they want to prove that we have failed in our mission.'

His voice rose further. 'What about the floods?' he asked. 'Did Sheikh Mujib hit the clouds in the sky so that rain came pouring, causing the rivers to overflow? Did he make this summer hot, hotter than all previous summers, so that the crops dried before the harvest was ready? Certain people actually believe all this. Certain people who admire these heinous conspirators will never accept Bangladesh as a stable nation – not even fifty years after our independence.'

He looked at Nur Hussain's Mujib coat and became upset. 'The coat does not look black,' he said. 'It does not look pure black. Have you overused it? Nothing is really useful if it is not pure. Let me give you an example. What do you feel

One day he arose early in the morning, drank tea with us, gathered his bag and guitar and sang one last song before stepping out.

'I'm leaving,' he said. 'Don't look for me.'

That was all.

I suppose Shah Abdul Karim gave him what I could not: ease and friendship. He made him feel at home in my home. By contrast, I crushed Nur under the weight of life's obscene necessities. I reduced him to a shiny coin on which I engraved my own portrait. He was mine, I thought. His energy was mine. His words, his silence were mine. His future was mine. It was my future now. He had nothing for himself. He would be mine – the same stuff, the same creature, the same nothingness – as long as I needed him. That was not what he had expected when he came here. Probably he was at a loss with me, and did not know how to get out of the situation – if he had known, he would not have come to me in the first place. All these things made him silent around me.

At the same time, I also did not know what else to do, what else a person could do at such moments. I had lost much of my self-respect. If an accident were to occur during one of Moina Mia's assemblies – say, an explosion – and I was killed, newspapers would publish feature stories on how a journalist ended up accumulating wealth by taking advantage of society's most destitute people. They would print my picture with a caption: 'The most unpredictable end of a very predictable man.' This was not what I had believed my life would be like. I had never thought that one day I would have to accept such a pitiful condition.

What was happening to me? I asked myself this when Nur Hussain was not around. I sat before the window and reflected on how abrupt and impolite I was to him. My responsibility was to give him courage, to inspire him, to make a better human being of him, or at least to try and get him to explore his potential so that he could attain his own goals. In times of crisis we needed to cultivate virtue with greater perseverance than ever; we needed compassion and generosity. Instead, I seemed resolved to do the opposite.

Abdul Karim lived with us for only three weeks.

He behaved strangely during his last few days. He began cooking for us, and gave us some beautiful advice about life, as though he was our father and had just rediscovered his role after an early retirement.

'Do not burden yourself with problems you do not understand,' he said. 'If you do, then only the problems win. Human life becomes a tragedy.' Or: 'No man is more of a stranger to you than you are to him. Receive him with trust.' Or even this, which he said as he took us by the arms: 'Look beyond your self-importance and pain. You will know yourself better.'

I could not stop myself from asking him about Sheikh Mujib. He said: 'Love or hate for Sheikh Mujib will not end this. Who is Sheikh Mujib? Is he imperishable? Can he tell when seeds will wake up, when the sky will shine? The answer to hunger is in our hearts, not in food. It is not in politics, but in our feeling, in divinity, in the very essence that makes us human. Our hearts must weep to end our tears. Our minds have to be free in order to end this suffering.'

I understood there was a sphere beyond politics and famine, where he lived as a man free from illusions. When he sang, he came down from that sphere, became an ordinary man, soiled his feet and crawled in the dirt willingly, after which he raised himself again to his ideal dwelling place. There was no government in that sphere. It was not cluttered with human complaints and sighs.

19

A GUEST IN THE HOUSE

Abdul Karim loved sleeping on the couch, leaving his bag and guitar next to his pillow. He relished the tea that Nur Hussain or I made in the morning, and with great appetite he ate every item of food we put on his plate. We would leave him at the flat when we went to work for Moina Mia. Upon our return, we would find it clean and tidy. He wanted to show his appreciation by providing small services for us. I turned to Nur Hussain and said: 'See? I told you. He's a person with a conscience. He knows how to be courteous. How many people of this stature do you see around here, and how many of them are as humble as he is?'

Frequently, he entertained us with new songs. In one, he sang: *How shall we escape the claws of misfortune? The snake is there, waiting / and the rhinoceros, its rocky mouth eager to strike.* And in another: *What evil is this? The heart, stiff, and memory, mechanical / the ceremony of formal feeling is over / what continues is eternity, with all its great pain.* He had an outstanding ability to compose serious songs with very ordinary words that, in his voice, became musical; they came out of the gloom we had imposed on account of the sad life all around us, and

119

became beautiful. He played the guitar with one hand and slapped his forehead with the other; he sometimes also hit his chest, as if by torturing himself he might evaporate the expanse of sorrow inside him. A few times he woke up early and left the flat for the refugee camp, to see his new friends there, to sing for them under the morning sky. By singing and talking he was able to erase much of the dismal mood of the day. He forgot to return home at night; he returned only when we went to look for him. He saw us and instantly remembered he was living with us. We could tell by looking at his face he had not eaten the whole day. That his friends always fed him was a lie. At home we would give him food, and then he would take up his guitar to sing for us out of gratitude. Nur Hussain or I would take the guitar away and prepare the sofa for him. 'You are tired,' we would say. He would fall asleep within minutes.

Nur Hussain and I did not speak to each other a great deal. I should say, rather, that we did not speak much outside our business needs or small, everyday matters. He knew his job and I knew mine. We trusted each other so much that our silent physical presence was sufficient for communication. But he spoke a lot with Abdul Karim, and I guess he also bonded deeply with him within a short period of time. Together they sat in the living room, ate meals and drank tea. They went out together; from the window I could see them walking side by side, talking, stopping in wonder to look at each other. I would watch them until they were lost behind the walls or trees. At night, sometimes Abdul Karim started a song, and when he returned to the intro Nur Hussain would add his own voice. He swung his head while following the notes of the songs; the songs seemed to pierce his heart.

22

A Coat for All

Abdul Ali was waiting for us at our door. There was no chair or stool in the passage, so he must have been standing the whole time. 'Where have you been, so long?' he asked, almost angrily, as soon as he saw us climb the stairs. He had come to call us to an urgent meeting with Moina Mia; one we mustn't miss, he said.

As we followed him silently, he drew our attention to his Mujib coat. How did he look, he asked; did he look like a real supporter of Sheikh Mujib? He told us that because of a step taken by Moina Mia recently to strengthen public support for Sheikh Mujib, from now on he would have to wear a coat; the gatekeeper, Ruhul Amin, would also have to wear one, and Basu and Gesu would have to wear coats as well. Moina Mia's initiative did not end there, he said. Although it was not election time, new measures were being taken to raise huge wooden boats – the insignia of the Awami League – in the market, at important intersections, at the gates of the refugee camps and at other significant public venues. There would be at least sixteen boats across the constituency, and the first one would be raised over the gate of Moina Mia's residence.

I could not tell if he looked like a real supporter of Sheikh Mujib or not, I said, but I could tell for sure that he looked interesting. 'What do you mean by "interesting"?' he asked immediately, sounding concerned. 'Are you trying to insult me?' He stopped and refused to walk any further until I explained myself. His expression of delight was ruined, and I imagined I could cause him immeasurable trouble with such a comment. Where this trouble came from, I could also guess. He should not worry, I said softly; if Moina Mia knew what a person felt in a coat when wearing that coat was compulsory, he would not have imposed it in the first place. He wanted to arrange a pageant, with hundreds of people across the constituency wearing the coat. His purpose would be served. He could boast to the Awami League council that he had gone beyond traditional means of popularizing the party; he had made an extra effort to protect Sheikh Mujib's legacy. Nobody would bother to read what was written in the hearts of those wearing the coat. They might be real supporters, but if they were not, it did not matter. Abdul Ali could look like a monkey in that coat, or a crow without a tail, but to Moina Mia he would still be a loyal colleague, a valuable fighter for Sheikh Mujib, an indispensable element of his pageantry.

'Do I look like a monkey in the coat?' Abdul Ali asked, as he took the first step onward. 'Do I really look like a crow, so ugly?'

I asked Nur Hussain what he thought. 'Why don't you answer him?' I said. 'After all it is not a meaningless question.'

He took a moment and then said: 'Protect your heart. Forget the rest.'

Did he learn that from Shah Abdul Karim, I wondered?

a tent next to a burial ground under the open sky, knowing that one day after my death from acute starvation I would be buried by strangers in a strange place, or left on a street corner to be eaten by dogs and vultures? Would I be able to think clearly about such a long and critical journey? Would I do something else entirely, like killing people who stood in my way, or who hid food in their backyards and did not sell their wares because they waited for a price hike? It was good that I was alone, with no children or elderly relatives; good that I had no parents to look after. If I had, I would have left them behind. I would have snatched their food to feed myself. *Every life has a duty to live, you know; every life is precious, but at this moment my life is more precious than yours* – this is what I would have argued. It would have been reprehensible.

I became exhausted whenever I asked myself these questions. I struggled for breath. I struggled to look normal, to appear to Nur Hussain as though I was perfectly fine, fit to accompany him to Moina Mia's gathering, although I knew in my mind that I was falling into an endless abyss.

In 1974 alone over one and a half million people died in Sheikh Mujib's liberated Bangladesh. How big was that number? Five times the number of Bangladeshis killed by Pakistani forces during the entire period of the Liberation War in 1971. No natural disaster had claimed so many lives since the beginning of our national calendar. No ruthless tribal landlord or maharaja in our history had been the cause of so many deaths on the Subcontinent. No religious clash, territorial disagreement or deadly disease had subjected our people to witnessing helplessly the untimely demise of such an astronomical number of lives.

21

THE NEWCOMERS

A new wave of refugees came to the city in September 1974. It was probably the worst thing they could do. In the villages, they could collect herbs, catch birds in the fields, steal eggs from turtles and uproot a banana tree to extract its white skeleton. There were hundreds of thousands of canals and ponds full of fish. Such opportunities were not available in the cities. Still, they came.

What pushed them to set out for Dhaka at that critical moment of our national history, I asked myself once again, if not a conspiracy of Pakistani collaborators, as Moina Mia had said? I came up with several answers. First, they were not landowners. These people were rootless, so it was easy for them to decide to set out for a new place; they had nothing to lose. Second, they were not going anywhere. They were just wandering the way they had wandered year after year, generation after generation, before the liberation as well as after it. And in the course of that wandering they found themselves in Dhaka, which happened to be the capital of the country. Third, they were scared of seeing more death. Death came every day. They looked for the most densely populated area in the country. They thought they would be able to hide themselves among Dhaka's crowds, where death would not find them. Fourth, they did not want to die meaninglessly; they did not want to be shadows of lives without enjoying the promises of the new country. They had lived year after year in slavery, burdened by discrimination and shame. Now they were free. If they could survive a few more days, they might be able to live with honour. By going from place to place, they wanted to buy time.

I revised my answers again and again, until I believed I knew exactly why the refugees chose to come to Dhaka. For other refugees at any other time, I would not have used the same arguments. I was sure these refugees set out on the road to Dhaka one morning compelled by a higher cause.

They wanted to get as close as they could to Sheikh Mujib. That was it, I thought; definitely. That was why they were here. He was their man. They wanted to draw his attention to their suffering. What better way was there to do that than by coming to the capital, becoming his neighbour, burying the dead at his doorstep, bowing down before him and saying with unshakeable conviction that even after thousands of deaths they would not lose confidence in him? He was not going to go see them in their villages. They had waited and waited and seen death after death; still, he did not come, even though he had promised in his speeches to look after them. So they came to him.

I saluted them. They were strong people. They had made it this far through the famine. Soon they would be at his house; they would be his uninvited guests and speak their minds, calling for his attention.

If I lived in a village and the famine had hit, I asked myself, would I have the courage to come to Dhaka as they had? Would I dare travel those drought-stricken miles and raise sitting before a colourless sunset – excited? It is not to be seriously admired, is it? If an Awami League representative does not know how to keep his clothes in order, how will people think that his party will be able to keep order in the country? We have to be more cautious about everything we do, especially about small details such as wearing a coat, keeping our shoes shiny, hanging the portrait of Sheikh Mujib in a spotless and expensive mahogany frame, choosing an effective typographic style for banners, choosing images with warm colours for the posters. These are things that are easily overlooked, though they make the first impression.'

He asked how many coats Nur Hussain had.

Why, just one, we replied, was that a problem?

'Only one?' He could not believe us. We were to buy half a dozen immediately, he said, if possible that very day, so that if one was damaged or discoloured or lost, Nur Hussain had another ready to wear to work.

'It is his voice that is important, not the coat,' I said resolutely. I did not hesitate to argue, as I felt a bit embarrassed by his interrogation. 'It is the way he delivers the speech. Anyone can buy a coat if there is money; but hundreds and thousands of beautiful coats would not enable people to serve the Awami League the way Nur Hussain does.' I looked at Nur for support. He was as lifeless as a yellowed picture in a frame. 'Besides,' I said, 'coats are worn over the *punjabi*; they are meant to be discoloured, aren't they? There is the sun. There is humidity. And a world of dust out there. They cannot glisten all the time, can they?'

Moina Mia understood my point. He brought out some money from the soft interior of his pocket and handed it to me. 'The purpose of having money is not to save it. It is to complete a job efficiently.' He asked if we understood what he had just said. We nodded. 'Good. Also, buy a pair of *punjabis*. A new coat without a new *punjabi* is meaningless. It means we respect neither the coat nor the *punjabi*.'

pronunciation and modulation, so that the question did not have to be repeated. He said he had understood me, and that he would remember all that during our visit. But now he seemed lost.

Sheikh Mujib often completed Nur's sentences by relating his own experiences of life in a village. He was born in Tungipara in the Gopalganj district, he reminded us, which was more or less the same as Gangasagar or any other village in Bangladesh. When he was a child, the only fun they'd had there was jumping into the canal from a bamboo bridge. Then he looked at Nur Hussain as if to enquire whether or not children still did the same in Gangasagar. When he did not receive a response, he began again. He spoke about crickets in the chickpea fields, butterflies among pumpkin flowers, thirsty crows drinking from date-juice pitchers and chasing the full moon in the evening across the fields. He would have loved to visit the place where Sepoy Mostafa Kamal had sacrificed himself for the country, he said at the end. He would be happy to have Nur Hussain beside him at that time.

It was such a serious point, but Nur Hussain only smiled.

What are you doing, you little insect, I said in my mind. *You are embarrassing me. Don't just smile, show some manners! Say, 'It would be an honour, Mr Prime Minister. What a beautiful idea!' Make your life a bit easier by showing some enthusiasm. What a leader like him could not do for you! He can direct his people to offer you a motorway construction contract. He can mould your life with gold. There cannot be any better prize than being in his good books during such a difficult time.*

Sheikh Mujib continued in his usual easy manner: 'Would villagers appreciate a monument in Gangasagar in memory of Mostafa Kamal?'

151

Nur Hussain nodded, though I had warned him specifically against nodding to the prime minister. Only people with little or no self-esteem would nod to a proposal instead of expressing their consent verbally. Yet Sheikh Mujib accepted his answer as valid. What a wise leader. All-forgiving. 'So be it,' he said. 'A monument to Mostafa Kamal.'

He repeated the sentence as if trying to register the decision in his mind, or trying indirectly to extract some response from Nur Hussain.

At this point Nur Hussain cracked his knuckles. He cracked his knuckles! *I am going to kill you, Nur, at home tonight; I am going to drink your blood.* The thumb first, then index, middle, ring and pinky fingers of the right hand, and then of the left hand, producing sharp popping sounds. Sheikh Mujib noticed but remained silent until Nur Hussain had popped his last finger. Then he continued the conversation with ease. 'The people of Gangasagar deserve to be honoured for their resilience,' he said in conclusion. 'They are great people.'

Then it was Moina Mia's turn.

He was the complete opposite of Nur Hussain. While Nur Hussain withdrew into silence and showed a degree of detachment and disinterestedness, Moina Mia spoke a lot, with intimacy and fervour. He addressed Sheikh Mujib as *Mujib Bhai*, which spoke of the cordial relationship they had. 'I called them to my residence, told them Mujib Bhai wants to talk to you, you must go,' he said. He pointed at Nur Hussain. 'This one argued that we had schedules for public meetings in the constituency. People would wait. Continuity is a big factor in a political campaign, he said. I told him that when Mujib Bhai wanted us to see him, public meetings – even if there were hundreds of them – could not stop us. They were irrelevant. As you yourself have said, Mujib Bhai, there are things that can be sacrificed for things that cannot be sacrificed, so long as someone is alive. Now here we are, sitting before you.'

Sheikh Mujib thanked him quietly, probably trying to remember the occasion on which he had said such a thing, and asked him about his wife and children. He asked how the children were doing at school, which school they were attending and why he had not brought them along, for they, too, would have had a good time. He must bring them during his next visit.

Moina Mia's answers were prompt. He always made sure he behaved like an ideal follower of his leader, one who knew what he would be asked and what the best answers would be. When asked if the school buildings were adequately renovated after the war to make students comfortable in the classrooms, Moina Mia said they had not only been renovated but also adorned with state-of-the-art scientific equipment and study materials. 'Mujib Bhai, you'll be surprised to hear that a new generation of students will soon graduate from these schools with exceptional skills and analytical ability. They won't be like our forefathers, with one foot in the mud, closer to death than life, always tired and whining; they'll make us proud in every possible way.' He became emotional when he narrated how his own son had learned the classifications of mammals within a week thanks to the illustrated textbooks introduced the previous year. Those books even featured a picture of the first human footprint in the moon dust. 'Can you believe,' he said, 'after only three years' work we are only three years behind America?' He lowered his voice as if giving away secrets. 'We're thinking of at least half a dozen Nobel Prizes in the next two decades in the fields of science, medicine and poverty alleviation. The day is not far off when we will overtake India and China as the most prosperous nation in the East. We may even start a transcontinental competition with Liechtenstein in the fields of investment and banking.'

'*Likh-tan-stine?*' Sheikh Mujib asked absentmindedly.

'The largest country in Europe, Mujib Bhai, larger than France and Germany combined. The whole country is a bank, and the whole world stores its money there. People in Liechtenstein do not need to work to buy something.'

It was my turn now. I was ready for it. I had been ready, in fact, from the moment I decided not to ask him anything. He was not the enemy, I said to myself. He was a friend, our most reliable friend. Those who said he was an enemy said so to *create* enmity between us – between him and his people. They would love to see us fall apart. He could not go to every house and give lessons in citizenship to people who were letting their countrymen down by being selfish. It was not possible. He could only guide. Accepting his guidance was up to us citizens.

After one of the members of the *Rakkhi Bahini* who had escorted us appeared at the door, I understood my time with him would be short. It did not matter, I said to myself. It was not important how much time I had with him, how many questions he asked me or how many of them I understood and answered successfully. That I had sat face to face with him was good enough for me to give him a permanent place in my memory. I could live with that for a long time to come. Perhaps my whole life. I wished every Bangladeshi could have a chance to sit with him

He looked at me, and I sensed immediately that he knew he had besieged me with that look. He could see through me, analyze my fears and doubts and interpret my thoughts and misconceptions. Then he took his pen from his breast pocket and carefully put it in my own. I would need it, he said; I would need it when the time was right. Then came the embrace, that soft, caring embrace, and a sweet goodbye to the three of us. He bade a special goodbye to Nur Hussain, whom he kept in his embrace one moment longer and whom he called 'my brother' again.

26

A TRANSFORMATION

I could not sleep that night. I could not sleep the following morning either, nor the afternoon after that. Whenever I closed my eyes, I saw Sheikh Mujib's face. I saw him sitting at his window wondering what to do about the famine, about all the people who loved him but who now questioned his leadership. I saw him suffer at the news of every single death in the country. He had a tear for every departed soul. It was a sad, sad face I saw – sad and anxious and exhausted.

I imagined he could not sleep, either. How could he? Our institutions were not functioning properly. His colleagues in the government did not value his trust. They were supposed to work hard to make the country's institutions strong, so that the country itself could eventually become strong, but they took advantage of his dependence on them. It was they who had sold aid relief on the black market, multiplying people's sufferings. If anyone deserved a bad day today, it was they, not he.

I wore my Mujib coat every day. I wore it whenever I went out – even if only for a few minutes, say, to buy turmeric powder or a pack of chickpeas, or to take out the rubbish – as a tribute to his heroism. I said hello to people whom I had seen on the street for years now, but had never wanted to speak to. I did not care how nasty they were as individuals and neighbours, or how young or old or politically indifferent and inexperienced they appeared.

'We have already lost over a million people,' I told them. 'If Sheikh Mujib is as strict as we would like him to be at this time, to bring the country back onto what we consider the right track, he will have to kill another million. Is that what you really want? More deaths, mounting anger, madness and mayhem? Who among you can stand before me with your hand upon your heart, your mind free of clouds, and solemnly announce that you have put your country before yourself? Who among you can claim you are not tainted by bloodshed or violence of some sort? You may choose not to answer me, but I know the answer right away; it is here, in my own heart. Sheikh Mujib will have to kill our friends, our neighbours, our relatives, siblings, parents, husbands and wives, our children, because every house, every family, every neighbourhood has contributed to the making of this mess.

'If all of us are not cured, the country cannot be cured. Maybe he does not want to see any more blood on the road after all the blood we have to shed to free the country. If he does not, my belief is that he is still the most patient person around here, our wisest and greatest person. He knows blood cannot be washed away with blood.'

I shook hands with rickshaw-*wallahs* at street corners where they waited for passengers, began easy and sweet political conversations with them, grabbed their palms until they spoke at least one or two good words about Sheikh Mujib. I asked shopkeepers the price of mustard oil and garlic cloves loudly, so that everyone could see I was in a Mujib coat and understand that Sheikh Mujib had not lost his voice despite everything: at least one Bengali was standing firm for him.

At home, I bathed regularly for the sake of the coat. I shaved my beard with the sharpest straight razor available on the market, and smeared coconut oil on my hair so that it did not look unkempt. Working morning and evening, I kept the flat clean and the stairs and the yard shiny and spotless. There were dry weeds in the shadow behind the gate; I removed them with a spade, and sprinkled water on the ground so that the dust settled down quickly. I opened all the windows to let in fresh air and light and regularly played the patriotic songs of Dwijendralal Roy on my two-in-one stereo, sometimes until late into the evening. If every house was uncluttered like ours, I believed, Sheikh Mujib would be successful. Great leaders, too, need strong public support at critical moments.

Nur Hussain did not wear his coat when we went out for groceries or to attend burial prayers. He was merely following my suggestions, I remembered. He was improving. He was improving exactly the way I wanted him to. But I wore mine with great passion. He might have found that contradictory, but I did not care. My priority was my leader. Shallow and unimaginative as Nur Hussain was, it would take me a thousand years to explain the real worth of a leader like Sheikh Mujib to him. Sheikh Mujib needed people like me who could evolve with time, leave behind their individual vendettas and serve some greater purpose. To appreciate Sheikh Mujib's worth required generosity and intellect. I understood what he was for us, and what would make him complete in the new era.

As I spoke to people, I gathered that most of them genuinely believed the famine would cost Sheikh Mujib dearly. It had already made him somewhat unpopular. Who knew where it was going to lead the Awami League as a party? If the present course of events could not be thwarted, as some predicted, the country would soon fall into the hands of those who opposed independence. They meant the Islamic fundamentalists, who still lived among us like predators and wanted to reunite our country with Pakistan at any cost. The defeat of Sheikh Mujib would mean their victory and the eventual extinction of the Bengali nation. That could not be allowed to happen. Not on our soil.

I hugged people again and again, patted their backs and whispered to them in consolation, saying: 'Let us not doubt it – the bad days will end. They will end because we still have people like Sheikh Mujib among us who can see beyond the present. He knows what is going to happen to us next year or ten, twenty years after that. It is not the first time in our history that we have faced hardship, and the problem now is not sovereignty: it is something as mundane and essential as food. We will get over it; after all, we have already attained precious sovereignty. We shall kill all the fish in our thousands of rivers to feed our hungry people. We shall collect all the leaves from the jungle, and all the grass from the fields to fill our stomachs. We shall live on simple rainwater, if nothing else is available. But we won't have to do that because Sheikh Mujib will soon be victorious. Sheikh Mujib has always been victorious, hasn't he? People of this country have known one leader alone: that's him. He is a legend in our land. People will not desert him simply because we happen to have a temporary shortage of food that has brought us to our knees. The Bengali nation is not so fickle. *Joy Bangla!*'

BOOK TWO

1

THE DISHONOURABLE DEMISE
OF TWO BURGLARS

Abdul Ali visited our flat one afternoon. He was in his *punjabi* and Mujib coat. The clothes were still new, but it seemed he had already lost interest in them. He had no interest in talking, either. He just sat on the sofa, silently drank the tea that Nur Hussain made him and looked around. After a few sips, he pushed the cup away.

'Is the tea not good?' I asked. 'Do you want some more sugar? Perhaps a few more drops of milk.'

That was not it.

Ruhul Amin, the gatekeeper, had shot two people dead the previous night, he said.

They had been burglars, and had come in the dark, grabbed two sacks of rice, hurled them over their shoulders and then tried to leave the premises by going over the boundary wall. Surprisingly, they had come wearing Mujib coats, and seemed to know exactly where the rice was. It was not immediately known if they had accomplices or acted alone out of sheer desperation. Moina Mia had advised the *Rakkhi Bahini* to look into the matter.

163

Although it was an unfortunate event, I told Abdul Ali, it was actually the dead men's fault. True, we were enduring a famine, but that did not give us the right to break into people's houses to steal from them! 'Where is morality? Where are social values, common sense and our desire to protect each other? Are we all turning into animals because we did not have a meal last night, and do not have any rice left for tomorrow?' I told him the matter was not too complicated for someone with a stable mind to understand. Ruhul Amin was only doing his job.

'Like the police. Will the police allow someone to leave with bags of banknotes from the vault of a bank just because the criminal needs the money? Not at all. Gatekeepers have to be gatekeepers.'

I waited for his approval. His concern was sincere, I could see that. I was sure his confusion would soon fade away.

Nur Hussain had followed neither Abdul Ali nor me. Standing at the window, he must have thought we were talking about professional matters with which he need not concern himself. He moved to the kitchen and stayed there, leaving us alone.

Abdul Ali sat motionless. He looked at me for such a long time that I felt uncomfortable under his gaze. So I thought some elaboration might help. I had seen many dumb people working at the party offices. The dumb became dumber there within a short while. The party sucked the intelligence out of them. It diluted their personality. Besides, he was not a properly educated person; it's likely he had no idea that there was a huge conflict between individual choice and the collective good. Individual choices must be set aside to allow the collective to prosper, even if that meant death.

'There is no place for burglars in our society,' I said. 'Today's burglars will be tomorrow's robbers, witches and demons. They will eat us up. Today they will steal our rice, tomorrow our sanity, the next day our country. The day after that, we shall look behind us and find that our thousand-year history has disappeared. We'll have no tradition, no moment of sacrifice to take inspiration from. Those burglars were enemies of us all. We are better off without them.'

Abdul Ali rose quickly, as if electrified, then took a few quick steps, then a few slow steps, and then stood still before saying that he was not there to talk about the shooting, but to inform us that we had more good luck in store for us. He gave me a forced smile. It was probably better than our previous good luck, he said. Knowing that he would not explain what this good luck was, I asked when Moina Mia expected us.

He was expecting *me*, not *us*, Abdul Ali corrected me, with one eye on the kitchen door. He added that Moina Mia was expecting me right away, and that I was to go with Abdul Ali.

I told Nur Hussain I would return soon and that I would inform him in detail what our meeting was about, that he should not worry. This was the first time I was going to such a meeting without him. He nodded.

Was the meeting about the two dead men? Was Abdul Ali trying to tell me something by only giving me the barest of information? He paced all over the room. If he was concerned, I consoled myself, it was only natural to conclude that he himself was associated with the burglary, not I. I was not a close enough friend about whom he would be worried

165

if I were in danger. I must take note, I thought. If I'm asked whether or not I've noticed any change in his behaviour, I could mention it. I could also mention the half-finished tea, and his indifference. I must not forget anything.

As I put on my Mujib coat over my *punjabi*, Abdul Ali watched me closely. 'In case I stay out late,' I told him. 'So many things can happen.' He did not reply. 'In case it gets cold,' I said, louder. He still did not reply.

Ruhul Amin opened the small door of the gate and stood aside for us to enter. If he could, I thought, he would have run away from us. Having shot two people, he was now a victim of his own guilt. He could not raise his eyes to meet mine.

'*Salaam,*' I said, finding him silent. 'How are we doing today? Are we all happy in this beautiful weather?' I noticed the .303 rifle on his back – not a technically advanced killing machine. It was old and had a rusty trigger, barrel and muzzle, as if it had been buried under the ground for a decade or more. But it had done its job.

He must have guessed that I knew about the shooting, especially as I was with Abdul Ali. Ruhul Amin must now think I was watching him minutely, wondering how he had hidden that killer instinct every time we had met and he had said *salaam* to me. He noticed me looking at him and realized that I could not do so without looking at the rifle as well, without associating it with the act of killing and concluding that it was only an extension of his unstable, repulsive inner self. 'Sometimes it is hard for a man carrying a rifle to dissociate himself from the rifle,' I said to myself. 'They become one. The ego of the person makes the rifle powerful, and the rifle makes a beast of the person, acting as a crude replacement for his spine.'

It was better to further clarify what was already clear. Instead of condemning him, I thought I would sympathize. The dead were dead, I would say. It did not matter if they were two, or two thousand. Whatever the reason, and however brutal it might appear to him, the truth was that they were no more, and therefore any regret was unnecessary. I could repeat what I had already said to Abdul Ali: it was not Ruhul Amin's fault. If the burglars had not gone to steal, they would not be dead now (provided they were not already victims of the famine). See, I am not dead, I would argue. My head is working fine, and I am not screaming for mercy for myself. He could see Abdul Ali was not dead either: that was because we had been able to control our most sinister thoughts the moment they raised their heads. We did not let them out to make us weaker individuals and endanger our lives. We were not involved in silly crimes.

'One does not need to work hard to see the truth in such a matter,' I said to myself. If the burglars were so desperate for rice, they could choose a house without a gatekeeper, or without a gatekeeper with a weapon on his shoulder. I could have pointed out lots of 'ifs' like this, which would have led to one logical conclusion: Ruhul Amin was not guilty of murder.

Then, on second thought, I stopped myself. What would my sympathy mean to him? Wouldn't he have to kill again tonight if he came across burglars crossing the boundary wall with sacks of rice on their shoulders? What if they came in the hundreds, in league with all the people who went hungry in the neighbourhood? What if they were from his family, people to whom he owed something? They might say they needed his cooperation now more than ever, and they wanted rice, only rice to feed their starving bellies, not money or animals or houses or plots of land in return.

I could not decide the destinies of men, I thought, not even burglars. Ruhul Amin must know what he had to do at a given moment in his given role. If he killed someone it was entirely his responsibility. He would have to work through his anxiety and guilt. If the burglars proved too many, and if they came every night, still it would be he who would have to decide what to do.

Standing at the small door I noticed Abdul Ali step towards Ruhul Amin, take him in a hearty embrace and pat him on the back. 'Brother Ruhul,' he said, in an equally hearty tone, 'my brother … o, my brother!'

I was confused momentarily. Was this show of affection for killing the burglars and keeping his employer safe, or to express sympathy with Ruhul Amin so that Ruhul did not feel bad for what he had done? I did not know.

Ruhul Amin wiped his nose on the sleeve of his *punjabi* and freed himself from Abdul Ali's embrace almost forcefully before going back into his gatekeeper's booth. From the gate I saw him standing against the wall with his eyes closed.

'He is in agony,' I whispered to Abdul Ali. 'Not every killer will feel the same way. Some will not look back, not for a moment. There is nothing called "remorse" in their book. Some will eat their clothes because they are not aware of what they are doing; the killing and its aftermath do not exist for them. Some will collapse in extreme fear. Will they kill themselves one day, like they killed their victims? Some will be so startled by their own actions; they will behave as though they are deaf and dumb. But this one here is different. He will be scared of the slightest things now. Don't talk to him. Whatever you say – good or bad – will embarrass him. Leave him alone. He will have to rip through his tormented soul before he is ready for a normal conversation. It is not easy. Give him time.'

2

SOLD

I sat on the sofa beside bundles of leaflets that covered almost half the floor, and waited for Moina Mia. There was a door on the right that opened into another room, inside which I could see a huge pile of boxes. Two workers were unloading a van in the yard and making another huge pile at the rear corner.

Moina Mia came through the door and handed me a leaflet that had two items printed on it: Sheikh Mujib's face and the words 'OUR LIBERATOR' in bold letters. I looked once and then left it on the tea table.

'So what do you think?' Moina Mia asked, sitting opposite me.

He had not told me anything about what Abdul Ali had referred to as 'my good luck', so I didn't immediately understand what exactly he wanted to know from me.

'What do you think of the leaflets?' he asked. 'Would they make people curious about the message?'

Although the leaflets looked like promotional materials from some therapeutic massage centre, I said I thought they looked good. I wanted to concentrate on our deal; maybe after the deal, if it went well, I would feel more enthusiastic about the leaflets.

'Only "good"?' he said. 'Then see this one.' He extended a new page to me, which was smaller in size but heavier. 'Peel n' Stick. Water-resistant, safe for any surface and restickable. Just came from the supplier. By the weekend, every bus stop, electricity pole, hospital door, school gate, restaurant counter and public library desk in the city will be covered with these. Thousands of boxes have already been dispatched to carefully chosen Awami League representatives.'

I held the sticker up. It had the same picture, though not the same wording. The new wording, printed in the same bold letters, read: 'OUR PROTECTOR'.

'We have to be innovative,' he said, sticking one on the tea table. 'The target audience of this campaign is the new generation – more specifically, those who did not fight in the war because they were too young. For future political stability in the country, it is necessary that they know who Sheikh Mujib is.'

It was an honour that he was letting me see these materials before public, I said, instead of commenting on their artistic quality. They inspired me. I now felt more involved in the campaign than ever. If there was anything I could do other than what I was already doing, he should tell me. 'Maybe I can take a box of leaflets with me and distribute them in the market,' I said. 'I can stand at the crossroads and campaign among young people who come there looking to steal food. There are so many of them, and if they are not brought into the party soon, they may get involved with drugs and addiction. It won't be a burden for me at all. I have to go to the market anyway.'

'Distributing one box of leaflets at a local market won't have much of an effect,' he said. 'It won't have the kind of significant impact we're thinking of. We've gathered together fifty-five different types of leaflets, twenty-eight types of Peel n' Sticks, sixteen types of banners, fourteen types of billboards and twenty different adverts to go on TV and radio, as part of our nationwide informational campaign. We have arranged twelve hundred exhibitions and forty-two thousand discussion programmes across the nation, all to be executed in the next twelve months. For our seventy million people we have printed a mass of three hundred and fifty million leaflets, so that each person receives five copies. We do not want to see a single mind in the country go against Sheikh Mujib and the Awami League.'

'Sheikh Mujib has liberated us – it is a historical truth,' I said. 'Who can dispute that? He can live a thousand glorious lives only on the basis of that fact.'

'We want every individual in this country to enquire about Sheikh Mujib when they wake up in the morning; we won't stop until children are refusing to go to sleep unless they are told stories of Sheikh Mujib, and until girls refuse to get married until their grooms promise to be loyal to Sheikh Mujib. We will invade every brain and plant the flag there of Bengali nationalism. Bangladesh will be a different country soon.'

He was happy to see my willingness to help, he said, but he needed me for something else, for something more important. He pushed the stickers aside, dusted his palms against each other and said: 'There is a price for everything, Khaleque Biswas; there is nothing that money cannot buy in the time of famine. In fact, the famine has made money more powerful, hasn't it?'

If I stayed with him, said Moina Mia, I would never have to worry about money again. 'Khaleque Biswas, believe me. This is it.' I should forget about being a journalist, he said, and let him guide me. He knew where the money was and how to win it. It was not any ordinary deal; it was a deal with Sheikh Mujib, the most powerful man in the country. Then he came to the point I was waiting for.

He wanted something I had, and he was ready to pay a price for it. In the same way Sheikh Mujib wanted something *he* had, so Sheikh Mujib must pay him a price if he wanted to have it for himself. Did I understand what it was that he wanted to buy from me?

It was simple. I told him I understood, and I was ready to sell. 'Not a problem ... not at all a problem. We are talking about our magnificent prime minister; when he wants something, he shall have it. Have I shown any sign that I would refuse him anything?'

'I knew you would not disagree,' he replied. 'I knew it the first day we met. Your eyes spoke of great cooperation. There was no sign of pity or revenge in them. You were as simple as water. But we have to maintain a certain decency in dealing with each other, don't we, especially when it is about such a sensitive product, so that our petty interests do not hamper our great future.'

My admiration for him had reached such a level, I said, that I could do anything for him. I was not teasing him. I really felt I had become a different person. 'I am a nationalist,' I said. 'I have duties to my motherland. I will bring my product to you. From now on, it is yours. Do whatever you want to do with it. I don't need to know anything.'

He heard me in silence; he did not answer.

172

I was aware of the quality of my product, I said calmly; I knew how much it was worth. I asked him if he knew he would have to come up with a competitive price. He said I should not worry about the price, as the amount he was going to mention would surely surprise me.

Thus I sold Nur Hussain once again. First I had sold him to the people on the street for their coins. Then I had sold him to Moina Mia, for his campaign. Now I was selling him to Sheikh Mujib through Moina Mia. I believed he would accept it. He had never disregarded me, never wanted to understand money, though it was for money that he had come to the city from that distant village. Besides, he would be doing the same job. What would there be to complain about? The only difference was that he would speak to a different and a larger audience now. We would travel across the country and speak for Sheikh Mujib. We would be sent a few days early, along with members of the *Rakkhi Bahini*. We would live in the areas reserved for VIPs. In due course, we would be advised as to when Nur Hussain should speak and for how long. He was to recite one paragraph of the 7 March speech, or a few more paragraphs from it, which would be edited and supplied to us beforehand so that Nur Hussain had enough time to memorize the text. Some new paragraphs would also be written to make the speech relevant to the subject matter of Sheikh Mujib's speech of the day. They would have a particular message for the nation, which must be articulated religiously.

3

AN EXCUSE FOR KILLING

As I left, I saw Abdul Ali waiting for me anxiously. He took my hand and pulled me aside to tell me that Ruhul Amin had decided to quit his job. He had a family with three children to feed. They would starve to death if he quit. 'Is he out of his mind to make such a horrible decision?' I said. 'What does he think he is doing?' Abdul Ali asked if I would be kind enough to have a few words with Ruhul Amin, to convince him to stay. He had tried his best, but it seemed the gatekeeper was adamant.

'Use your best words, Khaleque *sahib*. Be brutal, if need be. A person of that nature deserves to be punished. I suppose he does not understand that he has no right to make a family suffer by taking such an obscene decision. An ideal worker will never succumb to the pressures of his workplace, no matter what, do you agree? He cannot afford it. He will, in turn, force the workplace to succumb to him. He will fight until his last breath, because he knows if he loses his job he will die anyway. So be aggressive. Yell at him as loud as you can. Slap him right in the ears if you need to, so that he cannot hear even his own thoughts. Give him no chance to argue.'

I did not have any special relationship with Ruhul Amin, and I did not think my words would work either. I had no idea why Abdul Ali believed I might be successful where he had failed. But out of courtesy, I told him I would go to the booth and give it a try.

From his chair, Ruhul Amin saw me coming. When I closed the door behind me and stood with my back to the window so that nobody could disturb us in case he broke into tears or became agitated, he looked at me once again. I did not know what to say; I was afraid to be alone with him, so I stood silently waiting for him to begin. The rifle was on the table, within his reach. It was foolish, utterly foolish, to be there, especially on a day that promised me a better future. Just at the moment I decided to leave, he spoke up.

'They gave me no choice,' he said, 'absolutely no choice. They came to me, both of them, three, four times before last night, and asked me to leave the gate open for them, just for a few minutes so that they could escape quietly with the rice on their backs. I knew the house had a large rice storage room, and that it was full; losing two bags would not hurt Moina Mia, and they were burdened with a large number of close relatives who had recently come over from the village. My problem lay elsewhere. I am the gatekeeper; I am entrusted with the responsibility of safeguarding the house and everything in it, precious or trivial. I cannot leave the gate open and unattended for them, or for anybody – not even for a few seconds, so that they can steal from my employer. It would be a breach of my pledge.

'They refused to understand me; they knew nothing about pledges or promises or loyalty. They said, then, that they would have to leave the house by climbing over the wall. Are you following me? That is what they said. Over the wall. I showed them my rifle; I told them it was active and always loaded, although it was not. "You don't want to know what it is capable of doing. You really don't want to know." "Stop us if you want," they replied. "Perhaps it is better to take a bullet in the back once in a while than live in eternal shame."

'I swear to you, I have never heard anything stranger than that. I could not believe them. How could I, carrying as I was a rifle for such a long time on my shoulder, which I had always considered the source of such intense fear that no man would be able to conquer it? I did not believe they meant what they said. Would anyone with the slightest sense of responsibility actually be rattled by such threats from burglars? "Poor people do not want to be friends with poor people," I said. "They want to be friends with those who can provide. I am not your friend. When you need help, I will not be on your side." I spoke the truth, didn't I, though it was lowly of me? Sometimes it is acceptable to disgrace yourself if that saves a life, don't you think? I wanted to frighten them. A gatekeeper has to be tactical if he wants to avoid trouble.

'I had no idea how desperate they were. They told me the time when they would steal – the exact day and hour and minute. They even showed me which corner of the boundary wall they had chosen for their escape. I waited for them the whole day. I cleaned the rifle, loaded it and inspected it again and again to make sure it would not fail when I needed it. When evening came, I took my position along the boundary wall well ahead of time, aiming at the exact spot, with my heart beating, my legs shaking, my forehead sweating, waiting to prove myself wrong. They would appear only if they believed in miracles, I thought. You know, sometimes reality is too indistinguishable from miracles. Sometimes necessity is just too harsh.'

He knew his victims. He had warned them and tried to frighten them, tried to stop them. Yet they went ahead.

My head reeled. How could people be so reckless?

'You want me to stay here?' he asked. 'I guess that is why Abdul Ali sent you to me. He is such a wonderful person. I wish him nothing but well. But you tell me, tell me sincerely, can I stay here anymore after what has happened? Shouldn't I be ashamed of what I have done? Shouldn't I take the rifle, load it and aim it at myself, ending the power of miracles forever?'

I had never come into contact with a killer. I wanted to thank him, because he had told me honestly what he knew of the matter; but I found I was growing angry. 'You would not do that, mister,' I said loudly, moving away from the window. I thought it was useless to protect someone who considered it wise to destroy himself. 'You would not kill yourself or go to the police to surrender or even quit this job. You will have your lunch on time, relish your afternoon tea, say your evening prayers and abide by your duties, day in, day out. I guess I am a good judge of human character; I know exactly how far you'd go.' I bent before him and edged close to his face. 'You're a piece of dirt, you know. You're a cheap, obnoxious, miserable Bengali man who is completely immersed in desperate lunacy. Don't find my saying this outrageous, because even if I try and try really hard, I could not be as outrageous as you have already been. You're not only rude and unkind; you bring shame on all of us. You're worse than an animal.'

I opened the door quickly and rushed out as he stood up behind me to say something.

'No, not a word. You don't have to tell me anything, no further explanation of the situation, no excuses for your actions, no descriptions of the gloomy and dreadful night you've passed, nothing; not now, not ever. You knew what you were doing when you aimed at them. You could have made a difference by withdrawing yourself from your ego, by assessing your plans, your precautions or whatever you call them, but you chose not to. You had idle fantasies about being a loyal worker to your employer. You're a damned man. I can't help you.'

As if chased by crazy dogs, haunted by ghosts, I crossed the small street and came to the main road, where I entered a tea stall to drink a glass of water to the last drop and started walking again. Under no circumstances would I deny that I had compromised my integrity to a large extent because of my present uncertain financial condition – but killing a person was not a game. There was no excuse for it, including the fact that Ruhul Amin was paid to protect his employer. What did Ruhul Amin think of human life?

A thin fog descended. Through it came the sound of cries from the tent city on the school field. There was a fire there, said someone. 'So big a fire, as if from Hell. Tents cannot burn so high and so bright. Impossible. What do we have in a tent? A couple of pillows, a tattered quilt, some earthen cooking pots, empty bottles of sweetened syrup, a bit of rubbish in a bamboo basket, ailing children and parents sleeping on the floor. They can't burn for long. It is Hell. It is definitely Hell.'

I walked slowly up the filthy road. People ran any which way they could. Naked children ran, coughing, screaming, laughing like idiots, some standing back, throwing stones at the fire. Neighbours were fighting. Locals were chasing the migrants, and the migrants chased locals. Some woman blamed God for everything she saw. 'What kind of God is He, no mercy in His heart? Who will bring Him flowers? Who will bow down westward?' Biting her fingers, she watched as the smoke rose to the sky. Some other women, standing behind her, began to weep.

4
You, Not I

I did not want to waste my energy on Ruhul Amin. It would only end up filling my day with misery and thoughts of violence. It would tire me out. There were more important things to do with my time than focusing on other people's idiocy, their chronic hysteria, how they perceived their lives, and whether or not they had any real desire to remain sensible and noble. 'I am not that cheap,' I said to myself. I wanted to be assured that I really had at my disposal what I had sold to Moina Mia.

'We'll be speaking for Sheikh Mujib,' I told Nur Hussain immediately after I returned home. 'We'll be speaking soon.' Then I elaborated: 'Within three weeks or so. There is no specific date yet. We'll be informed in time.'

He did not respond, so I told him again. This time I said *he* would be speaking soon. I said it a little louder and more distinctly. 'Hello,' I said, 'I am talking to you, are you listening? Yes, you; there is nobody else in this flat.' I did not care if I sounded rude. He needed to understand that silence was not an answer.

He watched me for a moment and then said: '*We* shall be speaking,' which he immediately modified to: '*I* will be speaking soon. *I* will be speaking for *Sheikh Mujib*.'

181

His voice shook slightly. I enjoyed that. I enjoyed his weaknesses as much as I enjoyed his brilliance. I wanted him to understand perfectly when I was angry, what I would not tolerate and what I was allergic to. I did not want him to move even an inch from where I wanted him to stay. I did not want him to understand what I myself did not understand. I wanted him to smile exactly when I thought a little bit of smiling was acceptable, not before or after that. We would have a beautiful relationship as long as he did not do something that would force me to yell at him.

'Right,' I said. 'That is the deal. That is what we have promised Moina Mia today. Be ready for the call. Bath or no bath, food or no food, always on your feet. Always ready to serve. If you need anything in the meantime, let me know. Do not leave things for tomorrow. If you have any questions, let me know, so that they do not remain questions and do not affect your performance. Either you resolve them by following my rules, or I resolve them for you as I wish.'

He nodded. 'I shall be ready to serve,' he said, 'and I shall not leave anything for tomorrow.'

'Now, another thing,' I continued. 'If Moina Mia wants to see me again, and you are not a part of the meeting, which may happen more and more as the days go by and as more parties become involved with our work, I will pass on to you upon my return what I know. Like I am doing now. You have to know things. I feel you have to know what is going on even more than I do, and perhaps better than I do. That is because you are the showman, and my station is only backstage.'

'I am the showman,' he repeated obediently. Then I reminded him that he should be careful in his daily movements from now on, much more careful than he had ever been. A moment of complacency could complicate life seriously. He should not climb the stairs without maintaining three-point contacts, should not carry anything heavier than five kilograms by himself, should be careful with soap while having a bath so that he did not slip. What would I do with a Sheikh Mujib who could not stand on his feet?

When he got up to go, I stood at the door to be sure he followed my advice and held the railing while walking down the stairs.

'Good boy,' I thought. 'Very good boy. That is what I want from you. You will have everything if you follow me.'

The wind screamed at the window. The sun became pitiless.

Looking outside, I passed the time thinking. Then I walked across the room, listening to the silence, dusted the table and thought. I ate some lentil soup that Nur Hussain had cooked I did not know when, which tasted I did not know of what and thought, while heavy sweat ran down my forehead and into my eyes and mouth. I thought about Sheikh Mujib, Moina Mia, Nur Hussain and myself – what we were doing, and where we all now belonged. We seemed to have become bound in an intricate relationship, something I never dreamed was possible but was now a stark reality.

Sheikh Mujib was no different from Moina Mia or me; we were all fallible and delusional, we were all manipulating our own spheres of influence. Nur Hussain, who appeared like a ghost from a far-off village, was capable of doing certain things Moina Mia could never do, although he wished he could. And despite the fact that I was as ordinary as any man on the street, I could despise Moina Mia as much as I could despise Nur Hussain, and neither Sheikh Mujib nor any state technology or institution could do anything about it. We were all extraordinary, and indispensable to each other. The Awami League was facing serious publicity problems. If 1971was its best year, it was now a dying party. Its genitals were shrivelled; its collarbones were protruding; its soul had disappeared. Time was running out. But as long as the present situation continued, I thought, our relationship would become more active and interesting.

Then, lying in my bed, I thought about the price that Moina Mia had mentioned, which I had agreed to accept.

I was shocked.

5
A Thought in the Dark

The night grew deeper. Nur Hussain had returned a lot earlier than I had expected. He had eaten his meal by himself, without saying a word, and then gone to bed without practising the speech.

It was a few days now since he had recited it; some practice was necessary to maintain focus. But I did not insist. There would be time for practice tomorrow, and the day after tomorrow.

I tried to pacify myself by transforming my frustration into solid determination. I must find a comprehensive way of pursuing my interests. I decided not to see Moina Mia anytime soon.

I thought through what might happen if I did not see him. Walking, sitting, lying, I thought about what I might say if I saw him when I did want to see him, and then what I would say if I saw him after he sent Abdul Ali looking for me.

I was not afraid.

There was no wind to disturb me; no foxes screamed in the bush. But I woke up after an hour or two. After wandering aimlessly across the room for a few minutes, I chopped onions and chillies, washed potatoes in warm water, boiled them, prepared them in a paste and ate the meal with rice, sitting at the table. Nur Hussain's room was dark; there was no reason to think I would see him tonight, not in my present mental state; but I stood at his door for at least five minutes before going back to my room.

I woke up again before the night ended. I thought I heard some footsteps on the stairs, Abdul Ali's familiar heavy, slow and clear footsteps coming like beautiful music from the horizon. Moina Mia had understood his mistake and sent him immediately to mend it. It was too important to avoid or to be left for the morning.

In the darkness I opened the door and stepped outside to receive him. 'Come in, my friend,' I heard myself saying. 'Come on in; I have been waiting for you for a long time. Tea? Anytime, not a problem. Just ask. Don't we have an extraordinary bond between us, one that transcends political boundaries and social strata? You bring me important news, so you are an important person to me. You are – if I am honest and if I allow my instincts to speak – more important than any person I know, indeed more admirable than my father was to me. I know how to honour someone like you. Come on in, don't stand there, please; don't hesitate at all; think of this place as your home, you are welcome here any hour of the day.'

I opened the door a little more and stood aside, making room for him to enter. 'Have a seat, please,' I said, 'make yourself comfortable. Take a pillow for your lap, if that's what you want. Put your feet up on the small stool. You must have walked a lot today. That's better. It's my pleasure to press your feet. I shall be careful not to press them so hard as to cause tension in your muscles. No, I don't have any ego. It is ego that makes a man, I know that; but for me it is just the wrong component. I don't want to be characterized as inflexible, arrogant and extreme. Those who have ego are actually lazy. They do not know that man is not born with one passion only. No life would have survived more than one second if we were born with only one passion.

'You think I am doing well? Excellent. That is what I want to hear from a man like you. I mean it. If you do not like me, Moina Mia does not like me. If Moina Mia does not like me, Sheikh Mujib does not like me. If Sheikh Mujib does not like me, I am in torment, and after that I no longer exist. Mark, please, mark with kindness, that when you need to speak in my favour, you may say: *this individual is a gentleman, this individual has a genuine desire to promote the nationalist agenda across the country provided the country compensates him generously, this individual serves with pride until he is drenched in his own sweat.* Say this with me so that you remember it clearly. Say: *this individual has a genuine desire to promote the nationalist agenda.* Good. Say it again. *This individual* – pay attention, please – *this individual ... provided the country compensates him generously* (don't forget this part, it is very important); say it again ... *this individual ... drenched in his own sweat.*

'That should be enough. If not, let us begin our conversation by speaking of the interconnection between Sheikh Mujib and the future of the Bengali nation, so that you know how deeply I have entered into his soul. Let me say this emphatically: love him or hate him, tell me, who do we have without him? Who else can we entrust our country to? He is our Arthur, our Lincoln. He is our hero, our Menelaus travelling to Troy. Love him or hate him, come back to him to feel safe, come back every night for supper and honey and milk. Only he is the one who'll fight for us, and sing for our children. Love him or hate him, he lives in our heart. He is us.'

But there was only darkness and silence, and no man.

I woke up on the floor. Nur Hussain was sitting next to me, looking into my eyes.

My first sensation was of deep pain. I must have hurt myself during the night. There was blood on my nails. My neck was sore. My chest was hidden behind half a dozen long, deep scratches.

He sat quietly, like an image of the Buddha from Seokguram Grotto of the Unified Silla Dynasty, hands folded in his lap, in control of his urges, looking serene and unshockable.

'What?' I said, and rose slowly. I was about to begin coughing, perhaps from the cold of the floor, but controlled it by pressing my mouth.

'Don't you have anything better to do? Get lost. Go to your room. Stay out of here.'

No, I could not frighten him. He had known I would yell. He was prepared. Frustratingly enough, he had learned one or two things about me by this time.

I moved slowly. I did not know where my clothes had gone.

In the washroom, I found a towel to cover myself. Splashing a few handfuls of water on my face, I stared at myself in the mirror for several minutes, trying to remember what had happened, rubbing my chest with my palm. I had gone to the window, I remembered, and screamed at the dark neighbourhood: 'All you who are well-fed or unfed tonight, note this carefully: Sheikh Mujib is my father; he was the father of my father, grandfather and great-grandfather who died a hundred years ago; and he will be the father of all the future sons and daughters of this land, irrespective of their ethnicity and religious identity! It may be a matter of dispute who among our predecessors first believed in the creation of a nation based on the Bengali heritage, but let there be no dispute that Sheikh Mujib has risen more than everyone else and has fought more than everyone else to found that nation!'

I looked through the window and saw my *lungi* on the pumpkin bush below, flying like a windsock. A beggar woman was trying to pull it down with a stick.

'Don't you dare!' I yelled at her, and shook the window-panes to draw her attention. 'That's mine! Leave it alone!'

She watched me as I ran down the stairs holding the towel to my waist, and began to hit the bush more rapidly than before to free the *lungi*. I snatched the stick away from her. 'Shall I call them to shave your head for stealing my stuff?' I shouted. 'Shall I burn your face with boiling water?'

'I saw it first,' she argued, and came after me. Her stomach might have been empty, but her mouth was full with words. 'I saw it there since the morning. All doors in this building were closed. I even asked one or two people on the road if it belonged to them. Where were you when it lay in the fog? A bush is not a place where someone would hang his clothes to dry. Night is not the time when someone would spread his clothes in the bush. This is mine.' I was sure she believed I was not the rightful owner of that piece of cloth, that I was merely depriving her of an opportunity to make some quick money by selling it.

'It does not become yours because you have seen it first,' I said. 'You see that window? Look closely. Raise your head. You know who lives there? Your father. Sheikh Mujib. Not one. Two. If you don't leave this place this moment, you may never leave.'

She grabbed my arms aggressively to reach the stick, and tried to bite them a few times, but I pushed her back with a shove of my elbow.

Defeated, she punched my back and cursed me.

'Animal,' she said, loudly, to draw people's attention to her plight. None of the three or four pedestrians who had stopped outside the gate responded to her call. 'I thought I was bad, which is why there is no food for me in God's world, but now I see you're worse than me. You're worse than everyone else in the street. Was your mother bitten by a mad dog when she was pregnant with you? Was your father a dog?'

I collected the *lungi* in my arms and rushed to beat her for abusing me, but retreated when, as a defence mechanism, she lifted the front of her *sari* to show me her genitals. It was something I would never have expected. As I climbed up the stairs she came behind me and continued calling me 'dog' in an increasingly loud voice. 'Dog, Dog, dog,' she chanted. 'Dog, dog, dog!'

'Are you blind?' I said to Nur Hussain as he appeared at the door. 'Don't you ever look out the window? Don't you feel any responsibility to protect what we have in this flat?'

I doubt he heard me. He walked to the window and looked outside. He was not taking in the view; nor did the woman interest him.

A miserable calmness played on his face.

6

THE GLOOM IN THE FACE

As expected, Moina Mia sent for me within three days. Abdul Ali entered slowly, and sat idly on the sofa. He had grown old, ugly and lifeless in the space of a mere seventy-two hours. His forehead folded more frighteningly, and a dark cloud encircled his eyes. He had not had a shave recently.

Was it because he was thinking too much about the well-being of his fellow worker, the gatekeeper Ruhul Amin?

He denied it.

'He is doing well,' he said. 'He has proved himself smart by accepting your prudent suggestions. I am glad it crossed my mind that he might respect your words. Fortunately, you were there at the right moment. If he had not been convinced that day, he would have had more time to focus on what he had done, and then find more reasons to run away.'

My 'prudent suggestions'. I remembered the way I had abused him, and my angry exit from his small booth. It seemed Ruhul Amin had not shared any of that with Abdul Ali. I had doubted he would, but now I was sure.

I pressed on. 'You may confide in me,' I said. 'Let me be honest about myself. I am not the kind of person to report

191

one's minor sickness to his employer. I do not meddle in other people's business, and I am definitely not a spy.'

He said he felt heavy in the legs, in the waist, in the back and in his head. He felt like creeping to a dark and silent corner, sitting there endlessly, without food, without sleep, with no thought about the surrounding world.

What about his duties at Moina Mia's mansion, I asked. Did they tire him? Was there too much to do every day?

There was not – apart from a few more things over and above the regular routine due to the construction work and the new campaign. He would not say his duties were unacceptable or overwhelming. He had worked harder during the election, or even before it, when Moina Mia was restructuring the Awami League after the liberation.

Then why was his face filled with gloom? What made him so quiet?

If only he knew, he said.

'You should ask Moina Mia to grant you a few days' leave,' I said. 'That will give you the opportunity to get some fresh air. Some people go to the countryside when exhausted; some prefer a new city. Some just stay home to enjoy the domestic blessings, the beautiful companionship of family.'

He became absent-minded, let out a little sigh and sat with his head down, as if the very name of Moina Mia had poisoned his world. Was he feeling guilty about something?

As I put on my Mujib coat, I saw him quiver with some hidden pain, some unexpressed anguish. All at once a supreme quiet hung over him. He forgot my presence, and in no time fell asleep on the sofa only to wake up almost an hour later.

'Shall we?' I said.

He yawned and followed me without a word.

Nur Hussain was in his room. There was something strange about him. He had not come out to meet Abdul Ali that day, but when I looked back from the road, I saw him watching us from the window. He stood unmoving, an iron man behind the iron grille.

I looked back again a few minutes later.

He was on the road, fifty yards behind us, walking slowly, eyes on the ground. I stopped to see if he had anything to say.

'I might meet the MP today,' I said when he came closer. I did not know why I said I *might* when I had been summoned to see him and was already on my way in the company of his messenger. 'Do you have any questions or concerns?'

It was obvious I was trying to hide my embarrassment. I had not asked him that before leaving the house.

I was surprised to see that although Nur Hussain did not greet him or even look at him, Abdul Ali extended his hand towards him graciously, and the two shook hands. Abdul Ali's sleepiness was gone. 'It's a real pleasure to see you again,' he said. 'How are you doing?' Then he brought his face close to Nur Hussain's and whispered something to him. Nur Hussain looked at him seriously. His look became more intense after Abdul Ali whispered into his ear again. I nodded when he looked at me, as if I knew what the whisper was about. Then I moved away, to give them some time together.

'I understand perfectly,' I heard Nur Hussain say. 'It is irritating. It is terrible. I can't stop myself from going to the window. I always feel something has happened, or is going to happen. Small people may not always think small. You get it, don't you? We need only one person. One person is enough. One person with faith. Who is not frightened. Who will not stop in spite of the suffering. Then it is going to be very, very noisy around here.'

'Of course,' Abdul Ali replied. 'I get it clearly. Thanks for helping.'

'Every man has a vision,' Nur Hussain continued. 'Whether he understands it or not. I would not be surprised if I see a lot of people on the road one day. Once in a while a person has to look at himself the way others look at him. If he doesn't and then something bad happens, it is nobody's fault.'

'Of course, of course,' said Abdul Ali. He whispered again, to which Nur Hussain replied loudly: 'Never lose your sanity, because you cannot be born again.'

We moved to the side of the street to make room for the rickshaws. One rickshaw-*wallah*, whom I had not seen before – he might have been one of the migrants working for the local rickshaw depot – stopped beside us. He was not carrying a passenger. He asked Nur Hussain where he was going, if he needed a ride. 'Nowhere,' said Nur. 'That is perfect for me,' said the rickshaw-*wallah* as he wiped the seat with his *gamcha*.

'Get in, please; I am also going nowhere. I will take you there.'

'How much do you charge for a one-way trip to the market?'

The rickshaw-*wallah* smiled. 'Since you ask, and the market is the nowhere where you are going, I have to calculate how far the distance is and think approximately how much time it might take me to arrive there, including the time spent in the traffic jam, any journey breaks, prayer times,' he said. 'But don't worry; it is free for you.'

That is a trick, I thought. Why would someone offer a free ride when starvation was acute? These rickshaw-*wallahs* would blackmail any distracted passenger by fooling them with generous words like: 'I believe you, pay as much as you can,' or 'You are an honourable person, how can I charge you at all?' But when they reached the destination, they would not hesitate to shame the passenger if he did not pay more than the fare they believed they deserved.

Yet Nur Hussain shook Abdul Ali's hand again and got into the rickshaw confidently. As the rickshaw moved on, he looked at me briefly, and said: 'No, no questions, and no concerns. Everything is all right.' Then he began a conversation with the rickshaw-*wallah*. 'Tell me something about your life,' he said.

'My life?' the rickshaw-*wallah* asked. 'I do not have one.'

7

AT THE CROSSROADS

On the way, Abdul Ali and I stopped at the crossroads. A woman had jumped from the roof of a two-storey residential building and killed herself. The owner of the building, a woman now running from one end of the yard to the other yelling at the crowd, said she did not know who the dead woman was. She was angry that the woman had chosen her property on which to commit such an unspeakable act. 'Couldn't she jump under the train like all the others? Couldn't she have chosen the government-owned City Tower to execute her horrible final desire? Now people will say that mine is the House of Suicide. Now I'll have to pay someone to clean all the bloodstains from my yard, to burn incense to remove the smell and invite a *maulana* to bless the house so that incidents like this never happen again. Is it easy to waste money on such things in these times?'

She pleaded with everyone she found to remove the body as quickly as possible – including small children who could hardly hold themselves upright because they were so skinny – but only one person, a shaky, barefoot, ailing elderly woman, followed her. The old woman believed that suicide

---

was not the main objective of the woman who now lay dead. 'Look at her,' she said, drawing the owner aside; 'look at her fingers, her palms, her wrists and elbows; what do you see? Are they shrunken, as my hands are? Now look here, look from this side. See the toenails? No cracks, no fungal infections; all clean and well-trimmed. If she was starving, she would have been weak; if she was weak, she would not have had the energy to climb all those twenty-two stairs to go to the roof and jump. No, I don't think so. A starving person does not move upward.'

Her voice fell because of physical weakness, but her enthusiasm became stronger.

'She wanted to achieve something other than death,' she said. 'You have to find out what it is. Maybe death was going to happen – she knew. Death is not the most surprising thing one may encounter these day. But she wanted something out of that death that was more important to her, and that may be more bitter and devastating to you as the owner of the house.' Then she lowered her voice: 'If you promise to offer me some rice, you know, any kind, white, brown, boiled, sweet, clean or husked, I can walk around the neighbourhood trying to find out for you. If you do not have rice, give me whatever you have – wheat, beans, potatoes, pumpkin, mangos, anything.'

The woman's body had been lying there for at least two hours now, said a rickshaw-*wallah* who had been there from the start. In fact, he had seen her when she was in the air, when she glided through the guava tree branches, when her body became still after a small cry and a few incomplete gasps on the dust. He had pushed the gate open and shouted in his loudest voice to bring the neighbours to the yard. Now he was sitting on a street corner, his rickshaw parked in the sun, narrating the story of his misfortune to anyone who would care to listen – but mostly to himself.

'If the wheels had moved faster,' he was saying. 'If time was a little bit slower, if God was not looking away for a moment today, I could have stopped that woman. I could have run and said: "If you want to jump, jump on me; finish me with you. I've seen hunger, and I've wanted to jump so many times, but then I didn't. It's so great to be alive, even when you can't stand on your feet, even when you cannot stop the thought of eating someone equally as hungry as you." I could have stopped her. Now she is no more.'

I observed the small line of blood that ran from the yard to the road. Someone had covered her with a folded fertilizer bag, which lay like an ornamented winter quilt on her body, the bloodstains a tribute to her savage death.

While I stood behind the crowd, listening to the rickshaw-*wallah* and thinking of what might happen at my meeting with Moina Mia, wondering if I would be able to voice my dissatisfaction about our deal, Abdul Ali moved forward. He looked at the body for several minutes, moving around it with slow, small, noiseless steps. At one point it seemed as though he was choking, and had difficulty breathing. I was surprised. Hadn't he been cracking jokes with Nur Hussain just minutes ago? Hadn't he taken the deaths of Basu and Gesu more easily than this? Having worked with the *Rakkhi Bahini* for such a long time, he could have considered himself a small Angel of Death with a reasonable measure of pride. Did a man's perception of the destruction of his fellow man, then, change from time to time without his knowing it?

'Take my hand,' I said. 'This way.'

I pulled him to one side, sat him down on the ground and took his head on my lap. The elderly woman came quickly.

Forgetting her bargain with the building's owner, she sat opposite me and began to fan Abdul Ali. Her elbow popped with every swish of the fan, but her face reflected such concern and dedication that nobody dared offer her help.

'What is going on here?' the owner said. She took hardly ten seconds to assess the situation. 'My God,' she said in despair, raising her hands in the fashion of praying, 'why don't I go to the roof and throw myself off as well! Why am I still standing on my feet! I wouldn't have to see two bodies in a single day right at my doorstep!'

'You want trouble?' I yelled at her. What was she? I could not imagine it. A bag of vile selfishness? Living in a two-storey building, looking at the world through glitzy curtains, she knew nothing about what went on around her. She thought this famine, this endless line of hungry people, including the one who was now dead, were all conspiring against her to turn her comfortable life upside down. 'If you want trouble, you'll have it,' I said with firmness. 'I'll fill your yard with yet another body, you understand me? I don't care what connections you have, or where your relatives come from. Look at him. Not with those hollow, suspicious eyes. Look at him closely, with your mind and heart. Look at him the way you would have looked at yourself. He is my friend, and he is not dying. He only has temporary nervous trouble. Who wouldn't be anxious upon seeing a body lying two yards away? He is going to be all right soon. For God's sake, how can you talk about death so easily? Go back to your little room and scream as much as you like. We need some quiet here.'

The woman looked around in embarrassment and reluctantly found her way back to the building. From the yard I saw her watching us through the window.

After a few minutes she came out with a glass of water, which she offered to Abdul Ali. He returned the glass to her after drinking the water and looked at the body in the yard. 'I work with Moina Mia MP,' he said. 'I'll send someone with a van to clear out your yard. You don't have to pay anything. Thank you for the water.'

The woman's eyes filled with tears. Her lips trembled. She gathered the ends of her *sari* and covered her mouth.

8

TODAY FOR TOMORROW

We had left the crowd only a few yards behind us when a young boy – at best, fourteen years old – came running up. He needed a few moments to collect himself before speaking. He lived in this neighbourhood, he said; to be more specific, he mentioned the holding number of the house. '36A Jagadish Road, just behind the market; the third hoarding from the ditch where they throw remains of animals.'

'I know where it is,' Abdul Ali said clearly. 'What can I do for you?'

The boy hesitated, then said there was no need to send a van to remove the woman's body; he would do it himself.

'I will clean up the area, scrub the floor and the walls, disperse the crowd, make it like nothing has happened there; give me only two hours.'

Abdul Ali looked at me with concern before saying: 'Why do you want to do that?'

The answer was ready on the boy's lips.

'Because I live here, and it is my right. Before you send someone to work in this neighbourhood, you may want to enquire if we are available. Pay me what you would have paid the van driver.'

I wanted to reach Moina Mia's house as soon as possible, and so did not want to be bothered. The woman's suicide had already delayed our meeting considerably. I pulled Abdul Ali by the shoulder, but he did not move even an inch. On the other hand, I noticed, the boy sounded very tough and determined.

'You are too young for this job,' Abdul Ali said.

'But I have experience,' the boy replied. 'Since the beginning of the famine, I have removed thirty-four bodies. Women, children, grown-ups, I don't care. Bodies are bodies, aren't they? I am strong and I love the famine.'

'It may be a homicide,' I said to Abdul Ali. I wanted to scare him. I wanted him to come with me, and quickly. I could not wait. 'Who knows who was with the woman on the roof. A body on the ground may not be as simple as it looks. We need someone who is mature, who understands how sensitive the situation is. Besides, if you think about the law, the body may also have to be taken by the police for an autopsy and an investigation.'

The boy continued speaking to Abdul Ali in the same manner, as if he had not heard me. When he asked Abdul Ali how much he was planning to pay the van driver for the job, I spoke again, louder this time: 'Don't you listen to the little devil, Ali *bhai*; this could be a never-ending issue. It could even damage your relations with Moina Mia, causing you to lose your job in the end. I don't know why you are wasting your time with him.'

'Who is this man?' the boy said resentfully, his eyes on me. 'Is he a newcomer to this country? Doesn't he know there is no homicide, slaughter or disappearance here at the moment, only death – ordinary, raw, uncomplicated death? Doesn't he know I have come to seek your permission only out of courtesy, and I shall do whatever I find suitable in this case to help myself?'

Abdul Ali wanted to say something, but I pulled him aside, saying I would deal with the matter. I confronted the boy face to face. He was thin and undersized, and I believed it would not require more than a blow to shut him up for the day. 'And what do you think is suitable?' I asked him. 'Give me an example, please. I want to enlighten myself with your experience.' He looked up at me with the same anger. 'Tell me honestly how many bodies you have buried: one, two, three? None?'

He remained silent, so I kicked him in the leg, to which he reacted only by taking a step back, and bending to grab his knee, his face contorted with pain. He was terrified. I asked him again if he was still willing to remove the woman's body from the yard. 'My darling, my little darling, speak up. Don't limp, raise your head, make a fist and smack me in the face!' When he still did not respond, I grabbed his hair, and shook him from side to side a few times, then let him go.

Abdul Ali did not have much strength in his legs, but came to the boy's rescue. 'Khaleque *sahib!*' he said, and tried to protect the boy with his own body. I ran around him and kicked the boy again. 'Please,' the boy cried into the dust, 'don't hit me! Don't hit me! I just wanted to do something to earn money. It does not matter if it involves burying a body. I have half of my family dead, and the other half starving.'

Although I had controlled myself to some extent by that time, I still yelled at him: 'Tell me whether or not you have carried any bodies before, or I'll break your spine! Tell me the truth!'

'Oh, God!' he cried as he collected himself under my gaze. 'I have not. Oh, God!'

Soon his cries became louder. His body shook as he drew in every breath with visible difficulty.

Abdul Ali crammed a one-*taka* note into the boy's pocket and pushed me towards the road.

'What is this world, Khaleque *bhai*?' Abdul Ali asked as we proceeded through the neighbourhood.

He walked beside me, holding my arm. He wiped his nose with a handkerchief I gave him.

'What is this time, this circle of seasons, this turn of years, this vanishing light, this insignificant yet inviolable conflict between life and death? What is this that we see and cannot react to, that we perceive and cannot explain, that we repeat and yet cannot recollect? Tell me, if you know; tell me today; tell me when this is coming to an end. I do not believe in premonitions, but I'll believe today. Tell me anything; I'll believe you.'

I was now at least two hours late for my meeting with Moina Mia. What excuse would I give him? That someone fell asleep on the sofa, and I saw a death on the road? That would only prove I was not sufficiently careful about my responsibilities.

'If you hold onto me like this,' I said to Abdul Ali, 'I will not be able to walk. You're too heavy for me to carry all the way; you're too dejected, too preoccupied to let me speak, and too immature to understand anything.' I pulled my hand away. 'Walk by yourself, please. This day says nothing any different to me than to you. This day says: look ahead; that suicide did not happen; the blood you saw was only the juice of the earth; that woman was a mirage; that boy was a ghost. Walk straight, go home, sleep, wake up, walk straight, look ahead.'

'Why wasn't walking yesterday enough for today? Why won't walking today be enough for tomorrow? Why walk then, if walking doesn't count?'

'Walking is always for tomorrow. Yesterday's walk, today's walk, tomorrow's walk – all for tomorrow. That is what this world is. Such are the times. Don't come near me; walk apart, behind me or in front of me. Walk quickly, like the wind. I am walking now, for tomorrow; I am thinking now, for tomorrow. I am going to stun myself now, for tomorrow and tomorrow and tomorrow.'

He stopped talking. He stopped walking, pressed his chest and fell to the ground before me. 'Come, hit me,' he said. 'You hit the boy; hit me too.'

'Not now,' I said, as I ran towards him. 'Not now. Kill me if you want to kill me, but we have no time for this. We have to go.' I shook him by the shoulders, by the head, and slapped him.

'I am tired,' he managed to say.

'On your feet!' I screamed. 'On your feet!' I dragged him a few paces in the dust, pain growing in my armpits, my legs feeling heavy; then I raised him onto my shoulder and ran towards Moina Mia's mansion.

9
A Long Talk, a Win

Moina Mia told me he had new information for us; it was about our pre-programme orientation. We would have to stay with the *Rakkhi Bahini* for a couple of days at a campsite, where we would be trained in the handling of small firearms. There might be someone who would want to kidnap us to embarrass Sheikh Mujib; if we were trained to use firearms, we would be able to protect ourselves.

'The price ...' I said. 'Before we begin discussing subsidiary matters like unseen terror lurking in the dark and the effective use of handguns, the price must be reviewed.' Although the nature of our work had not changed, I argued, its conditions had changed fundamentally. For example, Nur Hussain would have to memorize different passages for every new assignment. So far, he had delivered only the parts of the speech he had already learned. Now, suddenly, he would have to vary. If learning were easy for him, he would not have been a speaker in the first place; he would have found a job with a bank or an insurance company. He would have been a bus conductor or a mechanic – a weaver, at least. Therefore, learning new passages would not be easy for him.

I also explained that every time new passages were written, they would be written in a style different from Sheikh Mujib's because they would not be written *by* him, but by someone else *for* him – most probably by some tricky speechwriter using words as weapons. Those words would not be simple, either. The language of revolution is simple, whereas the language of governance is very intricate. Revolution just needs one short sentence – a slogan. Being the government, Sheikh Mujib would have to find a language with which to highlight his achievements and conceal his limitations as an administrator.

Then I spoke about myself. The new schedule would place extra pressure on me too, I said. How? I was the one who would have to read the passages to Nur Hussain, as his ability to read was limited and his understanding erratic. It was not Moina Mia or Sheikh Mujib or the *Rakkhi Bahini* who would sit with him in the dim circuit-house room to check which parts of the speech he missed or improvised. I did not mind doing something for Sheikh Mujib; in fact, I would enjoy doing it. But it would help me explain things to Nur Hussain logically if I could say that his payment demanded that kind of hard work or superior level of commitment, and that he could not give up just because he felt annoyed or did not understand something. Nur Hussain depended on me to explain things to him, I said, which, in turn, effectively depended on how comfortable I felt about performing my part of the job.

That was not all, I said, as I launched into the second part of my argument. Now that we would be working for Sheikh Mujib, I told Moina Mia most dutifully, we would not be able to avoid people – people of all kinds, especially from the media – who would follow us virtually everywhere. For example, I argued, they might want to put together photo-essays on his daily life; after all, he was the only person Sheikh Mujib had selected to deliver his speech. It would not be an advantage for Moina Mia or for Sheikh Mujib to let people know we lived in a small flat. Important people live in prestigious places: I made this clear to him. If we wanted to move to a place of even average prestige, we would have to pay a higher rent than we now paid. Even if we moved to a prestigious residence, I said, we would need to retain a gatekeeper who would keep trouble away. We would have to employ someone like Ruhul Amin, who was brave enough to shoot trespassers.

If earning money required talking, I was ready to talk. I wanted to push our deal as hard as possible. Being an MP was not easy. Being a speaker for a troubled prime minister was not easy, either. Moina Mia had to know this.

His eyes became small. He stared at me as if he had never seen me before. The creases on his forehead became deeper.

I managed to clear a generous advance from him, in cash. It came directly from the bank. Newly printed bills – they smelled wonderful.

The advance was a token of our trust in each other, I concluded. By taking that money I had given him my word. I was not going to make another deal with anyone else, even if I were offered better terms by another Awami League leader, as every leader needed propaganda during such a crisis. Money was not everything, I told him, but my word was my word, and he and I were both gentlemen with our honour to protect.

I did not care what impressions he had of me. Was he concerned about the impressions I had formed about him? Did he know I knew exactly who the two burglars were whom Ruhul Amin had shot the other night? Did he know I knew they were Basu and Gesu, the two servants who had brought us tea in his house – and that I did not speak about their unfortunate deaths with him simply because he did not speak of them with me? Two men just disappeared, two men wearing Mujib coats. They disappeared while stealing from their employer. They disappeared even though they did not steal jewellery, money, legal documents, state secrets or any valuable items, but only two sacks of rice. He had his way of exploiting a situation, and I had my own.

I felt good about myself. In fact, I was delighted to see my plan actually work the way I had hoped it would. Now I would not have to go to the editors looking for a job. Now they would not be able to look down on me, or dismiss me as trivial even after I hit them with compelling points about transformational leadership and how it might be applied to our nation. The ground under my feet was stable now, and my grip was firm. I had Moina Mia in my pocket. I had Sheikh Mujib under my control. Because of the Mujib coat I wore, I had the entire Awami League carrying out my wishes.

10

THE SWEET TASTE OF THE UNKNOWN

That night, I thought of my father.
He had been a small trader dealing in ginger. 'You will be a seller like me,' he told me one day as we sat on a mat in the crowded village market, spreading his little inventory next to our feet. 'How old are you – six, seven? I want you to know the twelve different tastes of ginger before you reach fifteen, so that when I am no more, you can carry on without trouble.'

He gave me a piece of ginger to taste. It was dry but very strong, and I had tears in my eyes within seconds.

He laughed and showed my tearful face to his friends. 'This is how you know ginger,' he said. 'By mingling it with your life. There is no other way.' He gave me another piece to chew, this time from a fresh root. 'Don't worry, soon you will feel better. Before you go to bed tonight, you will know a part of the Big Secret of the World. You will say: I have seen it – I know how awful it can taste. A piece of ginger is not an object of fear for you anymore.'

Before he died, a few years later, he advised my mother to grow ginger on his grave. 'At least six columns of it. Loosen the soil before watering. Put a fence around the grave to stop goats. Collect the ginger and dry it before it rots in floodwater.'

When the early showers came and the earth became moist and fine, we saw a dense clump of ginger plants swinging in the evening sun.

My mother died two years after him. She always said she had suffered during her life with my father. There was a chance that she could finally be free after his death. She would begin again. Surprisingly, she decided not to. She could not resist his loud call from the grave. I saw her thin arms getting thinner, her bloodless face becoming ethereal. She walked as slowly as an earthworm during her last few days, although her memory worked perfectly.

She left a basket for me. Wrapped with an embroidered quilt, it was full of dried ginger chunks, some sour, some sweet, some hot and spicy, some as hard as beef strips.

I threw the basket – along with her coconut broom, *saris*, wooden shoes and utensils – into a ditch.

I hated my father, growing up. I didn't know why. Probably I thought he wanted to imprison me in the kind of life he knew, while I wanted more; or because I believed that if I did not hate the life he introduced me to, I could never embrace another. Whatever the reason, I did not return to the village I left behind. I stood before my mother's grave for a few minutes only, and prayed: 'Let me go, let me go, let me go.' Then I did what I thought was good for me. I moved on. My education and creativity, my writing, communication and negotiation skills – all came through hard work, and at this moment, my life was not where it had been one year earlier. It was not even where it had been yesterday, full of hesitation and confusion. I was now in a situation that was larger than my normal life would have allowed.

I stood at the window and looked at the city. It was sleeping under a dark cloud. Small tin sheds looked like deep, bottomless tombs, cursed and silenced to the last heartbeat under the constant torture of time. The old streets lay in darkness, like dry veins in a body, never to wake again, never to be filled with human voices and footsteps. It was noiseless everywhere, except for the howling of some angry cats at the crossroads and a cricket calling incessantly from the bush.

It had proved very mysterious to me, this city. I had lived here for over two decades. My thoughts were formed here. My ability to fight for my place in it evolved under its very direction. Day after day I collected the necessary information about it; the names of its different areas penetrated my memory, and would not be lost in a lifetime. I was not interested in sports, but I had gone to the stadium once or twice to watch football matches with forty thousand other spectators, who jumped in excitement or cried in frustration with every goal. Then there were the processions, general strikes, throwing stones at government buildings, singing in praise of the motherland on days of historical significance, wearing clothes suited to the mood of the season, soaking in the monsoons. That was the city I knew – not the one that lay before me.

'But I know what to do,' I thought. I had come to understand that the unknown was not the problem – the problem was the known, the world in memory. The known had changed. Patriots had turned into enemies of the country. It had changed so drastically that I found myself on the street, fighting for an over-chewed bone like a hungry dog. It was ruthless; it shattered my pride as an individual, and placed me under the weight of a life without course.

In contrast, the unknown stopped before me most compassionately, smiled at me elegantly, cleaned me up, received me into its bosom, gave me ambition and dreams, and was ready to walk every step with me.

'I will go with it,' I said to myself. I was not my father, finding my future in a small bag of ginger. I would walk into the unknown with confidence and hope, and create a life without memory, without a sense of loss and anguish. And I would keep walking, right up to the end.

11

THE EYES OF GOD

The next day, I appeared at Moina Mia's gate – but not to meet Moina Mia. 'Take me to that building,' I said to Abdul Ali, who met me there, and who appeared to have shed some of his lethargy by that time.

'Which building?' he asked. 'Are you going for a walk somewhere?' He had not forgotten our conversation about walking the previous day.

'The one they are constructing. The one that is five storeys now. I want to see something.'

'Of course,' he said. 'Please follow me.' We crossed the yard, the fountain, the fence, and took a passage strewn with bricks and wood planks. 'Where in the house do you want to go exactly?' he asked.

'Anywhere,' I replied, but added instantly: 'Take me to the sitting room, please; I have heard a lot about it from the workers. I heard it was exceptionally spacious, and gave the house a special character rarely seen in Bengali houses.' He said it had been designed to accommodate at least one hundred guests at its long dining table.

'One hundred guests?' I asked. 'Why so many?'

'Why do you say that, Khaleque *bhai*?' he replied. 'Here is a man who knows what he is going to need in the next fifty or sixty years. A very practical man. He knows what a big house can signify when you are a political leader. People want to see you own something precious, so that they can be reassured that you are not going to steal from them. The richer the leader, the more respected he is.'

'He's not planning to hold party meetings in his sitting room, is he?'

'This man will grow old gradually, like we all will; when he grows old, he won't want to go to the party conference room for every little meeting. He would rather bring the party to his home, and have the meetings right here. Imagine a day when this yard will be crowded with hundreds of the country's leaders. They will compete with each other, argue, insult each other, throw shoes, leather bags, teacups, microphones and chairs at each other, break each other's necks and determination; and then, at the end of the day, they will compromise shamelessly with each other for the sake of the party, on the order of the leader.'

'This is what he said to you?' I asked.

He smiled. 'No, he did not. This is what I believe will happen. Based on my experience, I can predict some of the developments in the political culture of our country.'

We entered the sitting room. The doors and the windows had not been fixed; the floor was littered with blue plastic sheets, cement bags and paint containers. The smell of brick and sand was thick in the air. I went to the corner opposite the door and looked back.

The way Nur Hussain and I were advancing now, coupled with the opportunities that might come along very soon thanks to the prestige of working for Sheikh Mujib, it would not be unwise to think that before another election came we would have everything we needed. With my part of the money, I believed I would be able to build myself a multi-storey French-style Gothic mansion on twenty-five acres of land right here in this city; it would have a much wider lounge than Moina Mia's. I would buy a beautifully crafted Barbadian Heritage mahogany cot to sleep on, a Regency-style revolving dining table and sideboard, a set of magnificent Four Seasons English oak breakfront bookcases for the lounge and a six hundred and eighty-kilogram Holstein-Friesian black-and-white cow for milk. In time – and that would be before I turned forty-five – I would find myself a luscious Puerto Rican wife with pretty, plump hips, similar to the one I had seen on the cover of a travel magazine – a woman with youth, mystery, sensuousness and femininity. There would be a white Latvian guard dog at my door and a doorman with a handlebar moustache from Bihar to protect me. These were not unnecessary luxuries. A man with taste and a sense of adventure needed them badly. A man who did not have them could not declare himself successful, happy and free.

'It isn't as spacious as I believed it would be,' I said to Abdul Ali. 'They gave me wrong information.'

He agreed, and walked to the centre of the room. 'He wanted to make it more spacious than this,' he said.

I looked at the backyard through the window.

'Why didn't he? I can see there is still a big plot left.'

'He wanted to go higher as soon as possible.'

I was confused. 'What do you mean, "higher"?'

'You must have noticed in the last year or two,' he said, 'there is inertia in the country; there is only destruction. This building, along with some others of the same type, will change that. They will be considered symbols of activity and progress; wherever in the city you go, you'll be able to see them from your window.'

I looked into his eyes. 'This is what he said to you?'

'Yes, he did,' he said thoughtfully. 'This and more.'

'What more? Is he going to build another building behind it?'

'No, nothing like that. He said this building would go higher as the famine went deeper. It would stop only when the famine was over.'

I turned away from him. Suddenly I did not like his tone of voice. In fact, I felt quite unprepared to have this conversation with him. He was complaining now. I should not have taken him into my confidence. I thought that if he was unhappy with his employer, which was evident at this moment, he might be unhappy with me as well for having a good relationship with the man. Although he showed no sign of that, and rather took me as a friend to whom he could reveal his employer's secrets, I thought it was better for me to maintain my distance from him.

He stood at the back window and spoke with an ironworker welding outside. There was some laughter between them, and an exchange of information. At Abdul Ali's request, the worker tightened a screw on the window grille. Abdul Ali checked to see that it was rightly fixed. 'Someone must inspect all the screws before the painting job begins,' he said. 'We don't want any hazards to remain unattended to. Not a single one.' The worker agreed.

'Shall we leave?' I asked after a while.

He nodded. 'Sure, if you think you've already seen what you wanted to see.'

'I am done. At least for the time being.'

As we walked towards the door, I said: 'I hope I get a chance to come to this building again, when the construction work is complete. I would like to look at the city from the topmost window. It must look beautiful from there, very beautiful, especially on a day without dust or fog, when the sky is blue. It would be like looking at the world through the eyes of God.'

He stopped and stared at me for a while. Then he smiled suddenly. 'You'll have that chance, Khaleque *bhai*, I'm sure.' He passed me and looked back. 'Just pray that the famine stays long enough, so that we have a very tall building. The taller the building, the better the view.'

12

THE SCREW EATER

As we stepped into the main hall, I heard some laughter coming from a room to the right. The door was locked. When we had entered this building just minutes earlier, I had not heard anyone in there; nor had I seen anyone come down the stairs. I would have overlooked the matter if the laughter had not turned into an intensive coughing fit. Someone was choking in there.

I looked at Abdul Ali enquiringly. 'You don't want to see this, Khaleque *bhai*,' he said, sadder than he had been before. 'You really don't want to see this.' He doubled back to me and pulled me by my hand towards the fence. 'I am surprised that he lingered so long. He was not supposed to, judging by the way he was when I last saw him.'

I pulled back. 'Why don't you tell me what's happening here ... What's the problem?'

'Don't worry,' he said. 'He'll be silent soon. Just give him a few more hours.'

The coughing became deadlier now, and then stopped and turned into laughter.

'Who'll be silent soon?' I asked him. 'Who's there?' Abdul Ali began to walk away, but I told him I would not leave until he opened that door for me.

'You're very stubborn,' he said. 'Very stubborn, and sensitive. A handful of trouble. Not like the man I thought you would be.' He returned and opened the door reluctantly, using his key ring. 'You go in, I'm not coming with you; it isn't going to be a pretty scene, I can tell you that,' he said. But he followed slowly when I stepped inside.

There was a small middle-aged man there, bound to a chair. Blood dripped from his mouth. He had blood on his naked chest, and on the *lungi* at his waist. He grew shy seeing us, and kept looking at the ground.

'Don't ask me anything,' Abdul Ali said. 'I know nothing.' But when I insisted, he opened his mouth.

Construction workers had caught the man on the previous evening. They had their building materials in a van parked outside the gate. He had come from nowhere and begun eating tiny iron screws from a box. When they chased him, he started gobbling the shiny screws faster than before. His throat was jammed, so they brought him within the boundary wall and began hitting his jaw to release the screws. Then they used a knife to prise open his mouth. They removed some of the screws, but most of them went down the man's throat. On Moina Mia's instructions, he was bound to the chair and left in the building for the night.

'The end of the world is here,' said Abdul Ali. 'When men become too powerful, God stops thinking. What can we do? Look at him. Look at his face. See how he smiles, how he enjoys the last few moments of his life, as if he is God and has unearthed the final secret of his existence. I don't think anything human is left in that face.'

The man raised his head. He observed us quietly. He had no complaints about being bound, I imagined. There was no sign that he would be grateful to us should we volunteer to untie him.

'*Bhaijan, mone kichhu koiren na; boro bhok lagchhilo, ja paichhi khaichhi,*' he said, without any visible distress: 'My brother, don't take it too hard; I was very hungry, and ate whatever I found.' He added: 'It was not meant to be dramatic. I'm not a thief. I'm not mean. You see, I couldn't stand on my feet because my stomach was empty. It had been dry and light for quite some time. I ate from the workers' lunches, but soon I realized I needed something heavy in my stomach, heavier than regular rice and egg and potato and milk. I did not want to go to bed only to wake up a hungry man in the morning.'

He coughed and spat blood on the floor, then smiled. 'I can tell you this: those screws were really delicious. They were exactly what I needed. You can imagine, if I don't have anything to eat for the rest of my life, I will still be able to stand straight and walk tall and spend a beautiful evening watching a sunset over the river.' He lowered his head to get a view of his stomach. 'God knows I'm feeling so good now; I'm feeling wonderful since yesterday evening. This is blood, I know, and I am coughing, I know that too, which may sound terrible to you – but believe me when I say there's no pain in my stomach. It is all quiet now. I've satisfied it for a long time to come.' He blushed for a moment, and then the coughing began again, twisting his thin body; more blood came.

'I can't believe this is happening,' I said. 'I can't believe you have bound him to a chair instead of cleaning his stomach.' I took a step forward to release the man, but Abdul Ali stopped me. 'Don't, don't!' he cried. 'You can't help him. Nobody can help him. He is not in the land of men anymore. Those screws were sharp. They've probably already cut through his stomach. They'll cut everything as far as they go and as deep as they go, unravelling all his mysteries. Relax now; he's done; no sympathy is necessary. He's done, and he knows it. That's why he doesn't care, don't you see? Leave him in peace.'

Hearing this, the man smiled at us before lowering his eyes once again.

That was his last smile that day, and forever.

Abdul Ali untied the ropes. The body fell from the chair with barely any noise.

'So this is what famine does to a person,' I thought as I walked back home. 'It does not bring one to his knees only; it eats one alive. It is hungrier than a hungry man.'

My confidence was shaken. I could not stop staring at people along the way. Most of the men and children wore no shirts. Their scrawny stomachs, determined to expose their ribs, looked ugly at first, but when I thought about a stomach with dozens of sharp screws in it, they appeared beautiful. They were real. They shone in the daylight, every one of them, though I knew they were empty or half-empty, or dry, as the man had repeatedly said.

'These images are everywhere,' I said to myself, as I entered the gravel yard. 'Live, concrete images that cannot be misinterpreted or denied or eliminated or undermined. They dance and wink lustfully at you. They do not believe in a man's capacity for idling. They are sharp. They love blood. There is no good or evil in the world, only images. Learn, Khaleque Biswas, learn; learn and face the truth. Do a necessary service to yourself, or this is your fate, this sickening trap, this absolute darkness, this moment of never coming back, this irrational game of unconditional, slow but certain disappearance. You will break. Choose before it is too late. Set a goal. Set another goal beyond that goal. It isn't the time to be gentle and contemplative or likeable, or to wander without purpose. It isn't the time to be innocent. The famine has shot a dart aimed at you. Learn, and live.'

13
My Fear

For obvious reasons, I was compelled to be more attentive to what I was doing. I needed to evaluate and re-evaluate my present position in terms of the deal. I needed to identify my weaknesses before they broke. I was doing fine, I thought, except for one fundamental problem, and I needed to attend to it more seriously.

I had to recognize that I had fears about Nur Hussain. True, he had maintained his silence consistently when it came to our business; he had not argued or contradicted me over payment. I had enjoyed his loyalty throughout, but at this critical point I really needed to know who he was, what he was thinking, what his plans were for the future, so that I could trust him or suspect him or at least keep him seeing reason. I wanted to know how I could adjust to him for the sake of survival, or make him understand why he must adjust to me for the sake of a meaningful future. Despite all our conversations, our meals together, our experiences of working together, and considering every thread of communication we had had, I found that I still did not know him.

His loyalty to me might come from his helplessness. He was nothing without me. He was one of the millions of lost young boys who would end their lives pushing bullock carts in busy waste-management centres. His loyalty might come from the fact that he was sent to me by Raihan Talukder. If Nur Hussain did not respect me, it would mean he had no respect for Raihan Talukder, either. As long as Raihan Talukder was alive and Nur Hussain needed to return to the village, he could not harbour any disregard for me. If he did, he would dishonour the conventional system of respect.

Wouldn't he be a different person – egocentric, incomprehensible, impertinent – if he knew he needn't be dependent on me, at least as much as he thought he had to? What would happen if someone like me – or smarter – came forward and offered him a more lucrative deal? He did not seem to know what money was; he did not ask how much he earned, or how much I earned because of him, or even how much his talent was worth. Someone could explain to him what kinds of extraordinarily beautiful and momentous things he could do if he were more organized in his life, or worked with more self-confidence in his profession. Someone could easily lay out his future, in the flash of an eye. It might also happen that one day he would disappear, just disappear, without a word or message or address. What would I do? I would look for him everywhere: at the market, at the tea stalls, in the refugee camps, throughout Dhaka, in Gangasagar, and still not find him. What would I do then?

I walked the streets harbouring these deep, silent vexations. I walked for a long time, passing the smelly stalls of the meat-sellers, the dried-up well in the market, the laundry house with its coal-heated iron. When the tailor who had made Nur Hussain's Mujib coat waved at me from his door, I moved on without waving back. At the corner of the road, where the council had placed a massive rubbish bin, two beggars blocked my way and extended their tin plates. They did not speak a word, not even when I pushed them to the ground and threw their plates aside. No, I did not look back. The beggars would not come after me, I knew; they were too weak to attack anyone and too used to being beaten regularly.

When I felt worn out and unable to take one more step or speak a word, good or bad, I found myself on the premises of the Mrittunjoyee Primary School. I sat on the veranda where Abdul Karim had once given me peanuts, looking at the sea of tents before me. I felt disgusted by the human cries coming from the passages criss-crossing the field. There were people everywhere, standing idly or sitting on the ground like corpses, quarrelling, fighting, chasing or cursing one another. At least two dozen children crowded the corner of the field where there was a mountain of rubbish from the tents, from people who would throw their babies away before throwing away food, but still the children turned every piece of dirt, every can, every bottle upside down, looking for treasures.

Then a woman, right before me, fell to the dust in a feverish hallucination, telling of her sorrow at losing her son and drawing a large crowd around her. She looked like a spectre of evil, a repellent, amputated monkey, jumping up to burn itself while loudly cursing its unavoidable misfortune. I wanted to run and hit her on the head to relieve her of her pain. Any person so overwhelmed with hardship had no right to exist. The famine was a time for the able and the

231

strong-willed, I thought. It was a time for the intelligent to reign, to introduce new ways of life. They can make their own laws to protect themselves from non-existence, the way I have found my own path. They can create a religion of their own, if necessary, which will define success and morality in a completely different language. The famine can set apart the fit from the weak-hearted.

It was not necessary, I thought, for a society to have people so vile and given to filth instead of grit and ambition. What would these people do with themselves, if suddenly this field before me were to turn into a beautiful mansion, and all the tents beautiful suites, and the heap of rubbish a dining table with plenty of delicious food and drink? I could not imagine a different scenario: they would still find something to condemn in one another, chase one another and cancel one another out. All the able and intelligent men in the country, the creative people who did not surrender to the demands of hungry stomachs, should rush to this camp and burn these tents down, peel the skin off these shameless human animals. Sheikh Mujib should order his *Rakkhi Bahini* to dig a deep trench in which to bury all the faint-hearted people alive, thus ushering in a new era in which the intelligent can grow up with beautiful minds, and help advance this country. It did not matter how many unfit people were buried to nurture the fit ones; those who could not fight for a sustainable existence should perish without mercy.

Sheikh Mujib was right to turn a blind eye to these people who insulted the human spirit so extravagantly, I said to myself as I walked off the school premises. He was right to block the images of death from the media. If it were not for him, more people would have died watching those images than from the famine. If they did not die, they would be blind or infertile or eternally beyond control and correction.

As I came nearer to the tea stall, I saw a man crawling after a shiny coin thrown two yards away by another man. He had gangrene in both his legs. Repulsed by the stink from his sweaty body, I went inside the stall, and looked back only to find that the second man was engaged in a game with the crawling man. He turned out his pocket to show he had plenty of coins there, and that the gangrened man could win them all if he was ready to please him by crawling. The man crawled after coins and the crowd around the two men applauded.

Although he won't walk again, I thought, this man is more transparent than Nur Hussain; more readable, more considerate. This man is trying to live; reaching for every coin makes his face brighter and his desire to crawl stronger. He is doing exactly what he needs to do at this moment: exercising his right to degrade himself, and to enter a voluntary madness for the sake of a stable tomorrow. Suffering is not an otherworldly affair; it will never be the case that a person can't unearth the mystery of his suffering in his lifetime. This man is not acting like a phantom, accusing metaphysical abusers and creatures of the shadow world of working against him. It is better to be mad than dark. He is doing the impossible, I thought; he is a human jewel in a heap of human rubble.

By contrast, I thought with utter frustration, Nur Hussain did not say anything about himself; he did not say how engaged or disengaged he was to and from his commitment with me. For the sake of gratitude to me for everything he had now, he could have opened himself up to me once in a while, and taken it as his solemn responsibility to tell me he had no rage against me, that I would not need to growl or bark at him to know his mind. He was killing me with his silence. He was insulting me with his lack of distress, his imperceptible rashness. If I had a prison of my own, I thought, I would surely have locked him up using the Taiwanese lock, bringing him out when I needed him to speak for Sheikh Mujib. I would have starved him of food, of sleep, of conversation, of all human contact, had he refused to deliver the speeches. I would have beaten him morning and evening until he gave in, until he learned to refuse to admit he was in pain when he was indeed in severe pain, until he had licked my shoes more abjectly than Basu and Gesu had taken the dust of his own feet to their chests, until he had served me with the last drop of blood in his body.

The truth was, I did not have any such prison, and he was a citizen of a free country as much as I was. If he decided to create fences around himself, he could do that. I only hoped he would not.

'It's a gift from me,' I said, placing the box before him. It seemed my only option was to make an effort to enter his imagination. 'A simple thing, not very expensive; it looked beautiful on the shelf.' He was going to speak for Sheikh Mujib; nothing could be more delightful for us. 'We must celebrate the moment. We must celebrate our success.'

He did not ask what was in the box, so I sat on the sofa and told him to open it and see. He did so indifferently, and then put the pair of black shoes inside on the floor next to his feet. He thought his old pair was good enough, he said. Weren't they?

'Try them on,' I said, instead of answering. 'Don't be so serious now. See if they fit you.'

He tried only one shoe, the right, and took a few steps.

'Any good?' I asked. 'If not, we can return them.'

He looked at me. I could not read his eyes.

They were impenetrable.

14
NUR HUSSAIN PUTS ON RAGS

Our first speaking engagement for Sheikh Mujib had yet to be scheduled. We were to look for a new house, well-protected with high boundary walls as I had described to Moina Mia, and with enough space and furniture for our new life together – although I still didn't really know Nur Hussain, either as a person or as an accomplice.

Within a couple of days I no longer saw the new pair of shoes on his feet or anywhere in the flat. Nor did I see the pair I had bought him when he first started delivering the speech. He was using the ones he had arrived in from Gangasagar: dark-red rubber sandals with blue laces.

Had he donated the shoes to someone? Everything could be sold in these times: blood, bones, organs, babies, virginity, honesty ... everything. A pair of shoes would be one of the more sophisticated items. They had more market value than the newly printed Constitution of the country. Shoes could be sold and resold, unlike a Constitution.

I would buy him another pair, I thought to myself. It was only a pair of shoes. Not a huge loss. Perhaps he did not like the colour but felt he could not tell me so, for the sake of keeping me happy and satisfied. Perhaps they did not fit him properly, and he had known it the moment he had opened the box, which was why he hadn't even tried on both shoes. Next time I would take him to the shop when I bought him shoes, so he could choose a pair he liked. A man should have the right to choose his own shoes.

The following day I did not see a bedsheet on his bed. I asked him where it was, if he had soaked it in soapy water to wash later – though I had already checked every corner of the flat, including the toilet. The buckets were empty. The soap was in its place.

I could be stubborn, but this was a time during which I wanted to be least stubborn with him. It might cost me dearly: he could leave me. It might begin with something as simple as a conversation about a pair of shoes and then take the shape of a yes/no question about the deal. He might say he did not want to be under anybody's thumb, that he did not want to deliver the speech even if Sheikh Mujib himself stood before him, begging. Was it his problem that the country had fallen into disarray? If Sheikh Mujib suffered for his own faults, nobody could save him.

I asked if he had thrown the bedsheet away because it was old. He knew we could do lots of things with such a bedsheet; we could use it for darning the quilt, cut it into pieces to make rags or, at the very least, use it as a kitchen curtain. But it was definitely not a big deal, I said; I didn't mind, and would buy him a new one when I went to the market next time. In fact, I had not done any shopping for a few months except for buying food; I should have walked around the flat and made a list of things we needed. Now that we were doing better financially than when we had started, there was no reason for us to keep dragging our old life along. A new life deserves new elements. I would buy him a pair of high-lustre, super-soft, wrinkle-free satin bedsheets.

Then one day I saw him wash his *punjabi* and Mujib coat, dry them and wrap them in paper. I followed him as he left the flat and walked towards the refugee camp, raising dust under his sandals. I walked quickly to keep pace with him, and stopped when he stopped. Then I saw him handing over the package to an elderly, dejected refugee, who unpacked the coat and the *punjabi* and sat immediately on the street corner to sell them while Nur Hussain stood a little apart from him. After a few minutes, a man stopped and bought them. The refugee ran towards the nearby grocery with the bills in his hand, and Nur Hussain took the road home. Now he walked slowly – he had all the time in the world. He was satisfied. He had accomplished the most glorious thing a human could ever conceive with his disgustingly small mind.

Within a couple of days he was in his rags – the clothes he had worn when coming from Gangasagar. He looked impoverished. He looked as if he had never spoken in public, never had that loud, inspiring voice, never been to Sheikh Mujib's residence as his guest. He went out at all times of the day, walked without direction and stood or sat anywhere hour after hour, watching and thinking. A few times I had seen him actually go into the refugee camp to speak with people he did not know, listening to them attentively. A few times I had seen him come back home late, very late, and then lie down in the dark with soiled feet. He did not ask if there was any progress in terms of our schedules with Sheikh Mujib. He did not bother to check if I was home, if I was well, if I needed anything. When he cooked, he cooked a lot, but did not sit with me to eat. 'I'm not hungry now,' he would say, when I insisted. 'Maybe later.' Then, immediately after I had eaten, he would go to the kitchen, put food in a bowl – much more than he could eat – and cover it with a plate. The next thing I knew he would be out in the street with the bowl, walking quickly towards the refugee camp.

I knew to some extent how he felt. Of course I did. Anyone who had a human heart knew we were living in an inglorious Hell. But, I suppose, I had not known how deeply he felt it, how seriously the demoralizing scenes of death had affected him. Had he reached the point of delirium? Would he fail to calm his nerves?

I thought it would be wise for me to participate in some of these humanitarian activities with him, to go among people to talk about their suffering instead of preaching in Sheikh Mujib's favour. Just to let him know I was on the same page. These were very unfortunate days for a man with a beautiful mind; I understood that, though he might have noticed that I resisted my sense of compassion and refused to encumber myself with other people's burdens.

In the afternoon I took him to the local market. He walked like an apparition; the wind could sweep him away, he was so thin and weightless. I told him he could buy anything he wished to donate. He only had to consider whether or not it was within our means. What our means were, he had to decide for himself. There was no pressure from my side.

We stood on the pavement next to an electricity pole and looked around. The market was full of food, fresh and clean, colourful and expensive, exquisite and exclusive; food from local producers and from abroad, from dealers and black marketeers. But what food to choose, I asked. Choosing the right food was essential. I spoke briefly to Nur Hussain about the eating habits of the starving generation. Did they wait for expensive, delicious food, like those red, succulent strawberries? Did they have any question about where the food came from? In both cases I answered 'no' so that he knew we were not there to spend money for the sake of spending it. We were looking to help as many people as possible – something he wanted, something he badly wanted – while staying within our limited means. We must be more tactical and useful than simply charitable in our effort. We would count every bill as if we were buying something for ourselves.

Finally, I said it was not up to us to consider whether we were generous or miserly. Individuals such as us were too insignificant; we would not be able to stop people from dying. The famine was on such a massive scale that without proper administrative intervention, the situation could only be aggravated. What was required was an enhancement of security and order. We could feed people one or two meals. We could feed only a few families, even if we spent all the money we had earned. That would not accomplish anything in the midst of such endless desperation. We would buy whatever we could, but if we could not do a lot, we should not be unhappy.

He did not buy anything. He had no money on him; I had it in my wallet. He followed me as I moved from the grocery to the vegetable market to the restaurant. I bought ten kilos of rice packed in half-kilo paper bags, five kilos of beaten rice, cabbages, potatoes, onions, green chillies, bottles of mustard oil and some *samosas*. I gave him a bag to carry so he would feel involved. Then we hired a rickshaw to the refugee camp. We did not have to distribute the items; refugees of all ages stumbled upon them as soon as we said they were free. They grabbed the rice, tore at the packages, fought over them, hit and yelled at each other. Cabbages rolled on the ground.

Nur Hussain sat in the rickshaw, saying nothing, touching nothing. His eyes were lowered and moist.

That day he did not go out again. But the next day he did.

15
MY FRIGHT

This time he went straight to the Shaheed Minar, where he had first delivered the 7 March speech, where Shah Abdul Karim had sung his songs and where starving refugees gathered day and night for nothing. He walked the cement courtyard from end to end, watching the undemonstrative crowd in silence. Some of the refugees had made the place their permanent home. It was better than the camp at the school field. At least the ground was hard and dry, and rainwater did not pool there.

He saw me standing on the corner, ten yards or so away, but said nothing. With an uncertain look he sat down on the cement and hid his face in his palms.

Though he was in his rags, some of the refugees recognized him. I heard one of them loudly asking the man sitting next to him if Nur Hussain was the person who used to deliver Sheikh Mujib's speech, if he was the man in the fine *punjabi* and the Mujib coat they had seen the other day at Moina Mia's rally. The man took a few steps towards Nur Hussain and watched him, raising his right hand over his eyes. He then looked back. 'He is,' he said.

'Are you sure?' asked the first man, who now stood up and, in tandem with the second man, moved towards Nur Hussain.

'He is.' He was sure.

I sensed some desperate ferocity in their attitude. They were plotting something.

These hungry people could be really nasty. They did not need a reason to start a fight.

I ran at them with a thundering warning, telling them to stay away from Nur Hussain. 'You hear me,' I shouted and ran fast, fast, stepping on sleeping refugees, hitting children who played with sticks and plates, undoing the corners of several *sari* tents. I grabbed the two men by their necks just when they were two yards away from him. 'You ill-begotten bulls,' I said, 'you'll never walk again!' I squeezed them under my arms, pressed their heads to my stomach and kicked them in their legs while they tried to wrest free. I pushed one of them down and kicked him again and again, until his nose bled and he started crying in loud yelps. As the one under my arm gave in, I pushed him towards the other and breathed hard.

Nur Hussain watched the whole affair. Although a large crowd had gathered around us, he did not move. Nor did he show any interest or concern. It all happened so fast that he probably did not know what to do, probably felt numb; I made him numb with my arrogance, and he could not do anything but sit calmly. He watched as my two victims pulled each other to their feet and nursed each other as I walked away from this scene of massive embarrassment.

I was not in my Mujib coat at the time. I was not in my clean, white, neatly pressed *punjabi*. There had been no time to put them on.

Had I been wearing my coat, I asked myself that night, would I have done what I did? I knew some refugees in the camp had assaulted an Awami League supporter wearing a Mujib coat when he went there to tell them to join Moina Mia's rally, and I knew members of the *Rakkhi Bahini* had come that night to set fire to their tents. I saw the ashes the next day. Some refugees had burns. Some had bruises all over their bodies.

Then I asked why it was that I had not waited until the two men reached him to see what it was they intended to do to him. I could have. I could have waited a little bit, instead of ambushing them. I could have just walked over to them as any reasonable man would, a man who remained composed even in the face of the most serious danger. That way they would have had enough time to reach him before I grabbed them. Then I could have asked them if they had any objections or grievances against him. Thus I would have been able to win their confidence as a mediator. Maybe I would have realized that they had no hostile intentions at all. Why didn't I do that? Why had I run towards them when I saw he was not running away from them?

Nur Hussain did not return home immediately. He returned when it was late, and went straight to his room. I heard him close the door behind him. Then everything was quiet.

Later that night I heard him cough a few times. Then I heard him snore.

It would not be an endless night, I said to myself. There would be a morning for him, a morning with glaring light, giving shape to things. Morning would begin for me too, within a few hours. Weren't we going to see each other and get on with our regular lives, I asked myself, and forget what had happened today?

16

HIS MONSTER SPEECH

I opened my eyes. I must have slept for several hours, for I could see the white sun through the window and hear the bells of rickshaws from the street below.

I could hear his footsteps. I could hear the jumbled sounds of utensils, washing, sweeping. Those small sounds gave me hope. It really was a new day.

He had washed his clothes and put them on the line to dry, swept the sitting room, the kitchen, his own room. This was the man I knew. This was the man who cared for himself and for me, and for the place we lived in.

I brushed my teeth, went to the kitchen and sat at the breakfast table. He had prepared *paratha roti* and potatoes and eaten half, leaving the other half for me on a plate. Then I heard him practising the 7 March speech. I stopped eating and pricked up my ears to be sure the sound came from his room.

My brothers, he said, then cleared his throat before beginning with '*My brothers*' again. *I have come before you today with a heavy heart* ... He started the way he had always started. The pace was slow, but the old determination was there.

He did not go out for two days. He ate, slept and recited the speech. Sometimes he looked out the window, but the street scenes did not make him desperate to run outside with bowls of food to the refugee camp, to sell whatever he found near to hand. He did not look absent-minded, either. When he kept his mind occupied with the speech, nothing else could enter it. It all depended on what he wanted to do with himself, how he wanted to deal with the times.

I did not go out, either. I cooked for us, but ate alone. I must give him a comfortable space in which to think, I said to myself. He needed that space to recover. By practising the speech, he had already begun the process of healing.

Sitting on the bed I read some old copies of *The Freedom Fighter*, which I had read many times before. I read the reports and looked at the pictures, holding the paper up to the light from the window for a better view. Some of the exaggerations were amusing, some of the details baseless, some of the jokes obscene, some of the conclusions extremely hypothetical. They had made sense during the war; that was why we had written and printed them. Now, looking back, they seemed appalling. They were rubbish. We were not ourselves when we were at war. Something bigger than human reason guided us from day to day. It was not always beautiful.

On the third day I had to go out for groceries. Our kitchen was empty with only a few onions left, no *dal*, no vegetables, no protein whatsoever, no cooking oil. I thought I would buy a *hilsa* fish; the appetizing smell of fried *hilsa* right from the hot pan would improve his mood. I would also buy some fine rice, long, thin rice washed in wax. It was expensive, but famine or no famine, I would buy some – at least a kilo, for his sake. Beyond that, I planned to buy him a *punjabi* and a coat.

On my way back from the market, I hired a rickshaw to carry the groceries. I sat in the seat with my feet on the sack and told the rickshaw-*wallah* to navigate carefully. I specifically advised him to avoid the 'manholes' that could gobble up a man like me easily, and suck me into the dark underground sewer in seconds. Plenty of manholes on the streets remained open. The whole country could disappear through them.

We left the main street to enter the neighbouring lane, then came near the small market where we would turn right for my flat. Before we did that, I thought I saw someone like Nur Hussain walking in the crowd. I told the rickshaw-*wallah* to slow down so that I could get a closer look at him. He stopped in the shadow of a shop.

It was him. He looked around suspiciously, as if plotting something, and walked past the confectioner's, the pharmacy and the rickshaw garage before crossing the opening where amateur sellers sold various household items every week. He was heading to the Shaheed Minar.

The Shaheed Minar area was as crowded as always. A woman had hooked one end of her tattered green *sari* to the columns of the Minar while draping herself with its other end. The *sari* flew like a giant flag; its flapping produced the sound of rogue waves in the sea. A few more refugees had moved to the cement yard from the school field. They were raising tents and setting up ovens in the sun. A small girl cried, holding her empty tin mug; she wept while sitting and then lay down on the cement, weeping more shrilly. A man wearing a *gamcha* around his waist came running – probably her father. He smacked her in the face, snatched the mug from her and thrashed it until it was flat under his feet. A little boy came to her rescue. The man smacked him too. The girl stopped crying. She got to her feet quickly and watched with surprise as the man threw the mug into the bush behind the Shaheed Minar.

The woman pulled her *sari* from the columns and ran to the children. 'You pig,' she said to the man, and gathered the two children in her arms. 'Get lost. Get out of our lives, or you will see the last of me!'

I was still in the rickshaw. As Nur Hussain moved towards the centre of the yard, walking through the scattered crowd, I watched the surroundings more cautiously. I wanted to be sure nobody ran to attack him. He was man enough to protect himself against any surprise attack; still, I felt overcome with my usual sense of insecurity. The Shaheed Minar was a ghostly place today. I could feel it; it was a place taken by a very powerful force. That was why Nur Hussain had to come back here; that was why more refugees were crowding it, why the small girl cried, the *sari* flew, the cow dung smelled so heavy. I envisioned something coming, something I had suspected for a long time; wanton destruction was galloping towards us, gathering speed, becoming vaster and raising its head to absorb Nur Hussain's simple mind.

'*Joy Bangla*,' he began. He said it twice, enough to draw everyone's attention. The second time was longer than the first: '*Joooooooooy Bangla!*' Those who recognized him got closer. Among them I saw the two men I had assaulted the other day. They looked meek, like two kids. Those who did not recognize him followed the others. He spoke a few sentences, including: *We have given lots of blood; but if it needs more, we are ready to give more.* Then he stopped and looked around, giving the crowd time to understand the meaning of those words.

I laughed at myself. How could I think of such abomination! Force, destruction. The seduction of a simple mind. I must have abandoned my own mind somewhere, without knowing it. 'I know nothing about this place' I thought. 'I know nothing about him. I know nothing about these people.'

'Move on now, will you? Come on, let's go home. I've fish in my bag, it will rot,' I said to the rickshaw-*wallah*. 'Take a shorter route, if you know any. Let's get out of here.'

He pushed the rickshaw a few feet backward before dragging it into the street. Then he rang the bell, seeking a passage through the crowd, and got in the driver's seat. Before his feet had completed a full circle, I heard Nur Hussain speak again.

'My brothers,' he said, in the most memorable tone of the 7 March speech, 'I have stood here many times before. But I have not felt what I am feeling today. Today I can tell you that there is no hope in the words that I have spoken for so long, that they were words unconnected to our lives, to our dreams, our future. Look around you and tell me truthfully: where are all your brothers, your sisters, parents, children and neighbours? Where are they, why aren't they here with you now? They were not as lucky as you were, because of the famine? No. We won our luck in the victory of 1971. We have written our claim on hope forever by winning freedom. This is the mistake of one person and one person alone. I have struggled with myself, but today I can tell you the truth: Sheikh Mujib has become a monster, and as I speak of my emptiness here, he is coming for you.'

17

A Conversation and a Warning

It was late December. Still 1974: a very long year. A year that did not want to end until everything else did.

Refugees who had found no hope in the city began to leave. The ones who decided to stay were adjusting to the new sorrows, difficulties and riddles of city life.

I had jumped off the rickshaw and reached Nur Hussain in a few long, swift strides, pushing the crowd aside. I knocked him down immediately by pushing him violently in the chest, and silenced him by shouting more loudly and shrilly than he, right in his face. Then I carried him on my back and got him into the rickshaw. 'Go, go!' I said to the rickshaw-*wallah*. 'Faster, faster! What're you waiting for, you creature?' Several refugees ran behind the rickshaw to see where I was taking Nur Hussain. I looked back and shouted at them. I would kill them, I said; I would break their necks with a lethal blow, if they got any closer.

He was calm. He looked like a small boy, innocent by nature, enriched with an innate ability to overlook danger and threat, a boy who was facing the world for the first time in his life. He had no idea what he had just done. He sat next to me without a fight or an objection or any bitterness, squeezing himself into the corner.

Later that night I explained to him that it was no good blaming Sheikh Mujib for all the starvation and death. Nobody in the country was sadder than him to see people die. 'One cannot expect an intelligent government in a country that does not have intelligent citizens. Citizens have to know clearly what they want. Our people are shameless. How many directions do we have on Earth? Ten. But they will move in any direction they want without bothering about decency and meaning. Seventy million people will propose seventy million solutions to the same problem.' If Nur Hussain thought he could not respect Sheikh Mujib because of the famine, he should show some restraint; there were millions and millions of people in the country who respected Sheikh Mujib. He had no right to insult those people. Besides, the harvesting season had already begun; new crops had appeared on the market, and more food aid had entered the distribution system. A new pricing policy had also been declared to beat inflation, and special measures were being taken to tackle corruption. Soon the famine would end. The famine was a test for us to see if we would fall apart, if we would forget our solemnity, our pledge to future generations. Unfortunately, we failed that test. But life would not stop there. It would go on.

It was a conversation with myself, to speak truthfully, as if I was trying to understand why I was not like him – savage, dangerous, hysterical; why I was frustrated, yet calm; what strange power occupied my head. Wasn't I more upset than him just months earlier? Hadn't I ridiculed him for being silent and emotionless despite seeing death all around? Under the pretext of disarming him, I knew I was actually satisfying myself with my own arguments.

He listened attentively, but did not give the faintest sign that he actually accepted anything I had said. It seemed he could stay in the same pose for ages without moving his feet or hands, without raising his head, without blinking. I stayed with him, softly repeating myself, waiting for his response. There was none.

So it was time I became strict and gave him an either/or choice. He was to speak only what I had taught him to speak, I said clearly; that was the speech, the words of the 7 March speech, with *'Joy Bangla'* at the end – *'Joy Bangla'* only once, not twice, so as not to confuse anyone in the audience. Personal observations and emotions could not come between him and his work. There was a deal in place, and that deal had to be honoured as expected.

If he did not do as advised, I warned him at the end, if he spoke more than what I had allowed him and dropped something that the speechwriters considered important for reinvigorating the sense of Sheikh Mujib's personal heroism and the Awami League's image, I would not be able to protect him any longer. Any unforeseen consequences would not be my responsibility.

18

A REACTION, AN OVERREACTION

The following day I was called in for a meeting with Moina Mia.

The news had reached him. It had reached him in its entirety. He knew more than I did. It seemed that Moina Mia had people at the Shaheed Minar who informed him exactly what had happened – perhaps people like the two *Rakkhi Bahini* members who were sitting on two small stools on both sides of the door, holding rifles. I had never seen them before.

In addition to calling Sheikh Mujib a *monster*, Nur Hussain had called him a *disgrace*, Moina Mia told me. Nur Hussain had said that Sheikh Mujib was worse than all the Pakistani rulers in our history, because none of them had cost us so many lives. That Bangladeshis should gather against him, put him on trial and sentence him to what he deserved for clinging to power while the country sank into chaos – perhaps lifelong imprisonment: that would be his minimum punishment.

Moina Mia asked whether or not I found these words distasteful, and whether or not I was aware that Nur Hussain was going to speak like that. Had I noticed any sign that might suggest he was changing from being a supporter of Sheikh Mujib to becoming his brutal critic?

I said no, I had not seen or heard anything objectionable. Whoever had reported the matter to him must have had a pre-planned agenda to condemn Nur Hussain in Moina Mia's eyes. Just the day before the incident, I had heard him practise Sheikh Mujib's speech with profound dedication and passion.

Then Moina Mia asked whether or not there had been another incident just a few days earlier in which I had injured two refugees as they approached Nur Hussain at the Shaheed Minar: I had hit one of the refugees on the nose and kicked the other in the stomach. What had made me do so, if I had not thought some danger was approaching, if I had not believed Nur Hussain capable of doing or saying something that might turn a whole lot of people into his enemies, including those two refugees? I must have known something about him; I must have observed he was going through some kind of bizarre delusional period. What was it?

'An overreaction on my part,' I replied. 'Simply proof of my lack of judgement.' I was mistaken, I told him. I had not thought properly before attacking the refugees. I just wanted to protect Nur Hussain from any harm, because I loved Sheikh Mujib and did not want Nur Hussain hurt because some refugees had lost their minds. By attacking the men before they could harm Nur Hussain, I was making sure he was available to serve Sheikh Mujib faithfully and completely when the opportunity came.

It was disconcerting, Moina Mia said, very disconcerting indeed, to learn that, first, I believed some refugees had lost their minds and then, that I associated the matter with

Sheikh Mujib's leadership. He could not understand why I had brought the two things together to describe a problem, when there was no problem with either of them. Refugees were being fed full meals regularly at various relief centres across the city. Hadn't I seen this? Didn't I watch the TV broadcasts, which began and ended with bulletins about how the government was helping the destitute? There were deaths; Sheikh Mujib had acknowledged that. Those deaths were caused by natural calamities; Sheikh Mujib had admitted that, too. It was expected that some people would die in the new country, because some people always died in a new country. If it was expected, it should not come as a shock. If it was not a shock, why would anyone lose his mind? Why would anyone be so violent as to attack Nur Hussain for delivering Sheikh Mujib's speech?

He was calm. The two *Rakkhi Bahini* members stood. They knew what they were expected to do. They were trained. But he restrained them by glancing at them briefly.

'Go down the road,' he said, 'ask a man, any man, young or old, if he is hungry; give him food, delicious food, give him as much as he can eat, wipe his mouth, leave him to relax, to enjoy a moment of fulfilment, to pray to God in gratitude. Go to him the next moment, the very next moment; ask him again if he is hungry. He is. What did you expect? He is hungry, terribly hungry, for he has not eaten in a month, in three months, he is so poor – even though you can see his hands are still yellow, greasy and smelly, that there are bits of food in his teeth. You uncover your bowl, he jumps on the food with both hands, fills his mouth, pushes unbroken chunks of food down his throat forcefully; he eats and eats as you watch him with wonder, anger, fear and disgust, he eats and eats and eats and eats, until he explodes, himself becoming food for dogs and crows and unnameable insects, making you believe firmly that an act of generosity can bring a lifetime of misery to someone. He will overlook the fact that it was you who fed him a full meal a moment ago. He will overlook it even if he is eating the same food from the same bowl.'

Moina Mia looked at me sharply. 'That is the reality here, Khaleque Biswas,' he said. 'Desperation is the rule. Desperation guides us in life. Rationality does not.'

Then, he asked, how could I explain the matter of Nur Hussain donating the Mujib coat? He could have donated as many *punjabis* as he wished. If he thought he had money to waste, he could have bought all the stores in the country and donated their goods to whomever he wished. But he could not donate a Mujib coat. Giving away a Mujib coat to a destitute person to sell in the market insulted the coat and the man behind it. Why hadn't I recognized, after living with him for so many months, that Nur Hussain actually hated Sheikh Mujib, hated him badly, though he practised his speech as a livelihood?

I remained silent for some time. I had no answer. I was astonished to see that he knew everything. Who else was there in the road the day Nur Hussain had donated the clothes? The old man who received the clothes from him? The man who bought them? Who had reported the matter to Moina Mia? Were they *both* undercover Awami League informants?

I remembered that the old man had sold the clothes to his very first customer. I had considered that a sign of his utter desperation to buy food. Members of his family might have been extremely hungry. At the same time, I also remembered the customer had bought the coat immediately. Why was he ready to buy the clothes at the price the old man had asked for? I had seen no bargaining. There had hardly been a conversation. Those two men were connected to each other; I was convinced. They were connected to Moina Mia. Only Nur Hussain did not know he was entering their trap by his simple-minded act of compassion.

'What's the use of asking me these questions?' I said. I was becoming very upset with Moina Mia, not only because of what had happened with Nur Hussain but because he seemed to have prepared himself for some time to accuse me of fraudulence. If he wanted his money back, I remarked as a last resort, I would give him his money back. Then we would go on our way.

He explained that the money was not the most important part of the matter. Why was I behaving like a beggar or a schoolboy, he asked, who understood neither money nor honour? If it were between us, he added, we could have come to a deal, or sorted things out in a few seconds. Unfortunately, it was not between us, and it was not about us. Although the incident we were dealing with did not involve death or bodily harm, he said, it demanded infinitesimal analysis and infallible interpretation.

'What do you think I should do?' I asked timidly.

'Something has happened,' he replied. 'That something must be solved. It must be solved immediately and clinically, before it becomes the cause of much wider harm.'

19

AN IMPOSSIBLE OPTION

Sending Nur Hussain away to Gangasagar was the only option I could think of. I could take him back to Raihan Talukder and say I was sorry, that I could not find employment for him in the capital. He would not be my responsibility any longer. I would come back and begin a new life. I would rent a flat in another city, or in another part of the city, find something to do or just disappear one day so that nobody could find me, not even Moina Mia.

But Gangasagar was a long way from Dhaka. It would not be a pleasant journey if Nur Hussain and I were not on good terms. What would I do if he resisted getting on the bus in the crowded inter-district transport terminal, and then screamed for help? Some freedom fighter turned radical nationalist might lose control and attack both of us.

I decided to be cordial with Nur Hussain, if that was at all possible. I wanted to remove the distance between us that had grown in the last few days. I wanted to speak with him again, slowly, to make things clearer to him, to make him understand why what he was doing was taking us in the wrong direction.

He did not give me a chance. He was obsessed, terribly obsessed. He began by chanting 'Joy Bangla', then quickly moved away from it and spoke his mind. 'My eyes are open now,' he said. 'My heart is sad no more.' He was sincere. He was like the underground artists who painted the graffiti on city walls. 'I have made a pledge to myself, and nothing, not even Sheikh Mujib, has the power to shake it.'

Suddenly he was like God – so arbitrary, yet so passionate. Everything was in his power, huge or trivial. He could make the whole famine-ravaged country disappear with a small blow, and create a beautiful, balanced country in its place, putting a new army of gentle, honest, responsible, charismatic, intelligent and patriotic people there. He spoke, then slept for a while, and then woke up only to speak again.

No, I could not think of taking him anywhere – not even to the local streets, let alone to Gangasagar. I was not as confident as he. He was wiser than I, firmer and better. He was an idealist; pursuing noble principles suited him. His perceptions were sharper than mine, deeper and possibly quieter and finer than mine; perfect. But this was not the time to consider who was better. It was time to understand who was more practical, better suited to survival over the others. I knew I would not be able to turn back time or heal it. Sheikh Mujib was trying and failing, despite his long and outstanding record. What I could do was pass through life without noise. For that reason, I would have to take care of myself. Wasn't that why we had liberated the country – to understand our priorities and fulfil them, undisturbed, untarnished, as earnestly as possible? Let us face the truth: why should I feel guilty for being alive? Why should I sacrifice my life in order to prove that I am strong? No, I would not accept that either. Life is not supposed to be complex. It is about unwinding things by giving simple answers to simple questions. Besides, individuals have to be more cautious about their lives during moments when governments do not seem to respond sincerely to their needs. A government ought to be sincere to its people: this felt like a distant, unnatural thought to me now. It might be appropriate elsewhere, in countries where people did not need governments, where governing was a spiritual need rather than a political imperative for leaders, but not in our land, not in a hundred years.

I guess he still had some respect left for me: he ate silently when I offered him food, slept or lay down quietly in his bed when I went to sleep, and did not flee to Gangasagar when the door was open.

20

THE RETURN OF SHAH ABDUL KARIM

The next day when I saw Shah Abdul Karim at our door, I almost wept. Although he had grown extraordinarily thin and old, and did not have his bag on his shoulder, I had no problem recognizing him. His tired face broke into a smile as he embraced me.

Immediately I called Nur Hussain to come out of his room to greet our dear visitor. 'Where are you? Are you listening? See who's here,' I said. 'Isn't this day a blessing for us?'

He appeared at the door slowly, then ran into Abdul Karim's wide embrace.

'Good God,' he uttered in whispers full of pain, as though his heart was breaking with joy. 'God the Generous. My God.'

Shah Abdul Karim was not one to eat a lot, or to be happy to see lots of dishes appear on the dining table. I had observed that during his last stay.

Still, I cooked up a storm that evening: rice, chilli fish, chilli eggs, tomato, *dal* and cucumber salad – an array of food that would have been called inappropriate in those days. Nur Hussain helped me. He chopped onions, turned the eggs over in the pan and washed glasses in warm water before drying them with a kitchen towel. From time to time I looked at him, engaged him by asking if he thought the *dal* needed more salt, if the chillies were too hot for us. No, he said, they were perfect; no, not that hot, we could digest them. He asked me if he should remove the water from the rice, or was I planning to do it myself. 'Go ahead,' I answered, 'please, just be careful.'

He grabbed a chair from his room and placed it at the kitchen door. 'This is for you,' he said to Abdul Karim, and stood holding the back of the chair until Abdul sat on it.

Asking Nur Hussain to serve dinner, I went to the toilet, where I washed my face and hands repeatedly. Several times I grabbed the handle of the door to come out, but did not. I sat in the corner as my body shook with emotion, something I had not allowed to happen in the clear light of the kitchen. I opened my palms and found them shaking. My eyes filled with tears; they became heavy and painful. I let a few drops flow down my cheek.

It had been a long time since I had felt such comfort in my heart, a long time since I had cried. I saw people weep standing during burial prayers, and when volunteers came with trucks to carry the bodies away, but I did not cry then. My eyes had been made of sand. No tears could form there. No hardship was difficult enough to melt me. But now I wept shamelessly, pressing my mouth with both hands, biting my fingers and the back of my hands. Then I washed my face again and took several deep breaths before returning to the dining table.

Abdul Karim tasted every item of food at our insistence. Everything was exceptionally delicious. The smell was hugely appetizing. The colour was good. Nur Hussain ate more than he usually would. 'This is fabulous,' he said about the tomato. 'Excellent!' His hunger had awakened. He enjoyed the *dal* with relish, and raised the almost-empty plate to his lips.

As evening fell, we asked Abdul Karim the same questions again and again, as if we were afraid to be alone with ourselves, and he gave us the same answers, but each time with a new enthusiasm and sadness. His stories concerned the same topics: starvation, disease, death, burial, and then, again – starvation, disease, death, burial. Sometimes starvation was so vivid and penetrating that the subjects of his stories died before moving to the next point in the cycle: disease. They went straight to death.

He told us about his travels through Narayanganj, Dhamrai, Tongi, Comilla, Chandpur and Mymensingh, where he had stayed quite a few weeks before moving back to Dhaka. A picture of any city could be a picture of all other cities; in famine, all localities looked the same. He sang in every place, made friends – many of whom he also buried – saw many births and saw news of the birth turn to news of grief for the parents.

Within the hour, he grew sleepy. I thanked him for remembering us, for being our guest again. Nur Hussain made his bed on the sofa.

'Good night,' he said. 'Sleep well.'

He must stay with us, I said to myself as I went to bed. Abdul Karim must stay here at least for a few days to keep us company and give us a sense of purpose, which we appeared to have lost.

I was a much happier man at the end of the day than I had been at the beginning. The mood of the flat had changed forever. I was thankful for that. God bless Abdul Karim, I thought, he could not have chosen a better time to come back to us.

Abdul Karim woke up with a fever. I touched his forehead: it was burning. It could be a symptom of a serious illness, I thought. Maybe he had caught something by starving day after day. He needed immediate medical attention. I knew that many diseases started off with a high temperature before escalating into something worse.

But I kept silent. I did not express my concern. I was happy when he said it was nothing, that he had seen worse, that it would disappear after he had slept a few more hours. 'You'll see,' he said.

That would be his usual reaction, I knew. He did not believe that minor illness or disease should overtake one's mental strength; I remembered this from one of his songs. For a body to be ill, its mind had to be ill or dead first, the song went, and once the physical illness was recognized there was no use looking for an unadulterated mind or spirit in a person.

An illness might compel him to reconsider his decision to get back on the road immediately, I thought, thus prolonging his stay with us and giving us a chance to heal. It would be good for him to stay, I told him after breakfast, adding: 'Most people in the city are suffering from one or more incurable illness. It wouldn't be wise to let a simple fever develop into a more complicated illness by picking up something else from them.' I wanted to stop him from going to a hospital, so I explained that hospitals could not be considered institutions for health care anymore. They were ghostly places where death slept on the floor, the operating table, inside the coffins in dark rooms, on the veranda. Death showed itself in the eyes of the doctors, who prescribed cholera medicine to smallpox patients, smallpox medicine to typhoid patients and typhoid medicine to cholera patients. Sometimes they gave the same round 500 mg yellow tablets to all patients suffering from cholera, smallpox and typhoid, because that was the only medicine they had. Did he want that kind of treatment?

'The best solution,' I finally said, 'is to stay indoors, eat well, sleep well, wipe your face with wet cloths ... things one traditionally does for fevers.'

He accepted my suggestions and stayed in bed the whole day and night. Nur Hussain and I cooked barley, carried it to the sofa and fed him, spoonful after spoonful. He moved his head a little when he did not want anything more, and pointed at the toilet when he needed to use it. We carried him on our shoulders and stood by the door, leaving him inside, before carrying him back to the sofa after a few minutes. We washed his head three times – afternoon, evening and at night – and dried his hair well, so that he would not catch cold. We ate together, whispering to each other to eat more, because unfed or insufficiently fed bodies were more prone to illness; also, we had an ill person in our flat who had walked through many diseased places and crossed many rubbish-strewn streets and neighbourhoods before arriving at our door. Then we sat together by Abdul

Karim's side, ready to help him immediately if he needed anything.

I could not remember when, if ever, our flat had been so quiet, or when Nur Hussain had spoken his mind so clearly. He responded to every question, expressed his likes and dislikes, did not leave things for me to decide and did not prove his existence with only a dull, hateful, unreadable and strenuous silence. I could not remember a moment when he had shown he was capable of such extraordinary care. I left him with Abdul Karim because he seemed to suggest he would not go to bed until I did.

By the afternoon of the following day, Abdul Karim felt better. His temperature fell. The dry skin of his lips became soft again, after a bath in lukewarm water. He walked little by little to the window to look outside, to the kitchen to drink water, to Nur Hussain's room to start a conversation about simple things like buttons, nail clippers or razors, and sat with his guitar to mend the string. He had seen enough, he said, enough for a lifetime; now he was tired. He wanted to return home, prepare for something new. 'It is time,' he said.

As he was not going anywhere new, I asked if he would consider living with us for some time before moving back to his village – even if only for a few days, until he felt totally cured. 'Please,' I said.

Surprisingly, he agreed. 'Maybe two weeks,' he said.

Two weeks? Did he say two weeks? 'That would be great; I said. 'Wonderful.' I embraced him and looked at Nur Hussain.

21

THEIR OBSCENE TALK

We were now well into the middle of the second week of January, 1975. The days were shorter, the nights longer. The sun could not be seen until 10 AM; a dense cover of fog descended as early as 4 PM; and the sun set a little while after 4.30 PM.

Abdul Karim repaired his guitar, but did not sing for us even once in those last few days. When we requested a song, he found a way to avoid singing. He would write a good song for us later, a new song, he said, his best, and then sing it. It would take seven days to set it to music, but we wouldn't forget it for seven years. Then, his throat wasn't clear; he felt something in it even when he spoke. Singing was out of the question; singing might cause his condition to deteriorate. A singer did not have anything if he did not have his throat under control. Then again, the guitar was not in the best of shape. It had tuning problems. It needed to have its string replaced ...

Actually, it was whenever *I* requested a song of him, not *we*. Nur Hussain never insisted that he sing for us. Did Abdul Karim not sing because only I wanted to hear him? Who could tell? We all have perfect reasons for not doing things on someone else's schedule.

On the fifth day after his two-week extension had begun, I knew what that perfect reason was. I knew it when I returned from the marketplace, when, standing at the door, I saw the two men sitting together, old and young, experienced and naïve, wanderer and apprentice. I knew it when I heard them talking about politics at the top of their voices: about the famine, about the Awami League, the *Rakkhi Bahini* and, finally, about Sheikh Mujib. They were not arguing but complementing each other, filling in each other's gaps, believing each had a responsibility to make the other feel good about his irritation and frustration.

Abdul Karim had recovered his health by that time. His eyes looked deep and alive. He called to me to sit with them when he saw me at the door.

'Come, join us,' he said. 'Let us honour this beautiful afternoon with beautiful conversation. There may be another afternoon tomorrow, but we might not have the same strength of mind.'

I did not. I turned my face, and with a few swift steps, went to the kitchen, where I left the groceries on the floor and continued to listen to Nur Hussain and Abdul Karim.

'How could Sheikh Mujib say that only twenty-seven thousand people have died in the famine,' Abdul Karim said, 'when the actual number is over a million and a half? Or that at least three million people died in the Liberation War, when the actual number was less than three hundred thousand? How could he do that? Does he love Bangladeshis, then, when others come to kill them, because he cannot kill them himself? Does he hate Bangladeshis when he himself is killing them, because he cannot hate himself?'

'Can a person *be* such a beast?' asked Nur Hussain.

'That is not the question to ask. Because he can. Because he will. The question to ask is: will a person *remain* such a beast? And for how long?'

Nur Hussain did not need any more confusion than he already had. What was Abdul Karim doing, rekindling his anger? Damaging him, instead of helping him?

Nur Hussain murmured something I could not understand. There was a distance between us, and he extended that distance by speaking confidentially to Abdul Karim, by whispering into his ear; his words were lost before reaching me. But I was sure Abdul Karim understood him.

'You can't predict anything about a ruler,' I heard Abdul Karim say. 'You can't predict anything about a ruler when he is aware that he is the only hero a nation has. He wants your unconditional loyalty: when he promises something to you, when he breaks those promises and even when he becomes barren and violent. He does not understand how anyone could believe loyalty is not cheap, that a ruler must attain it with his actions, qualities and insightfulness. Isn't he a hero, he thinks, isn't he the best?

'I have wasted a lot of time deciding. It is hard for a spiritual man to accept that only a private militia can protect a government that has lost its sanity. It is hard for a faithful citizen to believe that his government does not care about him. I ran from place to place to avoid confronting myself, asking myself a few harsh questions about Sheikh Mujib. I am ashamed of that. I now know that if there is any eternal God of the universe, there is no eternal leader for a country. No more doubt, no more procrastination; I know what I am going to do. But you, Nur Hussain, my pious friend, do you know what *you* are going to do? Do you know how to ditch a tyrant who hangs upon his citizens' fate like an unending curse, extinguishing their hopes, destroying their aspirations, forcing them to blame themselves for his inability to rule?'

I could not restrain myself. It was just too much for me. I felt I was dealing with my nemesis, a blind, and inconsiderate nemesis, who had vowed to make me dumb and to eliminate me at any cost. I kicked the grocery bag with all my might. A small cinnamon packet, garlic cloves, beefsteaks wrapped in newspaper and green lemons fell on the aluminium saucepans with a huge noise. Then I rushed to the corner and kicked the saucepans around a few times. Abdul Karim and Nur Hussain ran to the kitchen doorway to watch me, Abdul Karim more surprised than Nur Hussain, Nur Hussain more frightened than Abdul Karim.

'Khaleque Biswas,' Abdul Karim said quietly, 'is everything all right with you?' When I did not reply or look at him, he took a step inside saying, 'Is there anything I can do to help?'

That was enough to increase my anger. 'Out!' I yelled as I rushed towards him. 'I don't need a friend who stabs me in the back!' He did not seem to understand why I was shouting. 'Out! Right now!' I yelled again, and pushed him back to the sofa, handed him his guitar and pushed him again, repeatedly, until he was out the door. 'Don't you ever come back!' I shouted. 'Don't you ever think of returning to this neighbourhood!'

I slammed the door in his face. Nur Hussain watched as I went to my room. I screamed several times in extreme anger, and spoke whatever came to my mind: 'This is why I brought you in, you slimy pig?! This is why I respected you?! You cannot pollute what I have purified! You cannot take away what is mine! You know neither God nor men! You know nothing about politics! No government will ever surrender to the wishes of its people! No society will ever be free from the control of its government! Go rot in the camp, you old eel! Dig yourself a grave at the heart of the refugee camp! Take your songs with you! Don't leave them behind to misguide people!' The screams became weaker and feebler as my fury subsided, little by little. Finally, after a few destructive minutes, they were gone.

Nur Hussain passed the night without a sound. He did not eat supper. He went to the kitchen quietly, as if afraid to fill his glass. Then, whether he slept or stayed awake the whole night, I did not know. I did not hear him snore. And he did not practise the speech.

I had frightened him to the bones. He must have guessed why I had been rude to Abdul Karim. Well, he should have guessed that much earlier, before I lost my temper.

He was leaving. Nur Hussain was leaving my flat. He was leaving behind things he had learned, things we had promised to Moina Mia and Sheikh Mujib. He was leaving the way he came, without tension.

It would be a lonely flat again. There would be nobody to share food with, nobody to be angry with, nobody to compromise with. There would be no sound in the other room; it would turn into a storeroom again, lifeless and dirty. The flat would become a place full of spiders, a grave, a frozen piece of memory. There would be nothing to think, plan, prepare and accomplish; no good, no bad.

There would be no escaping my own futile, monotonous, agonizing presence. It would be only me there, growing old, watching my legs grow thinner, my head grow bald, my nails breaking every few months, winter or summer.

'Are you going to Gangasagar?' I asked, when he came to say goodbye.

'Where else,' he said, quietly. 'That is my home. That is where I belong.'

'Do you have any idea what you will do there?' That was not a meaningful question to ask, and I did not have the moral right to ask him that question anymore. Otherwise this moment of parting would not have come.

He remained silent. No idea. I understood.

'Would you like some company? Perhaps someone to talk to on the way?'

He stared at me.

I told him that I, too, wanted to go there; he only had to give me an hour or two. I had something to take care of. Once that was done, we would be on our way.

He believed me. He took a moment but he nodded, then went back to his room. I told him to eat his meal and pack some food in a bag so that we had something to eat on the way.

'Take some beaten rice, if you like,' I said. That was the only food that was left. 'And two pieces of gur.'

Then I went out.

22

A PUNISHMENT FOR ME

I was thinking too much, Moina Mia said when I explained the situation to him. I should not think so much. It did not help.

As an example, he referred to the Liberation War. If we had thought too much in 1971, he said, we would not have gone to war in the first place. Our weakness for the territorial integrity of Pakistan would have discouraged us. Our separation from West Pakistan would only benefit India, we would have argued, because neither West Pakistan nor Bangladesh would have the ability to stand against it in a time of regional crisis.

Then he spoke about the Prime Minister of India, Indira Gandhi. 'Did she fall in love with Sheikh Mujib only because he was a fiery orator, a tall and handsome man, as many people had alleged?' he asked. 'No. It was business as usual. A shrewd game of politics. Indeed, she did not fall in love with him at all; she helped him win the war by sending forces, because by doing so she was breaking up Pakistan; that brought her more pleasure than making love with him would have done. Women of that stature do not know what love is. They live their lives in constant fear of being disempowered.'

If we had decided not to play Indira's game, he continued, the war would not have taken place. But history would not have stopped there. Even if she had offered us Indian military forces, adequately supplied with ammunition and strategy, we could have thought for a hundred years about freedom – yet we would not have become free had we stopped to consider that we would be a failed state after Liberation. So, no, thinking was not the solution. That was why, although there were many thinkers in the country, there was only one Sheikh Mujib who inspired us. He took that very necessary decision at the most crucial moment. In the same way, Moina Mia said, I had to make a decision about Nur Hussain without thinking too much.

I had already made my decision, I said at once. He did not need to terrify me. I was under pressure because something had gone wrong, but I still had enough intelligence left in me to decide the best thing for myself, and for the kid. I was taking him to Gangasagar, I said. Everything that had happened in the city would remain in the city. It would be lost and forgotten once he left. Sooner or later, the refugees would be gone; the Shaheed Minar area would be clean and fresh. The school building would be renovated; its field would be given new grass. People would die and die, and then one day they would not die anymore. They would become immune to sorrow and hunger and disease. The makeshift camps would disappear. Besides, I argued, Nur Hussain had not said anything about Sheikh Mujib for a few days now. He was willing to go back to Gangasagar, and if I did not take him now he might start speaking out again.

'What makes you so sure he would not speak about Sheikh Mujib in Gangasagar?' Moina Mia asked. 'Is there any guarantee?'

No guarantee, I said. I could relocate him to a new flat, introduce him to people he had never met, take him to the zoo to study the behaviour of animals, but I could not change his mental patterns. He had to change his mind himself. For whatever reasons, he now believed in something. He would believe in it until he believed in something else, until his memory was obliterated or lost or damaged. We would be in the city, and he in his tiny, obscure village. 'He can do whatever he likes in his village.'

He can do whatever he likes in his village, Moina Mia repeated. By saying that, he said, I had committed two mistakes. First of all – he counted on his finger – Nur Hussain could *not* do whatever he liked anywhere in this country, not even in the village. Villagers must do what Sheikh Mujib wanted them to do. They must follow the system of Mujibism. Everyone in this country must follow Mujibism if they wanted to see the country prosper.

Second mistake. (His finger moved again.) Before he explained, he asked if I thought there were any Sheikh Mujib supporters in Gangasagar.

Yes, I said; there were, many, as in every village in Bangladesh; but unlike every other village, Gangasagar had shown great resistance against Pakistan's forces. If they did not love Sheikh Mujib there, they would not have displayed such resistance.

That meant that every word Nur Hussain spoke against Sheikh Mujib in Gangasagar would be properly recorded, reported and analyzed, Moina Mia replied. Then, either he would be dealt with locally if the allegations were minor, or he would be referred elsewhere, to be dealt with directly by the *Rakkhi Bahini*. Nur Hussain was not to be taken lightly, given what he had said at the Shaheed Minar – his 'monster' speech. The matter would quickly be investigated, and the findings would lead straight to me.

Moina Mia said he was making the matter easier for me to understand. In Nur Hussain's case, he said, which was now my case, there was nothing to investigate or establish; by becoming Sheikh Mujib's guests together, we had already established our relationship. 'Remember?' he said. The only thing that remained would be to make a decision about how serious the punishment should be, and when it would be executed.

'What's my role in this?' I asked. 'Are you being funny?' I felt my blood surge. He was not, I understood immediately. He looked at me frostily, his eyes like brass. If Nur Hussain was in Gangasagar and spoke there as he had spoken at the Shaheed Minar, nobody would know what had happened to us; we would just disappear.

But I had not advised Nur Hussain to condemn Sheikh Mujib, I said. What was Moina Mia talking about? Didn't he see how hard I worked so that Nur Hussain stayed ready to deliver the speech for Sheikh Mujib?

He flicked a particle of dust from his shoulder with the back of his fingers. I did not know what I was doing, he said. I did not have any idea about anything. He took a breath, then turned his face towards the window. 'Do you believe in Sheikh Mujib, Khaleque Biswas?' he asked me abruptly.

What did he mean? What was the connection between Nur Hussain's disapproval of Sheikh Mujib and my loyalty to him?

It would not have been possible for Nur Hussain to criticize Sheikh Mujib, he said, if somebody else had not criticized him first. 'Inspiration comes naturally, while condemnation needs systematic effort. Condemnation needs to be grown, tended and nurtured over time, with a purpose.' Nur Hussain had somebody with him, a collaborator, a radical and persuasive associate, a foolish mentor, a terrorist. Somebody ruthless and menacing must have entered his head and told him repeatedly what to think. Somebody gave him principles to argue with, the strength to contradict and the ability to withdraw, thus crippling him. I was the obvious suspect. I must have done something to him that had pushed him to his present impaired mental state. I had annihilated him and then reconstructed him to suit my dismal political experience.

How could I prove I had not done anything to make Nur Hussain turn against Sheikh Mujib? I could offer to bring him in to speak for himself, to admit that what he had said was completely his own invention and that I had no part in it. But I did not. That would not be enough. Moina Mia would say I had influenced him again, this time to get him to contradict himself, and that I had done so only to evade the Mujibist system of justice. By criticizing Sheikh Mujib so brutally, Nur Hussain had proved he could be influenced to commit any terrorist act, and by persuading Nur Hussain to take responsibility upon himself I would be defying the Mujibist system again. That would only double my punishment.

I was not just in an unpleasant situation now; I could feel the rage of the *Rakkhi Bahini* in my ears. I could already see the pair guarding the door paying wholehearted attention to our conversation. They would act and act clinically when their moment came. I could see them look at me when Moina Mia said: 'Answer me this: Where is your Mujib coat, Khaleque Biswas? Why are you not wearing your coat?'

I had left it at home, I said. Nur Hussain and I were preparing for our journey to Gangasagar within the hour.

The Mujib coat was not ideal travel attire. Wearing that coat on a bus crowded with sweaty bodies would not be to give it the respect it was due. I was aware of the honour it deserved, and that was why I had come to see Moina Mia before leaving. I had come out of my own sense of responsibility to request that he locate a replacement for Nur Hussain so that Sheikh Mujib did not find himself in an embarrassing situation. 'I am not a cheat; even though I am not wearing my coat, I have the Awami League and its social prestige right in my heart.'

He knew all about me. He knew I had bought my first Mujib coat only after I was invited to see Sheikh Mujib at his residence; I had not worn a Mujib coat before the war, during the war or after the war had been won. I had not begun wearing one even after I had bought one for Nur Hussain and taken him from meeting to meeting to deliver Sheikh Mujib's speech.

However, fighting was not his purpose, he said. There would be enough evidence against me to punish me in the most severe manner. I must come up with a more practical solution to the matter, and if I needed help, he could send a few *Rakkhi Bahini* members immediately. I would not need to do anything. I would not need to know anything.

'He has me,' I thought. 'The Awami League has me. I am dead.'

I would think about it, I said, although I remembered that he considered thinking unsuitable to progress. Then I moved towards the door.

'Sheikh Mujib has it all written out,' he said loudly, so as to make the two *Rakkhi Bahini* members look at me again. 'I am doing you a huge favour by being lenient towards you. If you follow me, you needn't despair.'

23

IMPRISONMENT BEGINS HERE

What would I do? There must be something I could do in this situation. There must be something. But what was it that I could do?

'Shut up!' I said, when I came back home and Nur Hussain told me he was ready, that the beaten rice was already in the bag and that we could start off anytime now. 'Shut up!' I needed time to think and plan. If only he understood what I was going through! If only he knew how I was suffering because of him!

He stood for some time with his arms folded; then his face suddenly grew dark, and he went to his room without further comment. He must have been terribly hurt and disappointed. I had shared many difficult moments with him, but at no time had my words been so uncontrolled and callous. Now I had lost myself, completely lost myself.

He came back, of course, with his bag on his shoulder. What did I expect? He stopped before me for a moment, wanting to say something – perhaps a courtesy goodbye – but he hesitated, and said nothing. Couldn't he give me one moment, just one small, quiet, simple moment?

He must have understood I was troubled. Within a short while I would be able to collect myself and say a proper goodbye to him, buy him a farewell gift and shake his hand, however difficult that might be and however inconsequential it might appear to him. It was not that he had bought a non-refundable ticket and the bus would leave if he did not show up on time. Buses departed every hour. There were newly introduced luxurious non-stop night coaches that would take him to Gangasagar early the following day.

Now that he would not be Sheikh Mujib anymore, we could sit in a restaurant and order a traditional three-course meal: rice, fish, *dal*. We could go to any restaurant and sit up front, without fear of people watching. He could talk about Gangasagar as much as he liked; I would not care. Then we would part, asking each other to stay in touch. That would be gentlemanly – a recognition of our respect for each other, and a fitting tribute to our mutual acquaintance, Raihan Talukder. But no, he behaved as if he had become strong suddenly, the last rebel on Earth, and could neglect me in a way that would be demeaning by any standards. Hadn't he learned anything about politeness after staying with me all these months?

He dragged his feet towards the door, slowly. I watched him with amazement and anger, and waited for him to stop. I counted: one ... two ... three. I expected him to change his mind and sit down, saying he was teasing me, that it was a joke, just a joke. Why in the world would he go back to a place he had so willingly left behind? He did not stop. I rose, and jumped upon him with an inconceivable lunacy. I snatched his bag, threw it onto the sofa, ran to the front door and closed it. 'You cannot leave,' I said. 'No way, not now, not until we are done with each other.' He knew it, but he stood still, more troubled than me, more troubled than ever, and could not find any words to dispute mine. 'I'll tell you what to do with yourself,' I said. 'I know exactly what you need to do.' I pushed him backwards, until he was in his room, on the bed. Then I closed the door and locked it hurriedly.

He said he felt suffocated, and asked me to open the door. 'Are you listening to me?' Although he had lived in that room for months now – since arriving from Gangasagar – suddenly it had become too small for him! He could not breathe, he said; there was not enough air in there. 'What a clown!' I thought. Then he screamed my name and kicked the door.

'Khaleque Biswas! Look at yourself! Take a very good look at yourself! What do you see?'

He was becoming desperate to get free. His kicks were now stronger and stronger, I noticed, but the moment I feared the door would break down, he stopped. A silence descended upon the flat. I was exasperated but did not move, fearing he might start kicking again once he knew I was there, just outside the door, afraid of him. He had become tired, probably, or was planning some trick. Perhaps he just did not notice how close he had come to breaking out. Whatever it was, I was ready for him. I knew exactly what I would do if he came out and attacked me. I had a steel shovel under the sofa that had been there for a long time, a perfect tool with which to face any intruder, known or unknown, who jumped into my world unexpectedly and shattered my peace, who damaged or intended to damage my property. Intruders are intruders – always enemies, never friends. One blow to the head would do it. I was not afraid to see blood after all the horrible deaths I had witnessed. Let there be blood. No madness comes to an end without some bloodshed. No stillness is ever achieved without some madness. I would ruin him before he could think of ruining me. If a single blow would not do, two would. Three or four, if accurate, certainly would.

I spent two more hours sitting by his door, then slowly rose, locked the front door and went to the market. There I bought two dozen sleeping pills, a long knife and some rope, and hurried back home. On the way I did not look anyone in the face. I had no idea how my own face looked. I went in and strained to hear any sound coming from his room. He was quiet; the door was locked, as I had left it.

I knocked on it. I was going to remove one of the small blocks of wood in the door, I said, so that we could see each other and talk. We must make a decent effort to close a deal, and I would let him out if he cooperated, if he was not violent. I wanted to tell him that he had been sold, that there was no point in resisting, no point in tears, that he could not possibly change the history of men selling men to other men, that it had always happened, and would always happen. But I did not say anything. What was the point? Did I want him to understand something? No. It was better that he understood nothing. That was why the past was better than the present, why we had seen a future together. If only he had remained the dolt he was when he came from Gangasagar!

I knocked a few more times; then, using the knife carefully, I created a small opening at chest-height. He was standing against the door. Grabbing the blade, he tried to snatch the knife – but I pulled it away quickly, cutting his palm. The blood ran; he pressed on the wound with his other palm. 'God!' he shouted. 'God! God!'

'Hold on,' I said, and ran to the kitchen. In one of the upper drawers, I found the box of Zam-Buk antiseptic ointment. I almost unlocked the bedroom door to give him first aid, but stopped myself: it would be too dangerous. Suffering and compassion could not bring us together anymore. I tossed the Zam-Buk into his room through the small opening.

'Apply the balm right on the cut,' I said. 'Apply it immediately. Then close your fist.' He picked up the round, white box and uncapped it. Then he threw it at me, fast. It hit the door; green Zam-Buk ointment splattered on the wood.

It was a relief that the cut was not deep. Once his anger abated a bit, he picked up the Zam-Buk and applied it after all. The blood had already thickened; the balm would take the pain away and help the cut heal quickly.

He was probably hungry. I supposed he had not eaten anything, even though I had advised him to do so before going to see Moina Mia. He had probably been so excited at the thought of going home that he had forgotten to eat. 'I am coming in,' I said. 'I am coming in with food and water.' Then I passed the rope through the opening and told him to move to the end of the room, where I could see his feet. He was to tie his feet together with the rope and stand with his hands on the wall.

He looked at me with blazing eyes, and did not move. I waited for some time, trying to read his mind. I had a deep headache. I pressed my forehead with my fingers and sat on the sofa. He came to the door, looked up at me through the window and did not say anything, good or bad. The silence became heavier. I tried to stay awake, but could not.

Several hours must have passed, for it was the dead of night when the noises coming from his room woke me up. He had broken everything: the mirror, the bookshelf, the small terracotta vase, the wall clock, books, newspapers, the mosquito netting, the pillow cover, his clothes … nothing had been spared. There was blood on his chest, face and hands; dry blood on the floor; small splotches of blood on the wall, on scattered newspapers and on pages of books. He must have hurt himself on the shards of glass arrayed on the floor and cried in pain, but I had not heard anything. I had slept like the dead.

When he saw me, he did not speak. He got up slowly and went to the back of the room, carrying the rope. He tied his feet with it tightly, without my saying anything. Then he sat on his knees, his back towards me, hands on the wall. He looked at me before turning his face to the wall again.

I opened the door just a few inches and pushed in a plate with some rice and *dal* on it, and a glass of water laced with four sleeping pills. He remained in position. Then I closed the door and locked it. I knocked several times to let him know he could now untie himself and eat the food.

What was I doing? So arrogantly, so wildly? I asked myself if I could reasonably explain any of my behaviour. No answer came to mind. I could not even remember where I had got the idea of buying the pills. What was I thinking when I ran to the market? *Why* had I run to the market?

Minutes went by. How had we reached this stage? I tried to understand it. Did I really push it this far? I looked at myself in the mirror, incredulous, puzzled. I was shivering. Had Sheikh Mujib scripted this, too? What was Moina Mia doing now? Had the *Rakkhi Bahini* guards been given any specific orders?

I opened the door again, only after he had eaten, drunk the water and fallen asleep on the floor, perhaps wondering why he was feeling so sluggish and why the cut did not hurt anymore. I walked cautiously, so as not to wake him up. Then I tied his feet with one end of the rope, and tied his hands together as well. I had the knife on me; I would slit his throat if he woke up and got clever. With a wet towel, I removed the dry blood from his face. I checked the cuts in his palm and on the soles of his feet, and applied a thin layer of Zam-Buk there. Then I cleaned the room, removed everything with which he might hurt himself and locked the door behind me.

It was my turn now. I needed some rest. I crushed four pills into a glass of water. My hands had no strength left, but I was able to mix the solution with a spoon and raise the glass to my lips. Now there was nothing else to do. He was there in his room, at the bottom layer of his quiet. I was now in my own room, in my own quiet. There was no one to visit us, except the *Rakkhi Bahini*. Abdul Ali would not come anymore; the matter was way beyond his negotiating power. It had to be the *Rakkhi Bahini*. It would be them. They would appear chanting the *'Joy Bangla'* slogan, and exterminate everything instantly.

24

THE DREAM RETURNS

'What is this place?' I said. 'I am in my bed, but I can see the sky above me; I can see the rice fields and the pumpkin bush with a kingfisher atop it. There, behind the old, timid, wavy, forgotten village path, I can also see some small houses under the green trees bathing in the sweet music of the river. It seems I am in Gangasagar. Am I? What am I doing here?'

The fierce battle had just ended, and Mostafa Kamal was victorious. Thousands of Pakistani soldiers lay all over the place, dismembered and dead.

He smiled at me. 'Don't think so wildly, Confused One. Discovering the depths of life requires endurance and serenity. Fantasy is only the beginning.'

I asked him why he was not coming to the point right away, why he wanted to confuse me with images that made no sense to me, if he knew I was already so confused.

'You want to sparkle all the time, don't you, Confused One?' he said. 'I am not surprised. All those in your situation do the same thing. They lie in their beds and think of me while falling asleep, and when they attain a certain level of stillness, they fly to me for inspiration. I do not sparkle, but they think I do; they want to sparkle like me. They want untroubled moments, an untroubled future, an untroubled last breath, without knowing I always considered life a trouble, war a trouble upon that – and that inspiration only makes one believe that no trouble is trouble without bounds. I hate you, Confused One, I think you are a defeated man; but I'll tell you why you're here. You're here to seek my advice.'

'What nonsense are you speaking?' I asked. 'Aren't you dead? Where is your shadow? What year is this? You died in 1971, I clearly remember; you died here, on this ground; those beaming baby bamboos and those hyacinths grew up drawing nourishment from your blood. Don't you remember we adorned you with a medal for bravery? He was a real man, we said, the man who loved us and the man whom we would always love. You should be satisfied with that. What more do you want?'

'I am as dead as you are,' he replied, sitting next to me, next to my pillow, placing his machine gun on the floor. 'And I am as alive as you are. But at this moment it does not matter whether I am alive or dead, Confused One. What matters is whether or not you consider yourself alive when *you* are dead.'

'Don't try to play with my memory, mister. And don't you try to trick me. Once I wake up, I shall shake you from my head. You are a hero today only because you have a machine gun in your hand. I don't have a gun with me, but I am not afraid of you. You're dead, dead, dead; I know that. I have walked in the field and smelled your bones; your thirsty soul whispered to me so many times, told me no hero wants to die, so cold, blind and fathomless is death.'

I held onto my bed as if I was falling. I thought, let me see what happens if I'm confused; let me be confused for a moment and see my fate. He may be correct, considering the fact that I live in Bangladesh, and it is no ordinary time.

'If you're alive, as you claim you are,' I said, 'I mustn't be myself; I must be dreaming now. If I am dreaming, I might not be asking you the right question to know exactly what you are doing in my bedroom in the middle of the night. Can the confused confuse someone? Can they confuse those who confuse them? As I confuse Sheikh Mujib, who does not remember anymore what he has become, a violent ruler? Can I influence him to protect a nation?'

'You're asking me how to confuse others,' he said, 'but I can see you've mastered the art of confusing yourself to the highest degree possible. You've so many questions that take you in so many directions. You want to stop somewhere, but you can't. You want to focus, but you can't. I shall guide you, so that you don't behave like the confused ones when you yourself are confused. That is what all great confused ones throughout history have done, including myself. Instead of asking me so many questions, you ask me the only question you have come here to ask. I know and you know that you know only one question; you've always known only one question, to which you did not have a proper answer.'

'I have no question,' I said. 'I never had a question about anyone or anything, not even about this famine. I am a happy man; I am satisfied with my meagre life. I know the famine is not here to stay, and eternity is just too long to keep one unfortunate year in mind.'

At this moment, there was thunder in the sky; somewhere, a lightning bolt broke the trunk of a palm tree. He asked if I would like him to remind me of the question, as I appeared to be out of my mind. I told him not to be smart with me. If

I knew I had only one question, as he was saying, I would not have forgotten it, would I? I would remember my question myself.

'You don't have to remember,' he said. 'It's so obvious. It has been the only thought you have been thinking. Your eyes, your movements, your sighs, speak of that hidden question. You can't sleep. You feel insecure. You think your plans in life are going to be washed away before you know it, and the only way to stop it is to know how you might answer that question.'

A man with a gun might be the dumbest man of all, but I felt he had hooked me already; he was not being funny, and he could read me very well.

'What is it you think I am thinking?' I said. 'Let me see how accurate you are, Soldier Oracle.'

He smiled again. He took his machine gun up onto his shoulder and said: 'Look around you, what do you see? The end of an era. I ended it. I'm right here on this Gangasagar battleground today, and I'll be here right until the sun has lost its light and the sky has fallen to the ground.'

The killer instinct can make someone really vainglorious: he was an undeniable example.

'Tell me, then,' I insisted, 'if you are so sure.'

He laughed a little and then began to leave.

'Don't leave so selfishly,' I said. 'Don't leave me to guess how pathetic you are. You may not get another chance. I may fly to other heroes for inspiration.'

He turned back. Another thunderbolt struck. The earth, my bed, shook a little.

'You're thinking about Nur Hussain,' he said, turning his eyes back upon me, his stare too heavy to bear. 'Your only question is what to do with him.'

'You might be right.' I tried to smile, though my breathing was becoming shallower. He knew my thoughts; he was not dead. 'How brilliant!' I said. 'Finally, I have met a clairvoyant human being. I have met someone who is aware, who thinks with style.'

'You can't admit your limitations, can you?' he said. 'Why do I even ask? You're not alone – you must have known that, by this time, Sheikh Mujib has joined you: the man you despise so much and yet force yourself to love. Don't worry; seventy million Bangladeshis, equally confused people like you, are with you.' He looked gloomy, even though it was the day he would attain his ultimate glory. 'I'll tell you what to do with Nur Hussain.' He turned. 'Kill him.' Then he started walking again.

'"Kill him?"' I shouted. 'What do you mean by "kill him"?' The wind began to blow, raising dust. A thin mist came down and gobbled him up. 'This is not fair,' I said. 'Come back; come back here right now. Where are you? You can't leave me here. You can't leave without explaining your answer.'

The mist became thick, then dark. The rice field, the trees, the houses under them were lost from my sight. The kingfisher jumped onto the ground, and from the heart of the hard soil caught a red fish and flew towards the village. 'Nur Hussain ... Nur,' I called loudly. 'Where are you?' I raised my head, looking for him. 'The whole country is full of traitors. It is a zoo; neither you nor I can live here in peace. Mostafa Kamal has lost his battle today. He has complaints instead of inspiration. He is just a vanished flame. There is no hope. Gangasagar is not an innocent place anymore. Don't go there.' I left my bed, walking through the black mist and looking for him. 'Don't go, Nur. Stay with me; I'll protect you. I'm the only help you have got. I am the only one left who understands you.'

Nur Hussain had woken up before me. How much earlier, I did not know. Hours, or minutes. I heard coughing. Then the dull, blackened world gradually became clear. The ceiling, the picture on the wall, the door all took shape. My fingers moved. I found myself back in the present.

It was the pain, I thought. A layer of Zam-Buk had not been enough for him. It cooled the pain momentarily but finally proved inadequate. Or he wanted to scratch and found his hands tied, like his feet. Then the anger returned in full measure, squeezed his heart hard and overpowered him, and he could not sleep again. The anger lingered, making him more awake than ever. He remembered everything that happened until the last moment, when he fell asleep. Or it was some nightmare that visited him immediately after he settled into the lethargic world of the pills. He woke up and believed the nightmare was real, finding himself tied up in a closed room.

I watched him through the small opening. He sat against the wall, his legs extended, his hands on his lap, and his breathing shallow. He heard my footsteps and looked at me.

25

THE GIRL, THE WOMAN
AND THE OLD MAN

A girl stood in the street under a massive new hoarding that featured a picture of Sheikh Mujib and which screamed: 'MUJIBISM IS THE BEST.' She was staring at our window constantly, until some noisy rickshaws distracted her for a second. She was fifteen or so, looked thoughtful and anxious and remained there as I cooked food and did not change her position, though it was midday and the sun was extremely hot. After watching her for a few more minutes, I raised my hand and waved to her, just to be sure she was not blind. She did not respond.

I closed the main door and crossed the gravel path to take a closer look at her. No, she was not from this neighbourhood. I had not seen her before. She must be from the refugee camp at the school field, one of the newcomers, a victim of the famine from a village whose name I had never heard in my life.

'Are you looking for someone?' I asked.

'Someone like who?' she said, instantly irritated.

'I don't know,' I said. 'You tell me.'

'What makes you think I am looking for someone?'
she answered quickly. 'Have I told you I am looking for
someone?'

'No,' I said. I did not want to scare her, so I kept my voice
low. 'You have not. But you seem to be lost, and I am trying
to help.'

'*You* will help me?' She smiled briefly. 'Have you helped
anyone in your entire life?'

It was no use starting an argument with her. She would
not understand how the adult world worked. I doubted
she had even learned how to speak respectfully to an older
person. If she were my relative, I would have never forgiven
her parents for not teaching her how to maintain at least
minimum courtesy with a stranger.

'Listen,' I said, suppressing my embarrassment, 'I know
this neighbourhood better than anyone else around here; if
you need to go somewhere, I can be your best guide.'

She smiled again, but quickly returned to attack mode:
'Have I told you I wanted to go somewhere?' Then, as if doing
me a favour, she added: 'Don't waste your time with me. Go
on your way. I have nothing for you.' That gave me the idea
that although she was young, she was not inexperienced or
foolish; she knew how to hide behind words.

'Why were you staring at our window?' I asked. 'Have
you seen anything strange happen there? Are you expecting
anything to happen?'

'I know you,' she said, faintly. She understood that she
had upset me, and that I would not let her go without some
harsh words. 'Nur Hussain has spoken to me about you a
few times.'

I did not want to mention Nur Hussain's name, considering
the sensitivity of the situation, but as she had mentioned him,

I asked what he had told her about me. 'You remember any of that? One or two words, maybe – the beginning, the end, the middle … anything?'

She narrowed her eyes as if she would never forget any of his remarks until her dying day. 'You have no heart,' she uttered clearly. 'There is only ash inside you.'

'And? He did not stop there, did he?' I took a step closer to her. I waited – with anger in my heart, but a vivid smile on my lips.

'Your tears are fake. Your words are lies.'

She watched nervously as I began to laugh.

'Anything else?' I asked. 'Tell me, even if it is trivial. Tell me, even if it is ludicrous. Don't hesitate. Don't hide anything. I am enjoying this moment.'

'You do not believe what you see,' she said, with a sort of obstinacy.

'What do I not see?'

'Yourself.'

'I do not see myself?' I raised my hands. 'I think you are right. I see a pair of lovely feet before me. Each has twenty-five toes, some of which are rotten, and some yellow and blue. I will have to crawl instead of walking on my feet.'

She did not find my retort amusing. 'You are a cheat,' she said. 'Those who cheat, suffer.' She took a step back and looked away from me. 'You will suffer for a long, long time.'

I could not determine whether or not Nur Hussain said that, or if it was her own conclusion about me based on his remarks. However, it wasn't necessary; I received the message. I was trying to understand how his words related to her staring at our window today. I asked if she was looking for him, what business she had with him now, if she had any news for him. Finding her silent, I changed my style.

'Little girl, speak to me,' I said. 'You are clearly uneasy, aren't you? Speak, speak.' She looked at me and again at the window, while her face became pale. 'What is he to you?' I asked, taking another step towards her so that she was within my grasp. 'Have you been sleeping with him?' She was not shocked, as if she knew I could be a little bit dirty-minded, and began to walk away when she spotted an approaching rickshaw carrying two passengers. I called to her. She did not respond. I called her three, four more times; then I had to stop, as the rickshaw-*wallah* and his passengers became aware of our quarrel.

I returned to the flat. From the window I saw her again, after two hours had passed, staring up from the same place with the same concern on her face. This time I did not go down to speak to her; I did not need to. *This was where all the food had gone*, I thought; Nur Hussain must have found a sweetheart. How enigmatic he was. He had never mentioned her, though he had shown her where we lived and spoken to her about me.

She would have to be warned, I thought. It was not a time for romance, and definitely not a time for romance with Nur Hussain. Love is only a clever investment for survival during famine. It will not survive. If she did not stop staring at the house, she would pay dearly. Yet I also thought warning her thus would make my life more difficult; people would want to know why I was complaining about her looking at my window, why I thought she deserved to be warned off. Some overcurious and stubborn people might want to see if I was hiding something in my flat, if I had started a brothel here and she was one of the disgruntled inmates.

When evening came, she left; but she returned early the following day and walked up and down the street, stopping for a while to look at our window. She looked quieter today, broken and smaller. 'Get away from there, brainless girl,' I said quietly; 'go away, go away! Or I'll bring you here, lock you up and make you share his fate!'

The sun rose higher and the street became dusty; she stopped walking and sat herself down firmly in the same spot as the previous day, bringing waves of sweat to my forehead. I feared she would stay there the whole day, that she would not leave as easily as she had done previously, that she would stay until I had unlocked Nur Hussain, taken him to the window and made him ask her to end her vigil. But after an hour she was gone, and never came back.

In the evening, however, an old woman took her place. She was not one of the beggar people, and absolutely not a refugee, I was sure. She had a long veil drawn down to her nose, and kept her hands inside her *sari*. It seemed she was ashamed of being in the street. I suppose she was some housewife from the neighbourhood who did not want to be recognized by pedestrians and rickshaw passengers. From time to time she raised her veil a little and glimpsed at our window. She stayed only half an hour and then walked towards the tea stall, following an old man with whom she had had a short conversation, and who watched the window for at least a minute before going on his way.

I saw the old man again the following day, towards the evening. He took up his position in the usual place and looked up at the window every few seconds, spoke with pedestrians and begged from them. He had a small tin can on which he made a rich, penetrating noise with a stick. He made that noise while looking at the window, which made some children look in the same direction. How devious he was, I thought; how crafty. He figured that if more than one person looked at the window, I could not accuse him of any special wrongdoing. He was having a conversation with the children now.

I should act quickly, I said to myself, before he said anything insensible to them. I put on my shirt and went down to the street. He noticed me and sensed danger; he began to walk in the opposite direction, looking backwards from time to time. When he saw me following him he began running, and threw the can to one side of the street. I took long steps to close the distance between us, and believed I would be able to catch hold of him before he became lost in the crowd now leaving the mosque after evening prayers. But he ran faster through the crowd, pushing people aside and, probably thinking the crowd ahead was thicker, took an alley to the right, heading towards the end of the neighbourhood.

He had just made my job easier, I thought. Only a few houses stood there, in between wet, cultivable plots of land; he could not go far. I ran behind him now, until I caught up and pushed him down on the muddy ground under a mango tree. I stood over his pale face. He was breathing fast; his lips could not pronounce what he wanted to say – some protest, some explanation, anything people say when they feel unsafe.

'I won't hurt you,' I said, 'calm down. You see, I have nothing in my hands, no knives or hammers or batons. I am not the *Rakkhi Bahini*. I am not interested in your money, either.' I kneeled, balancing on my toes, and asked if he knew Nur Hussain, if he had been waiting for him in the street.

He gasped for air, but nodded. 'Good man,' I said, 'very good man; now, wouldn't you like to be a little more comfortable, sitting straight, maybe against the tree, so you can answer a few questions?' I offered him my hand but he shrank back against the tree, disbelief in his eyes and his voice failing repeatedly. Extending my legs beside his, I sat in the mud. I must have been crazy to do that, but he was too important to me. Anything he would say was too important, and useful. I smiled to reassure him and asked mildly who the girl was. He moved his head from side to side; he did not know her. 'The girl,' I elaborated, 'who stood in the same spot yesterday. She spent a long time there, waiting and staring at our window; who is she?' He repeated his answer, which irritated me – but I was still a long way from learning anything from him, and could not afford to become angry.

'Is she your granddaughter? Have you been advising her to pursue him?' He shook his head more rapidly to deny my remark. 'I know your type of people. You would even push her under a speeding truck to escape the responsibility of feeding her. You disgust me. The moment I looked at you, I felt that somehow I would be contaminated by your sick fantasies.' I had to finish with him as quickly as possible, so I did not press the point. 'If you do not know the girl, it is all right,' I said. 'She is just a young woman with a little heart. She understands nothing. But perhaps you would like to tell me about the woman you spoke to, the veiled woman who followed you yesterday – who is she? What does she want?' He did not know her, either. She had asked him if ours was the house where Nur Hussain lived and he replied that it was, only this; she left after him but they had not talked about anything else. He did not know where she had gone, or where she lived.

'You don't know anybody in the world – I accept that; but tell me why you yourself chose the same spot? It wasn't a coincidence, was it?' If he did not want to talk about other people, I thought, he might be willing to talk about himself. Some people consider maintaining the privacy of others a great virtue.

'Don't you think it is impolite, terribly impolite, to stare at people's windows?'

Nur Hussain had told him to wait there, he said. He had told him to go stare at the window when he felt hungry and could not find anything to eat, that he would come down with food for him.

'Very good, you are returning to your senses. Your life is not a total waste. Now, try to make yourself a little bit better. If you knew the house, and if you were so appallingly hungry, why didn't you come to the door instead of standing on the street for such an awfully long time, making yourself more appalling? Couldn't you come to me, ask for some food, when you saw me at the window? I'm sure you recognized me. Why did you run away?'

He tried to speak clearly this time. 'I was told not to come to the door, at any cost,' he said and then watched me to see the impact of his small, deplorable revelation. I understood what he meant. There was an earthquake inside me; it was an unexpected twist. A cobra raised its head, hissing endlessly. It took me a minute to collect myself.

'Is that so?' I finally said, with a smile. 'That is terrible. But I can understand, yes, I can understand that.' I took his left hand in my right, clasped his fingers with my own. 'I appreciate that you are so forthright with me. Whatever you're saying sounds reasonable. My general belief is that you're telling me the truth. Nur Hussain could do something like that, easily. There is something mysterious about him, isn't there? There are layers, one upon another, one hiding the other; there are just too many layers, I lose count of them. Never says what he knows. But you are a transparent man; you say everything on your mind. I believe you.' He raised his head and leaned heavily on the trunk of the tree, with much relief. I shook his arm and released it in his lap.

Then I said, calmly: 'But I wonder why you would tell me the truth. Doesn't it sound unreasonable to you? Because of you, I now know what Nur Hussain did not want me to know. Why did you tell me what he'd said to you? Why did you tell me anything?'

He became still, and his relaxed mood disappeared. He was so baffled by my questions that although his voice had recovered by then, he did not find anything to say.

'Were you afraid of me?' I asked, to which he nodded lightly after a few seconds. He had hesitated to admit it, I saw. He considered the consequences of both admitting and not admitting his fear. That was what I wanted. 'Be very afraid,' I said finally. 'Do you know how many times Sheikh Mujib has sent for me to advise him about sanitation and relief management in the last few months? At least three times. And do you know how many times Moina Mia fell to my feet so that I would allow Nur Hussain to speak for him? More than you can imagine. Nur Hussain does not know these things. He does not know, because I did not let him. I did not want him to be frightened of me because of my power and capacity and connections. But I will tell you what you'll do. The moment I leave you behind, you'll do me a favour. You'll forget everything he has advised you to do or not to do. I am the king here. I rule this country. I don't want to see you around here.'

I smiled one last time before walking towards the neighbouring street.

Secrets, but no more. Not to me. I laughed as I returned home and watched Nur Hussain through the small opening. I laughed as I sat on my bed, and stood at the window. 'If only I could know what other secrets he has,' I said to myself, and laughed again. 'He must have spoken to many more people than these three; he must have spoken about many more things than just about food. If I could meet one or two more of these people, I would understand the origins of his present disorientation, and take specific steps to resolve it, bit by bit.' I grew tired. I needed to rest. Before that, I needed to wash myself and wipe the floor behind me. With a towel in hand I entered the bathroom, and suddenly burst into long, loud and painful laughter.

26

TEARS IN HIS EYES

A few days passed like this. I raised food to his mouth; he ate with gratitude. I raised a glass of water to his lips; he drained it completely in one go, in case I did not offer him water again. I ate what I'd cooked, then slept in my room after taking pills; he slept in his room, the door locked. I always gave him only half the food he required. I wanted him alive only, not strong – definitely not strong enough to overpower me – and I gave him only enough water to make sure the pills were absorbed.

Then I noticed tears in his eyes.

They were not on account of hunger, I understood, but because of the acute smell that had made not only his room but the whole flat unliveable. I felt like vomiting.

Within minutes I had unlocked the door and dragged him to the toilet, holding him by the collar. There I threw buckets of water upon him. He lay on the floor, tranquil, his face quivering with every splash. I would untie his hands, I said; he must stay on the floor, face down, and not move until I was out the door. He was to wash himself and change his clothes, then knock on the door so that I could tie his hands again before taking him to his room. I had the shovel in my hand, I warned him; it was sturdy, heavy and a good size for use in the small space of the toilet. If he tried to do anything stupid or became violent towards me, I would bring it down on him, and he would have to live with a far more acute smell for the rest of his life. Then I stepped on his neck, untied his hands, quickly ran out and closed the door behind me. He lay on the floor, terrified. There was a long moment of silence, then the sound of water splashing.

His hands were free now. I suspected he would untie his feet and not exit the toilet without a fight, or pretend he had no plan to attack me, behave politely, speak softly and in a friendly manner, do as I expected and then jump on me with all his rage the moment I opened the door. He could be ruthless, I had seen that. I had seen how he had broken everything in the room, whatever he could get his hands on.

I heard his knock in due course: two mild knocks, as I had advised. Then, a pause, after which two distinct knocks again. I told him to open the door only a quarter of the way. He opened it less than that, and extended his timid, shivering hands before I asked him to.

'Give me the rope,' I said, 'give me the end of the rope.' He bent to the floor, one hand still outside the door. With the other, he threw the rope out. He had it ready. It was clean: no blood, no smell of urine. He had washed it as he would have washed his handkerchief.

Then he extended both hands up to his wrists through the door. I tied them quickly. I could see the cut on his palm. I wanted to ask if it was still painful. If the Zam-Buk had not been effective, I would buy something else from the pharmacy. But I restrained myself. I did not want to begin an emotional scene before I was confident he could not harm me. I had to be safe before I helped him. I told him to move away from the door. He jumped a few steps back and stood looking at me. I pushed the door open further, and found his feet the way I had left them – tied.

I carried him on my shoulder and sat him on the sofa. There were several cuts in his feet, all open now, red and damp. Some of them, the deep ones, had swelled up. Others looked black. I told him to raise his feet onto the sofa so that I could examine the cuts better. He did – calmly, slowly. The skin on both sides of the cuts was whitish. That exposed the black line in the middle with a sharp contrast. I cleaned the cuts with cotton, dried them with a towel and covered them all with Zam-Buk.

Then I cleaned his room. I removed the quilt, put a new one on the bed, scattered some powdered bleach on the floor, washed it and burned some incense sticks. I removed the bloodstains from the walls and wiped the walls softly with a warm, wet towel. Once the white, sweet-smelling smoke had filled the room, I took him to his bed and placed a pillow against his back so he could sit comfortably. His face was dry. I poured four drops of mustard oil onto my palm and smeared it on his cheeks. Now he looked lively. I combed his hair, but did not bother to give him a Sheikh Mujib style. I trimmed his nails.

Then I prepared a full meal for him: rice, fish curry, vegetables, *dal* and chilli paste with spring onion. I kept my attention on his door, which I had not locked, and which could still be a dangerous outlet for his vengeance against me. An open door might give him the impression that he was free, though he was not free. He might be lulled into thinking he could escape easily. That, too, would be a mistake. I had the shovel with me all the time. I kept it next to the hot oven.

Sitting before him, I raised spoon after spoon to his mouth. He ate with great appetite and quietly, eyes down on his plate. Once or twice he raised his eyes to me, small glances. That was all. He asked nothing. I explained nothing. He spoke only at night, when I untied his feet. He said: 'Thank you.' I did not reply, and locked the door.

That night I did not give him pills, and I, too, went to sleep without them. They were no longer necessary. I felt he was coming back to me. Soon he and I would sit together, his hands free, my mind clear. We would forget the past, which would exist only as an idea on which we had compromised. These few days of suffering, his and mine, would have washed it away. Moina Mia, the *Rakkhi Bahini* and Sheikh Mujib would have nothing to do with it. They would not be a part of our world. They would not dictate anything. Let Sheikh Mujib be reincarnated with all the shortcomings of failed leaders. Let Moina Mia sing of him his entire life. Let the *Rakkhi Bahini* rage a war against all the hungry and disgruntled people because they blamed Sheikh Mujib for their misfortune, and as a result let people die in their thousands.

Let the whole country turn into a shameless tent city, never to be vibrant again. Let mothers hang their children, let the young starve the elderly and kill them. Let intellectuals become slaves of their own obscene complexes, because they love to be slaves. We would fight to live outside that insane, chaotic canvas. There must be space for us, a small place, somewhere in the living world.

He would grow into a complete man one day, a wise man, master of his own passions, I believed. He would use his mind creatively, and no longer need to turn to me for help. He would excel in some trade, earn a living by himself without speaking much. He was bright; he could easily acquire some technical knowledge if he wanted to.

And I would have a peaceful life, devoid of dissent against people and institutions alike. I would not brood over my dissatisfaction with life. A Puerto Rican woman would speak Spanish, a language I could not understand, so I would find a quiet, simple, warm-hearted and trustworthy Bengali-speaking woman from one of these neighbourhoods instead, and start a family with her. I would buy her wooden earrings, oyster-shell necklaces, fine cotton *saris* with lots of embroidery and bottles of aromatic haircare oil. On a moonlit night I would take her for a boat ride on the Jamuna River. When the boat went far out, and the cacophony of the port faded, I would tell her about this time. The thought of her, I would say, had saved me when I was most disoriented, and I had lived because of her. I would love her sincerely and make her the happiest woman in the world. A man like me could still do a lot of things in this country. I would create my own ideal world – little by little.

27

THE MADNESS

Instead of sleeping in the bed, where I had left him the night before, Nur Hussain slept on the floor right behind the door. There was fresh blood on his wrists, under the rope. He must have fought to untie himself at night. The knots were tight; the rope was coarse. It had damaged his skin and made him bleed. Now he was sleeping through his pain.

He had not gone to sleep with a delirious mind, I was sure. I had seen his face. It was calm. I did not think he hated me. There was also no sign that he had any objection to my tying him down. He knew why I had to do it. He knew it was not that I did not care about him. He did not need to be generous to recognize that. He could just look around the room. He could remember his wonderful meal.

So what had happened during the night? What had changed him?

His eyes were red. When he looked at me, his face spoke of horror, like the horror I had observed in him when he condemned Sheikh Mujib at the Shaheed Minar. He sat up, gathered where he was, felt the pain of the rope and told me to open the door. When I did not, he kicked it, took a few steps back and ran forth to kick it again. 'Open it!' he cried. 'Good citizens do not stand against each other; they stand against their government! Haven't you learned anything? Open it! Let me out!'

I walked across the room, not knowing what I should do, unable to concentrate on anything. Then I looked at him through the opening. He tried to kick my face, but his foot could not reach high enough – so he came at me with his head. His forehead hit the door and began to bleed.

If only I could give him some pills! If only I could tie his feet again! I was lucky to have locked the door before going to sleep. I was saved. With that anger, and with that brutality, he could have strangled me at night or used the knife, or the shovel, or anything of the sort, to kill me. If only I could send him to sleep again!

He saw fresh blood on the floor. Then he looked at me in disbelief, and collapsed.

When he recovered consciousness, he delivered the 7 March speech – just one line from it, in which Sheikh Mujib had said: *You cannot suppress us!* He said it again and again: when I watched him through the opening and when he lay down idly on the bed after kicking the door several times at a stretch and still failing to break out. Soon his voice became faint and his eyes became tearful. He whispered whatever came to his mind, as if speaking from the brink of a dream.

'Land of little villages, quiet nights,' he said, 'land of green leaves sleeping on the jute roof; land of white fish and golden evenings singing aloud; land of sweet smiles and warm embraces, filled with enormous blue skies, the sudden laughter of pride in the rice fields by the tiny river; land of sugarcane children, red pumpkin lovers, crowded lentil weddings in the night, awakening to a morning of beaten rice balls; land of dreams and promises and processions coated with mild wind and raindrops; land of celebrations, knee-deep happiness, drinking date juice all through the winter; land of life broken into loss, pain, tears, sighs and deceit; land of little villages, empty, dark; endless queues of bodies falling deep into the heart, forever.'

I could not resist the pull, so primitive was it, and so pure, so spontaneously beautiful. I could not turn myself away from the door, from watching him with sincerest astonishment; from sliding myself into a jar of silence, closed and asleep like a seed.

He could have done anything with me at that time, anything, had he tried. He had changed. He had grown up. He felt the pain of the nation in his being. He had shattered all the guises a man could wear in life and emerged as a true individual with an undivided mind. He was not to be defeated.

Cold and trembling, I stood behind the door as he continued to disappear into his voice.

He said: 'There is no question that cannot be asked in this land.'

'Nur,' I heard myself say, 'Nur! Nur!' I bent forward and covered the whole opening with my face. 'Let's go to Gangasagar. Let's start now. You show me the path, I shall follow you. I'm sorry for all this. The speech, the dress, the arrangement – they were all wrong; they were all a mistake, my mistake.

'I owe you a great deal. You see, I grew up in extreme poverty; I starved as a child, as a young man. Even when

I became an adult, I was earning barely enough to fulfil
my needs. I would not have agreed to let you live with me
unless I had known that *not* to do so would have been to
compromise my reputation with Raihan Talukder. I wanted
to save face because that was what I had. I couldn't even
buy you a mosquito net – remember?

  'Then the money came; it came from a place where I had
least expected it, and it came without effort and also without
the promise of continuity. It came with unfathomable
excitement, with my first unsurpassable feeling of real
success. I thought this was how I would fulfil myself; it
was supposed to happen a long time ago, but did not. I got
carried away. But I can see it now. I was not against you; I
was against myself. I am sorry. I really am. Give me a chance
to make it right. Let's go, you and I, to the little village of
green leaves and quiet nights, where the fish jump in the
air to kiss the sun. Will you promise not to attack me – not
here, nor in the bus stop, nor on the way, not in Gangasagar,
not ever, for this confinement, for being so cruel to you? I
have been cruel, I know. I was not myself. Will you help me
be myself again, Nur?'

  He watched me intently for some time, leaned his head
against the pillow and, closing his eyes, withdrew into his
semi-dreamlike state.

28

AN INSULT FOR A THOUSAND YEARS

His lips moved. 'The knot will undo itself,' he whispered from his solitude. 'The rope will disappear, the lock will melt like a chunk of ice; everyone will be alive again – those that are dead now, those that will die in the future.' Then suddenly he became aware of his surroundings, got up from the bed and looked at me. *You cannot suppress us!* He uttered it several times, his voice growing high in pitch, and he moved towards the door.

I suppose I had become too tired to listen to him, to make sense of his very presence, to correct that which could never be corrected. I felt a burden on my shoulders that I could neither remove nor overcome, which pressed down upon me more than the shame of living in acute poverty, for which, though continuously obsessed with my own powerlessness, I dared go as far as to be the creator of an unspeakable dishonour. I shed blood, found satisfaction in despicable viciousness and played with his life most obscenely to protect my own.

I took a step back and heard him say: 'I say "no". Not in my name. Not as long as I live and walk. Not as long as I speak.' He kicked the door a few times and looked at me through the opening. I was afraid, for he looked like a ghost, ferocious and repulsive, but I remained calm; I told him it would not happen again, that I was extremely sorry for what I had done to him, it was not in my plan. 'One world ends here tonight,' I said, 'and another world begins, a very different world.'

He watched me, then called me 'Sheikh Mujib'.

'Look at that little Sheikh Mujib,' he said, whispering. 'Victory to you little, rejuvenated Sheikh Mujib. Long live little, rejuvenated, indomitable Sheikh Mujib. May you be happy, little, rejuvenated, indomitable, indefatigable Sheikh Mujib.'

I begged, joining my hands together.

'Please,' I said. 'Why are you doing this to me? Why are you doing this? Please, please. Don't make me any smaller than I have already made myself.'

He was not speaking loudly, but I felt the whole world was listening to him, and would call me 'Sheikh Mujib' from now on. One generation would tell my story to another; every generation would add its disapproval and hate. It would go on and on and on, until all was quiet, cold and dead, until the Bengali calendar came to an end, never to begin again. But then, one day after thousands of years, the elements of the Earth will come together again and life will grow anew, little by little; a bright rainbow will arc over the Buriganga, and blue lotuses will smile in every pond and canal. I see strangers walking along a village road; I see men and women returning home after a long day's hard work in the fields. I see myself standing beside the walkway before a clump of bamboo, hoping to speak with them of beauty, goodness and generosity – but, my hands upon my chest, I can only say: 'One year we had a famine here, you know; one year, one and a half million of my countrymen died. But I, Khaleque Biswas, lived through it. I lived the next year, and the next, and the next.'

Then, before their tired but watchful eyes, I shall begin to suffocate myself with both hands at my throat, though I shall not be able to stop the story. I shall not be able to control the words, so speedily will they come. The strangers will come closer, with hesitant steps, and say, in wonder: 'But one and a half million died, and you lived! How did they die and you live? How did you make that happen! Were you a psychic, a magician? A prophet?' They will want to know if I, little Sheikh Mujib, am speaking the truth, if I really lived in 1974, for it will be too long ago now, it will be in the dark and frozen entrails of the past. I shall say I am indeed speaking the truth, that this was the best form of all truths, that truth could not look any better, not even with God.

They will laugh at me through their tiredness. I could not possibly mislead them, they will say; they are tired, but they are happy; their conscience is clear, they do not bear the stain of starving their fellow citizens. I shall implore them to listen to me; what they know will not be what it was, entirely, I shall say. There were huge floods across the country, I shall tell them; all the crops were damaged, the cattle carried away, infrastructure destroyed. Then came severe drought, and scorching heat cracked the soil like never before. Most importantly, there were just too many desperate mouths to feed.

But they will not listen. They will continue walking towards their homes and families, looking back at me with pity, as if they, too, had been present in 1974 and knew exactly what happened in Bangladesh under Sheikh Mujib's rule. I shall follow them for a few paces while tightening my hands around my throat. I shall have to suffocate myself a thousand times, because once upon a time one Nur Hussain had called me 'Sheikh Mujib' at the height of his delusion.

He realized that no other name or words could be more offensive to me, and that I would never be able to separate my life from the lives of those who now lay lifeless, that I would never be able to wash away Sheikh Mujib's sin from my own conscience. He called me 'Sheikh Mujib' in the voice of a boy, of a man, an old person, a hawker, a prostitute, a teacher, in every tone possible, moving his head from side to side. He called me 'Sheikh Mujib' while smiling, and pretending to sob. 'Little Sheikh Mujib, are you hurt? Shall I deliver the 7 March speech for you? *My brothers …*'

I could not take it anymore. I picked up the shovel from the kitchen, ripped the lock from the door and struck him, hard. He took a step or two back, I took a step or two forward. He fell to his knees; I looked down at him. He crawled, and said: 'You have betrayed us! You have betrayed us!' I bent over him and hit him and hit him, until his voice was heard no more, and his body stopped moving.

To be specific, I hit him only in the face; to be more specific, only in the mouth. I could have hit him anywhere on his body – his arms, shoulders, legs or even his head, if I wanted to smash him in one strike. But I hit him repeatedly and consistently in the mouth, because I had no anger against him, or his heart, mind or head: it was the mouth that had called me 'Sheikh Mujib'. It was the lips, the teeth and the tongue behind the teeth that had spat out that name at me. I wanted to punish them, and I did punish them, as long as they moved and produced words or sounds. I stopped only when the mouth became a dark hole gaping at me, hiding all signs that it was Nur Hussain's mouth or any mouth at all.

I laughed in satisfaction and sat on his chest to make sure he did not come back to life to ridicule me. 'You understand now,' I continued to say, 'what "little Sheikh Mujib" is capable of? I hope you dream of Sheikh Mujib in your afterlife, and are terrified.'

No moonlight shone that night; no spring breeze came through the window. I was alone in a flat I could not stand, but I was delighted to think that I had a glimmer of hope ahead, of leading a normal life. I would inhabit the beautiful, unsuspecting world for the rest of my life, now that Nur Hussain was no longer there to call me 'Sheikh Mujib' ever again.

29

GOODBYE TO MOINA MIA

As I walked the streets late the following morning, I saw no one in front of me or behind me. There were no rickshaws on the road. The yard of the mosque, which had always sheltered some refugees, was empty. The tea stall was closed, and the newspaper hawker next to it had disappeared.

I saw some children when I reached the crossroads, but they were not playing today. Looking at their sombre faces I imagined something fearful was happening somewhere very nearby. One of the children pointed to the tin gate of an abandoned house, under which I could see people's feet. I was the last person to be curious about anything that day, but I walked up to the gate, and before I could touch the handle to open it, someone from inside grabbed my hand and pulled me in quickly. There were a number of people there, leaning against the wall, sitting in the dust or watching the road through the small holes in the tin.

One of the men – none other than the *imam* of the neighbourhood mosque – whispered to me that a state of emergency had been declared across the nation, and that the parliamentary system of government had been dissolved in favour of a republican system. He said Sheikh Mujib had declared himself President-for-Life, with extraordinary power; the country's Constitution was no longer valid. 'I have also heard some very disturbing news on the radio,' he said. 'Sheikh Mujib has banned all political parties in the country but one; the only party that will decide the fate of the nation is the Awami League.'

One of the men there, sitting in a far corner, was the keeper of the tea stall where I had once entertained Abdul Karim. The Awami League would no longer be called the 'Awami League', he was explaining to another man; instead, it would be called the Bangladesh Krishak Sramik Awami League from now on. 'Why?' asked one listener, who looked like a factory worker, rickshaw-*wallah* or mechanic. 'Weren't *krishak*' – farmers – 'and *sramik*' – workers – 'part of the Awami League before? Then who did we support for so long?'

'Why do you ask me? Why?' said the tea stall keeper, irritated. 'I am not Sheikh Mujib. I do not make rules.' A man next to him touched his shoulder, as a request to keep his voice down. The tea stall man nodded, but when he spoke again he was louder than before: 'I am a shopkeeper. I don't know anything. If you have the guts, go to the President and ask him.'

I pushed the gate open and walked into the street. 'Come back,' said someone, probably the *imam*, but I did not care. As I walked, I heard him say, concerned: 'Don't go there – they'll shoot you. Come back ...' I walked on. After the pharmacy, I saw some people standing alongside the old brick wall, the newspaperman among them. He knew me as a journalist and gestured to me. When I went closer, he whispered that he had some bad news for me: many newspaper offices had been ransacked the previous night, and all national dailies and periodicals had been banned except four that were published under the guidance of Sheikh Mujib's intellectuals.

I started walking again. As I moved towards the main road, I saw a line of police cars there, now under the command of the *Rakkhi Bahini*. They were occupying the intersection to confront and disband any anti-Awami League demonstrations. All the cars were covered with numberless posters featuring Sheikh Mujib's headshot.

The *Rakkhi Bahini* had shot six dogs in the morning and gathered their bodies in the road, a bystander told me. He was hiding behind a large rubbish bin at the corner of the road, from where he observed the movements of the *Rakkhi Bahini*.

'There,' he said, pointing to a place twenty yards away. I saw the dogs' bodies scattered one upon the other. A few living dogs attended them, and sat nearby. 'Can you tell me what they mean by this?'

Another man who stood next to him grabbed his neck hurriedly to silence him. 'They mean *this*,' he said. 'Will you shut up now?'

The two men moved further into the shade to make room for me, but I did not want to hide. The fact that I could now walk in the middle of the road without being bothered by rickshaws, vehicles or pedestrians gave me unbounded happiness. I took a long breath, stretched my neck and arms and continued on. As I approached the intersection to inspect the dogs more closely, one of the *Rakkhi Bahini* members came up to me on his motorbike. He said he had recognized me (although I could not remember having met him before) and advised me not to be on the road on such a day, because someone who did not recognize me might take me for a troublemaker – which he was sure I was not.

He asked me where I wanted to go, and whether or not he could give me lift. I did not know where I wanted to go, so I stood before him, silent, looking past him at the dogs. He was called by a tall, middle-aged man with a finely trimmed beard, who I guessed was his commander, and who ordered him to leave immediately. Holding the clutch in the lowest position, the *Rakkhi Bahini* man said he was going to Moina Mia's, and that if I was also headed that way I could go with him. I looked back at the dogs – their mysterious silence chilled me – but the man on the motorbike pulled me to sit behind him.

'I did it,' I said, when I stood at last at Moina Mia's door. 'There is no need to send the *Rakkhi Bahini*. Nur Hussain is now sleeping in the depths of the earth, in some unknown grave with hundreds of others who have died from the famine. I did it; I did not procrastinate.'

Startled, Moina Mia took a few swift steps towards me, then stared at me silently. Perhaps for a moment he thought that Nur Hussain did not deserve to die for the crime he had committed, however odd and menacing the circumstances. Perhaps the massive man inside him quickly surfaced through the narrow buttonholes of his Mujib coat, and made his murky eyes glitter for a moment. It would be a moment only.

He invited me in and offered me a seat on the sofa. When I sat, he stood beside me quietly and put his hand on my shoulder.

I looked up at him. 'It is okay,' I said. 'I am not sad. Nobody could go unpunished after assaulting our Supreme Leader Bangabandhu Sheikh Mujibur Rahman.'

He was glad that I had come to him to tell him the news. He would find something to say to Sheikh Mujib, he said, and would not have to fabricate a story. Sheikh Mujib would understand if he was told that the famine had taken Nur Hussain.

'A leader like Sheikh Mujib does not depend on one person's genius to maintain his legacy,' he said, probably believing that I considered myself guilty for letting him down. 'It needs a whole nation of people to create a leader like him, and the same to keep him at the helm of power.'

Then he sat. His eyes deepened. He became the man I knew. He advised me not to talk about it, and to move on. It would remain between us. If I was asked where Nur Hussain was, I should say that I did not know, that he had lived with me for some time and then disappeared. *Why* he had disappeared was not a question to ask me; it was a question for Nur Hussain only.

I would not talk about it, I said. What was there to talk about? One body among a million bodies could get lost as easily as a sesame seed, lost without a trace. Then I said goodbye. I would see him again, I said, and I would not forget his generosity; he had given me a chance to serve my country.

'Would you like to mentor another speaker?' he asked, when I was at the door. 'One who is obedient? One who follows the rules? One who speaks only, and does not think or dream or analyze or speculate? One who does not have that troubling thing called a conscience in his head … a worthy and desirable citizen? One who does not transgress?'

'I will let you know if I do,' I replied and walked towards the gate. 'At this moment, one seems like enough.'

30
THIRTY-FIVE YEARS OF DARKNESS

When the last of the money was spent, sometime in August 1975, I left the city for a small community in suburban Dhaka where I lived among strangers. I became a salesman at a vegetable market; then I took an apprenticeship as a light-duty mechanic; then I became a digger for the city corporation, on its dam construction project. For two consecutive seasons I worked as a mosquito sprayer. I was good at it. At the end of the second season, my supervisor wanted to make me Lead Hand for the local unit. I said I did not want to be Lead Hand, nor did I want to take responsibility for others; would he please offer the position to someone else? He did not have anyone more efficient than I was, he said. I had to accept it. He would try to grant me more compensation for the extra duties and a few days' leave after the peak season.

I disappeared the following day without sending an explanation, and went to another community just a few miles away, where I became a schoolteacher. I taught history to children. I was glad the textbooks said nothing about the 1974 famine, though they did discuss what followed it: the assassination of Sheikh Mujib in 1975. In line with the syllabus, I introduced and reintroduced him as the 'Father of Our Nation'. I quoted from the 7 March speech while teaching the lesson covering Bangladesh's independence. My voice did not match his voice at all, but I found the students listening to me as attentively as the refugees had listened to Nur Hussain at the Shaheed Minar. There would always be an audience for that speech, I thought; it would never cease to raise one's hair.

Then I explained how unfortunate we were as a people. We had murdered our father; we had not given him even five years to organize himself, to take the necessary measures to make the country thrive. As a concluding statement, I said that although the assassins had murdered him like cowards in the dark of night, they could not kill his spirit; it would live on to inspire us in our tumultuous journey towards democracy. He would be available to us at any moment. It was history edited, lavishly distorted, but I enjoyed the fact that I did not have to speak about the famine – and thus nothing about the inheritance of an immense dishonour. I could teach history decade after decade in Bangladesh without ever remembering Nur Hussain and my sinful past or explaining why Sheikh Mujib was actually killed so brutally in 1975.

I taught history for three seasons and then quit. How would students know about honour if they did not know that dishonour was easier and more penetrating, if they did not know that people could die in the millions even if the earth did not move? These students would become judges, lawyers, executives, soldiers and, of course, leaders; they would be in charge of our nation, and guide it through time. It was important that they knew the problems of our past so as to learn exactly how to avoid them in the future.

I entered more humble professions in the days to come: cobbler, bricklayer, poultry worker; for some time, I was a boatman on the Dhaka–Keranigonj route. Often, I did not know what my job would be for the day. I stood in a queue with day labourers, waiting to be hired. I did all sorts of work – cleaning backyards, removing fallen trees, cutting harvests, drying jute fibre on the motorway, dyeing winter cloaks, rescuing drowning people from the river. Even these seemed satisfactory after a while; they gave me ample time to contemplate my life. I had my evenings free, and I had the respect of my fellow workers. They invited me for tea, brought sweets for me on religious occasions. The poultry owner gave me a dozen eggs every month; his mother repaired the sleeves of my shirt.

That was not what I wanted. With time passing very slowly, I wanted to be hated and tortured; I wanted something punishing, something to resurrect me from my own dead existence. I had sold my heart to the killer I was. I had sinned. In everything I saw and heard, I wanted to feel the pain that I had caused Nur Hussain in the very last moments of his life.

While working as a rescue worker, I saw a small vacancy notice in a local newspaper placed by the Anjuman social welfare organization. They were looking for a gravedigger. *Gravedigger?* That job was mine, I thought. It was mine, and would be mine until someone had to dig my own grave. Nobody remembers a gravedigger, neither the living nor the dead; nobody wants a relationship with a gravedigger. I thought it would be appropriate work for me, an appropriate punishment. Every corpse would remind me of Nur Hussain, and every evening I would cry for him, sitting in my lonely room.

I ran to the Anjuman office and told the recruiting
manager I was interested in the position, and that I was
strong and had strong nerves. I was a survivor, I told him;
I had seen many deaths up close; I would not become
emotionally involved while interring a body. I was not
allergic to bad smells either, I added, and he could pay
me a reasonable salary for my service. The manager asked
if I had used a shovel before. I had: spade, hoe, plough,
everything – particularly a shovel. I was born in a village,
and had lived there until I was sixteen, when I moved to
the city. Then, for a long time, I did small jobs that involved
lots of hard labour. I specifically mentioned the digging job
I had done for the city corporation. He watched me keenly,
as if he had never seen anyone with so much enthusiasm
for such a job. Then he asked if I knew how deep, wide and
long a grave was, and how much it could be raised above
the ground. I had done my homework; five feet, four feet,
six feet, and one foot, respectively, I answered at once. He
gave me a form to fill out.

The seasons changed, and the children who had survived
the famine grew up and had children of their own. Several
rivers ran dry; devastating floods and tsunamis killed
thousands of people. A few thousand more were shot dead,
hanged or kidnapped and tortured by dictators and elected
governments, including the Awami League. The population
of the country doubled; more mass graves containing the
bodies of nationalists who had sacrificed their lives in the
Liberation War were discovered. Half a dozen memorials
were erected in their honour. Surprisingly, the country's
archaeologists did not find the graves or remains of those
who had died during the famine; no memorials were erected
for them. Governments and political parties opposed to

the Awami League did not speak about them, because they themselves were ruthless like the Awami League; they, too, had much to hide and distort; they, too, needed protection against the truth. I myself had grown old and irrelevant because of my self-contradictions and my memory, which held the face of one Nur Hussain – who had cursed and loved me simultaneously.

When I was alone before a green, open field, I saw him sitting on his bed, his face between his hands, dark and contorted with some pain he could not digest or ignore or explain. Then I saw him speaking, standing at the Shaheed Minar and attempting to gather all Bangladeshis together under one roof. I heard his voice, with all its defects and in all its perfection. I heard him memorizing the 7 March speech phrase by phrase, sentence by sentence, trying to pronounce every word correctly, giving them the typical Mujibist enunciation. And I saw myself standing beside him, coaching him through the whole process of learning the speech, wearing the Mujib coat and disciplining him so he did not speak too much. I saw everything that happened afterwards, how one day things changed and I cut short his life with my ill-judged decision. Sometimes the images came with all the details; sometimes they were just outlines, one or two disconnected moments from the past. They came and went and came back again; they sat on my chest and tortured me constantly.

I lived in many places, so I did not buy very many things. I shed my needs gradually and came to be satisfied with a bare flat and a mat, quilt, pillow, saucepan, stove and plate, plus a cup in the toilet, two plastic containers for *dal* and salt and two sets of clothes. When I moved to a new place I left everything behind, in order to erase my past. Nor did I keep any copies of *The Freedom Fighter,* or any other newspaper published during the famine. They were not necessary. I had them in my head. I could easily remember how dark the water had been that the refugees drank to catch cholera. I could give a proper description of the night when Basu and Gesu were shot, and when Ruhul Amin entered a temporary phase of self-evaluation and decided that he had been right to pull the trigger.

Although the Anjuman buried around seventy unclaimed bodies every month – more during general strikes, elections and religious festivals – and I dug almost half of the graves, soon I understood that it was not enough for me. Gravedigging had piety, but could not save me. No act of generosity or kindness or punishment was adequate enough to make the wrong right. I could dig a thousand graves and cry a thousand nights, but doing so would not compensate for what I had done. I would still be avoiding the truth that I wanted to see reflected in our national consciousness: guilt for the dead. Only by admitting to the world that I had killed Nur Hussain could I finally deal with the matter, if dealing with it was at all possible.

EPILOGUE

The sun is setting. I can see the last glow of the day on the sprawling coconut leaves in the school field. The wind is slow. The dust is returning to the earth.

This is my last evening under the open sky. If I come here again, and stroll in these streets, and view these landscapes, it will be in my imagination – through the tunes, images and colours that I have gathered in my memory.

And I have gathered enough of them.

The cement floor of the Shaheed Minar is very inviting for a short and undisturbed break, before I finally withdraw myself from the world. With my cheek to the floor, I can hear footsteps, the noise of rickshaws moving frantically; they are returning home, carrying weary party workers. I guess Sheikh Mujib's birthday celebration is over now. His ghost will retire, at least for a night.

When I was a small boy, they said the more I ran, the quicker I would grow up. I ran mile after mile in rice fields, wheat fields, jute fields; I stumbled over hard mounds of earth and jumped into ditches and canals before learning how to swim. I think I grew tall before my time. After my confrontation with Nur Hussain, I ran again. I crossed vast distances, but this time to become small, to detach myself from everything I knew and wanted to be, and to become extinct. I wish I had never learned to run in the first place. Growing up is a curse, if one fails to grow a sense of responsibility as well.

I can see a flock of birds flying south. So many days, I have watched them until they became small, indistinct and finally disappeared in the flares of the horizon. Today, my sight is blurry; I cannot see far. But I can still imagine the shock that will surface in people's eyes when they find out who I really was. My colleagues on the city's excavation team, when they read my story in local newspapers, will be able to decipher the riddle of my sudden disappearance. They will say they knew from the beginning that there was something unpredictable about me. Gatekeeper Ruhul Amin, if he is still alive somewhere under the sun, will read my story only to condemn himself for showing me respect when I went to see Moina Mia. I was a cold-blooded murderer, he will say; indeed, so cold-blooded that even a killer like him could not stand a person like me.

From these stairs, I can see the floodlights of the Sheikh Mujib police station in Sheikh Mujib Drive; I can see several security vehicles sprinting down Sheikh Mujib Street, sounding emergency horns. Have they arrested one or two protesters at the square, who might have joined Sheikh Mujib's birthday ceremony peacefully but then, at the first opportunity, displayed placards portraying him with human skulls around his neck and called him our founding father but also our deadliest dictator? It would not be a surprise. It would not be a surprise, either, if all the Sheikh Mujib followers in the country came out into the street and, in their most hateful voices, demanded death sentences for the protesters.

I suppose they will do the same in my case. After my confession, they will turn the whole country against me, and together they will condemn me for good. Why make such a fuss after so many years, they will wonder; why bring the dead back to life? Is it because a sinner will always refuse to drown until other sinners have gathered themselves under his arms? I am not afraid of them. There is no room for fear in my heart. At this moment, I can accept only pain and remorse and despair. I must remember my cruelty for as long as possible, and as honestly as possible. I must relive it every day as a process of atonement, until I am done.

So leaving all details behind, and all debates, I say to myself: the story is long, but it is simple. I have carried excruciating guilt on my shoulders, which was pulling me to the ground at every moment. I have not admitted this guilt for a long time, have fought against it bullishly and have also won for a long time. I do not want to win anymore, especially by defeating part of myself again and again. Sheikh Mujib and the Awami League might not have recognized the deaths they caused by allowing the famine to worsen under their maladministration, but I shall recognize the death that I have caused with my misjudgement. Then I shall be free.

My heart beats faster and faster, and then becomes normal again when I stand before the station gate, and when I feel I am there, finally there, very close to the moment when I won't need to be thinking anxiously about my salvation anymore. I do not have any weight now but the weight of tears rolling up from my throat, looking for a way to come out. My life has been a waste. By destroying Nur Hussain, I have only destroyed myself.

'Good luck, my country,' I whisper as I proceed through the gate. 'Good luck, and goodbye, my misery; a very happy goodbye.'

NEW FROM PERISCOPE IN 2015

PRINCESS BARI
Hwang Sok-yong; translated from the Korean by Sora Kim-Russell
'The most powerful voice of the novel in Asia today.' (Kenzaburō Ōe)
A young North Korean woman survives unspeakable dangers in
search of a better life in London.
PB • 204MM X 138MM • 9781859641743 • 248PP • £9.99

LONG TIME NO SEE: A MEMOIR OF FATHERS, DAUGHTERS AND GAMES OF CHANCE
Hannah Lowe
Acclaimed poet Hannah Lowe reflects on her relationship with her
late father, a rakish Jamaican immigrant and legendary gambler.
PB • 204MM X 138MM • 9781859643969 • 328PP • £9.99

THE MOOR'S ACCOUNT
Laila Lalami
'Brilliantly imagined ... feels very like the truth.' (Salman Rushdie)
The fictional memoirs of a Moorish slave offer a new perspective
on a notoriously ill-fated, real-life Spanish expedition in 1528.
PB • 204MM X 138MM • 9781859644270 • 336PP • £9.99

DRINKING AND DRIVING IN CHECHNYA
Peter Gonda
A disaffected Russian truck driver winds up at the centre of the brutal
bombing of the Chechen capital, forced to engage with reality as never before.
PB • 204MM X 138MM • 9781859641057 • 240PP • £9.99

THE GARDENS OF THE IMAGINATION
Bakhtiyar Ali; translated from the Kurdish by Kareem Abdulrahman
A group of friends search for the bodies of two murdered lovers in this
haunting allegory of modern Iraqi Kurdistan.
PB • 202MM X 138MM • 9781859641255 • 448PP • £9.99

A MAN WITH A KILLER'S FACE
Matti Rönkä; translated from the Finnish by David Hackston
A detective's orderly life is upended when a missing-persons case draws
him into the Russian–Finnish criminal underworld.
PB • 204MM X 138MM • 9781859641781 • 288PP • £9.99

THE EYE OF THE DAY
Dennison Smith
'Remarkable ... beguiles and enchants on every page.' (Ruth Ozeki)
A privileged boy and a hardened fugitive cross paths mysteriously beginning in
the 1930s, across North America and on the battlefields of wartime Europe.
PB • 204MM X 138MM • 9781859640616 • 328PP • £9.99